Fossil Lake III:

UNICORNADO!

Edited by

Christine Morgan

Published by
Sabledrake Enterprises
www.sabledrake.com

A Fossil Lake Anthology
https://fossillake.wordpress.com/

For ordering information, contact
christinemariemorgan@gmail.com or visit us online.

ISBN-13: 978-0-9844032-7-1

10 9 8 7 6 5 4 3 2 1

For all the good ones taken from us too soon

... while so many shitbirds linger on.

Table of Contents

Foreword:

The Lonely Death of Sparkles the Unicorn

KH Koehler

Once upon a time there was a sad, sad unicorn named Sparkles. He was sad because even though his name was Sparkles, he was actually quite drab in appearance. And smelly. Very, very smelly. His lack of hygiene contributed greatly to that. He was pale and grey and unkempt from hiding in his underground grotto all day long. His mane was tangled from lack of care, his teeth rotted and crooked from eating crow, and his breath rank.

Sparkles spent his days writing nonsensical diatribes on banners that he flew from a flagpole atop his grotto and declared masterpieces, but because they made no coherent sense, even in the complex unicorn language, no one could read them. Sparkles, who believed his scribblings were magical in nature, only emerged briefly, and dramatically, to scream at the other unicorns frolicking in the fields around his grotto. He would shake his hoof at them briefly and snarl nonsensical and libelous accusations before returning to the sacred darkness of the grotto, where he would then proceed to wrap himself in a bondage sleepsack and stroke his own horn (a favorite pastime of his) until he fell asleep.

The root of the problem? The unicorns frolicking in the fields actually sparkled. They shimmered and shone, and everyone in the land knew their names and listened intently to their stories about people and places far off. Sparkles hated that everyone listened to the other unicorns and praised their stories. On top of that, no one ever wanted to visit him in his grotto and climb into his sleepsack with him. He was left stroking his own horn every night.

Stroking your own horn makes a lone unicorn very bitter indeed, so Sparkles took it upon himself to learn to breathe fire like his cousins the dragons. The problem? Even well learned unicorns didn't breathe fire very well, and Sparkles, being particularly retarded, couldn't learn even the basics of breathing fire. All he could do was fart into the wind (which he found greatly satisfying).

Suffice to say the other unicorns weren't very impressed by — or frightened of — his windy farts. A farting unicorn isn't very impressive, even to those unfamiliar with unicorns. Unicorn farts just produce brief, pretty rainbows.

Sparkles knew this in his secret heart, but he was determined to impress the other unicorns and strike great fear into their sparkly hearts. To accomplish this feat, he devised a plan to put the names of every one of the unicorns he was angry with on a card and slip it into a large, sparkly Rolodex. He would then spin the Sparkly Rolodex, and whatever name came up, that was the name of the unicorn he would visit and demand respect from.

The first name that came up in the Sparkly Rolodex was Brian the Zombie Unicorn. So, now having a name, Sparkles took his drab, smelly self to Brian the Zombie Unicorn's house in the deep of the forest. There he knocked on Brian's door and demanded his respect. Brian, of course, laughed. Sparkles, enraged, threatened Brian with bodily harm. He threatened to put Brian in unicorn jail. Brian the Zombie Unicorn merely laughed at the threat and sent the legion of angry, pastel-colored zombie ponies in his corral after Sparkles. Sparkles became very afraid of the angry, pastel-colored zombie ponies and ran away back to his grotto.

Once home, Sparkles locked the door and breathed a great sigh of relief. He had narrowly escaped being exposed for the pastel pony he was under his false outward gawthic unicorn exterior. But what to do? Such an affront could not go un-avenged!

Sparkly proceeded to spin the Sparkly Rolodex again. It fell on a new name — Mary the Unicorn Mare Who Had A Great Mane. Sparkles, realizing it was a female unicorn, rubbed his hoofs together in evil, gawthic unicorn glee and went off to find Mary and threaten her.

However, Mary, who lived in the city, wasn't impressed by Sparkles standing outside her window, yelling obscenities at her. She merely picked up her big black purse (her primary weapon) stepped outside, and hit Sparkles over the head repeatedly. Sparkled quickly developed a phobia of The Purse (which was large enough to swallow things like books and even other unicorns). Suffice to say, Sparkles ran crying like a baby all the way home.

Sparkles was livid with impotent rage. What to do? Nothing to do but spin the Sparkly Rolodex once more. This time it fell on Rusty the Baker Unicorn, renowned throughout the land for her rhubarb pies. Oh joy, thought Sparkles. Another female unicorn!

Packing up his meager, smelly belongings, he took public transportation across the Land of Sparkles to Rusty's door, who lived quite far away. However, Rusty, who was used to bothersome unicorns like Sparkles, simply shook her rolling pin and threatened to put him in one of her pies. Sparkles, who was naturally frightened of such things as mice, autumn leaves, and dust bunnies, began to quake with fear. He quickly made his way across The Land of Sparkles back to his grotto — though he did spend one night on a park bench, hidden under a pile of newspaper in order to hide from any potential gay unicorns who might be passing through the area.

Once home, Sparkles consoled himself by visiting Unicorn Jail (his favorite home away from home) and eating Porky Pig. Finally, frustrated, Sparkles spun the Sparkly Rolodex one last time. This time it landed on Christine the Magical Wordsmith Unicorn. Oh joy, thought Sparkles, one of the sparkly storyteller unicorns he was so jealous of! Gathering up his sleepsack (honestly, he was unable to peel it off himself at this point) he hurried to Christine's house, pounded on her door, and proceeded to threaten her, her offspring, and her fluffy house cats.

Christine wasn't impressed. She frowned, looked Sparkles up and down, and proceeded to slam the door in his face without saying a word. Sparkles pounded on her door for many hours, threatening her with Hovind dinosaurs, stick figures and blue-collar metal, but Christine would not let him in. She was busy at her writing desk, writing letters to the other storytelling unicorns frolicking in yonder hills.

Once the letters were delivered, the other unicorns paraded to her house and began dropping off their personal stories about their encounters with Sparkles the Sad, Sad Unicorn. Thus this book was born. And Sparkles cried and cried. Some say Sparkles is still in his sleepsack, crying, to this very day.

The end.

KH Koehler ~ December, 2015

Unicornado Miami: The Aftermath

Carl N. Brown

the hunting of the unicorn

morgan downie

The hunting of the unicorn

there is an understanding
in the savagery of the dogs
the stamping of hooves
and the terrible goring horn
the sympathy of beasts
the warp and weft
of hunter and hunted

no such pity in the furious pack
their cruel spears a stabbing phalanx
a nest of thorns to tear his side
and drop him to his knees
as gilded lords look on

of his blood they will
a mordant make
of his death a song

the unicorn falls
we turn our eyes away
all the rest is butchery

The Maven

Nikki Hetfield

Don leaned against a fence, admiring the rural North Carolina landscape one June afternoon when he glanced downward to see a horn burst through his chest.

When he looked back up at me with a stupefied look on his face, all the color had drained out of him. By the time he opened his mouth, as if to speak, he was already dead. He slumped forward, his weight resting on a single blood-drenched horn.

The horn shook back and forth with the body flopping like a rag doll and droplets of blood splattering on my face. Don slid forward and dropped off the horn, which — to my astonishment — belonged to the most beautiful white unicorn I could imagine.

To be honest, it was the first unicorn I had ever seen (not counting that one-horned goat at the circus), and I'd never even considered the possibility that unicorns could actually exist. But there it was, gleaming in the summer light against a deep blue sky. It was a tween girl's notebook cover come to life.

Of course, I still couldn't believe what I was seeing, so I tried to tell myself I was dreaming or tripping or

hallucinating. But when I reached out to reassure myself, I felt the beast's hot breath on my hand. He shook
some of my brother's blood off his horn, and a drop
landed on my lip. Then he reared back with a grunt
that echoed like a gunshot in the distance.

I don't have to tell you I got the hell out of there
and was back in my car before his front hooves hit the
ground. By the time I turned the key his horn shattered
the passenger side window, passing within an inch of
my eyes.

I floored it. The tires kicked up a tornado of dust
and gravel behind me as I sped down the dirt road. I
was almost back to the highway before I could bring
myself to look at the rear view mirror. Dust. All I could
see was that impenetrable cloud. I let out a deep breath
in relief.

Then the white demon flew — not jumped but flew
— out of the gray cloud and dive-bombed my pickup
with his hooves landing firmly on the bed. The weight
was so great my front wheels nearly came off the
ground. I yanked the wheel to the right, going off-road
in hopes of shaking the monster, but I could barely maneuver with him weighing me down. I gunned it towards a low-hanging branch. The truck lunged forward
when he flew off the back.

Back on the road, I made it to Highway 460 and
headed east, past Fossil Lake, and back to Black Rock.
I was going about a hundred by the time I looked back
again and saw he was still there, chasing me, gaining.

Who knew unicorns were such assholes? Could it
be everything I'd ever heard about these "gentle" creatures was wrong?

Questions flooded my head, but I couldn't formulate any answers — or a plan. All I could think of was a lesson I learned as a child: When being chased by a bunch of bees, you don't have to outrun them. You just have to find someone slower than you for them to chase instead. I was coming up on a car going fifty-five, so I flew past it. Sure enough, the unicorn went after it. All I saw was the beast thrusting his horn through the driver's side window and the car swerving off the road into a tree. Without missing a beat, the monster was back on my tail.

I blew through downtown Black Rock, which is only about three blocks long. He gored pedestrians left and right, sending the survivors fleeing into nearby shops. He broke through a plate glass window and jumped back out with two impaled children on his horn. One of them was still alive, still frantic to free himself until the unicorn skewered another child for his human-kabob.

That's when I stopped. I didn't know where he came from or why he was here, but I wasn't about to let that bastard kill any more innocent kids in my town.

Turning back around, I peeled out and tore down the street toward him. He jumped right over me. When I turned back around to try again, his horn smashed through my windshield with three kids still attached. One of their elbows knocked me in the jaw. I saw stars.

I heard three shots. Some old redneck was shooting the unicorn with a hunting rifle. Other hunters pulled the rifles off the gun racks in their trucks and started firing. That unicorn just thrashed around, sending little corpses flying left and right. With his horn free, he

used it to impale one hunter after another as if their bullets had no effect on him.

I ran into him, sending the unicorn bouncing off my grill. The truck was totaled, but the unicorn was fine. He was standing about ten feet from my door, staring at me as if about to charge. I slid across the seat and fell out the passenger side door as his horn tore through the driver's side door. I rolled out of the way just as the truck tipped and came crashing upside-down.

He stood in triumph on top of the capsized truck. Somebody shot the gas tank, and the whole thing burst into flames. The explosion shook the street, shattering store and car windows. But there he was, standing like a Stonewall in the midst of the fireball.

I scrambled on my hands and knees across the broken glass and bloodied bodies. Here was the corpse of somebody I'd known since high school. There were the remains of a friend, a cousin, and friend's kid. As soon as I got back on my feet I ran through the broken store window into Slaw's Restaurant. Shoving every table and chair out of my way, I made it to the back door and out to the alley.

If we couldn't shoot him, burn him, or run him over with a truck, how were we supposed to stop that monster before he wiped out the entire town?

Figuring the library might have the answers, I ran two blocks to the local branch, which was housed on the first floor of an old home. It was closed. Due to poor visitation, it was only open Wednesday and Friday mornings until noon. Damn! I tried the door, which happened to be unlocked (nothing in there worth stealing).

Checking the encyclopedia, I found out unicorns are mythical beasts that can only be subdued by a young girl who is pure of heart. Apparently, this unicorn didn't think any of the girls he'd slaughtered that day fit the bill.

As I continued reading, I couldn't find anything about unicorns being vicious killing machines. As a matter of fact, they were supposedly peaceful and completely harmless. That book proved about as useless as the rifles had been. There wasn't much else to do but call the National Guard, but how do you explain that there's a mad unicorn on the loose?

The screams and gunshots were getting closer as the unicorn's path of destruction spread. I couldn't think of a safer place than the public library, but I thought I would be just a bit safer if I locked myself in the basement. Down a narrow back staircase I found the windowless basement. Flipping on the lights, I could see dozens of file cabinets of various sizes and shapes lining the room. Closer inspection revealed the words "TOWN ARCHIVES" on each cabinet, and under these words were letters. Out of curiosity, I looked in the cabinet labeled "TOWN ARCHIVES/ U-W."

Sure enough, there was a file for "Unicorn." That's where I started to find some answers.

It turns out that, back before the Civil War, there was a secret cult on the outskirts of town, under the leadership of a nut job known by his followers as "The Maven." The group was known as the Plagiarists and, according to the documentation, "The signature calling card of the plagiarism posse is the sexual abuse of unicorns." The wording of the account was unclear, but it appears that the members reveled in committing unspeakable acts.

Apparently, one of the founding members, Phillip Campbell, had acquired a live unicorn from some Hungarian castle in the early nineteenth century and brought it back to his horse farm in North Carolina. The cult members kept the poor creature bound in chains in a cave on the old Campbell property past Fossil Lake, not far from where I'd first seen it.

The Plagiarists believed that learning the secret of the unicorn's legendary immortality would enable them to become immortal or some such nonsense. Needless to say, that plan didn't work. After the death of the unicorn's owner, the collective's leadership fell to his heir, Campbell's half-wit bastard son Lloyd, who demanded that his followers call him "The Maven."

After Lloyd's own demise, the followers gradually died off one by one. They abandoned the cave. And, it turns out, left one very immortal and deeply disturbed unicorn down there. He must have been waiting 150 years or more for his chains to rust enough for him to break free of them.

I hid in the basement until the horrible sounds eventually faded into the distance, and the unicorn was gone just as suddenly and as inexplicably as he had arrived.

I buried my brother, the locals mourned their lost loved ones, and the town rebuilt what it could. In the four years since then, people still occasionally claim to catch a glimpse of some gleaming white equine shape darting between the old growth forests near Fossil Lake.

Around these parts, we will always hate Lloyd Campbell the Plagiarist for the hell he unleashed on this town.

The Hazards of Owning a Unicorn

Lyn Godfrey

Tired of age-old boring normal pets? Are you frustrated with all the "fake" cyborg animals on the market these days? Have you been burned by crossed wires and so-called "intelligent" AI?

Well, we at the NoRobo Pets division of Genetisus understand. You won't find any electronic parts in our pets. And you'll certainly never find them boring.

Our scientists at the NoRobo Pets laboratory have been working tirelessly to produce new live Mini-Pets for our customers to enjoy alongside current customer favorites and top-sellers like those from our Fossil collection: Mini-Mammoth, Mini-Tyrannosaurus, and Mini-Sabertooth.

With our Mini-Pets, you can get all the fun of mega-sized animals miniaturized down to the size of a small dog.

Our lead scientist on these projects, Dr Thea Washington, is herself a devoted and loving owner of a Mini-Tyrannosaurus. When she was originally given the task of creating smaller versions of these large creatures, the job seemed insurmountable. However, she accomplished her goal and decided once again to take on the impossible.

Up until now, we have specialized in miniaturizing only the animals which have a fully-mapped DNA entry in our Genetisus database. Dr Thea Washington recently led our team in an all new mission: create a miniature version of an as-of-yet purely fictional animal.

This means that, in order to be able to minimize it, we had to start by genetically engineering a full-sized version of the animal.

Once again, she succeeded. Consequently, we are proud to announce the newest pet on our roster: the Unicorn.

It has long been speculated that we may eventually make the leap into full-sized pets, and with this newest animal, we decided to do just that. Both the Mini-Unicorn and our first venture into the full-sized pet market, the Unicorn, are now available for pre-order.

Current Gold or Elite members can order the Mini-Unicorn. Only Elite customers will have access to the full-sized edition. To those patrons that are not Elite status: don't despair! You can become an Elite member and own your own full-sized Unicorn for less than the cost of your own personal teleportation station.

Don't have the digital cash? We also now accept Bitcoin.

Both the full-sized Unicorn and the Mini-Unicorn will be available in multiple colors, including: Black, White, Chestnut, Tri-Color, Blue Roan, Dapple Gray, and Golden Palomino.

We have additionally designed both versions of the Unicorns in several varieties of pink: Bubblegum Pink, Baby Pink, Hot Pink, and our very special bioluminescent Neon Pink.

Last, but certainly not least, we have an extremely limited edition: Rainbow Sparkle.

Can you pass up this amazing opportunity to own your very own Unicorn? Don't delay. Upgrade your account today!

Legal Disclaimers:

We strongly recommend that you have your Unicorns trained. We've enlisted the help of a highly-qualified equine specialist to design a training program specifically tailored to our Unicorns. The training videos are available for free on our feed. You can also sign up to attend live sessions with the trainer at our NoRobo Unicorn Labs.

Never teleport with your pet, whether full-sized or miniature. Due to the complex process of rematerialization, it is always best to teleport one living individual at a time. All public Port stations operate this way, so we recommend using the same good judgement in your own personal and private teleportation lives. We are not responsible for anything that might happen if you ignore this warning.

In case of a storm, natural disaster, or other emergency, please attach the specially-designed safety horn-topper to your Unicorn's horn in order to protect yourself and others and to reduce the risk of injury or death by impalement. Though our pets are created to be docile and non-violent, accidental impalement can happen, so we advise you to operate with the utmost caution. It has been observed that unintentional Unicorn stabbings have a high statistical likelihood of striking directly through the heart. We are not sure why.

Do not try to nuzzle foreheads with either a Mini-Unicorn or a full-sized Unicorn. This presents a major eye-poking hazard. The Mini's horn may be much smaller than the full-sized, but it can still absolutely pierce and penetrate through the eye socket.

It is best not to have too many of our Unicorns in one place at one time. Preferably no more than ten. Because of the natural nervousness and excitability of the equine genus, this trait has shown to be exaggerated in Unicorns. They are rather excitable and may herd or swarm together if over-excited. Even Minis can become hazardous in a large group. If you absolutely have to group them together, be sure to use safety horn-toppers and keep each Uni securely reined and bridled.

Remain aware of your surroundings when out and about with a Unicorn pet. Our Unis have a tendency to recklessly chase rainbows and/or butterflies. We haven't been able to determine why they have this inclination, but they cannot seem to resist galloping after brightly colored or shiny objects. They may also become infatuated with their own reflection in lakes and other bodies of water. You can help curb these behaviors by bringing them to training sessions at Unicorn Labs where we will help your Uni learn to focus and not be so easily distracted.

Please maintain your Unicorn's coat, mane, and hooves. Our Rainbow Sparkle variety has shown to shed copious amounts of glitter, so frequent grooming is recommended. Matching combs and hoofpicks are available to complement each color of Unicorn.

Unfortunately, any attempt to breed our pets with other pets will be unsuccessful. All our pets are designed to be sterile, therefore you will need to purchase any extras directly through our website or from one of our licensed vendors.

Lastly, we will not be offering a Pegasus Unicorn as we were unable to design functional wings for the animal. Additionally, the FAA insisted that flying rainbow-chasing Unicorns would pose a threat to spacecraft, hovercraft, and dronecraft.

We thank you for your support,
Your Friends at Genetisus

Cosmic Unicorn Thunderfuck

Calum Chalmers

For Jo "Larry" McGee

The storm rumbled gently in the distance, clouds slowly creeping up to blot out the night sky and disappoint the crowds below.

For the first time ever, the local night sky was illuminated by the aurora borealis. An unexpected solar flare had sent the shimmering beauty of the northern lights as far down as Devon. The small coastal town of Dawlish had shut off all lights to allow the converging tourist hoards the chance to witness this phenomenon in all its glory.

"That storm's gonna be trouble." A small man holding various scientific instruments in the air waved aggressively at his companion. "Steve! Dude! You listening?"

Steve stood motionless in the middle of the gravel car park. His notepad rested on his side as he stared at the incoming cloud. "Beautiful, isn't it?"

The first man dropped his arms down; clearly tired of the acrobics they had been performing all day. He walked towards his friend and stood by his side.

"Looks like a big, angry, purple motherfucking cloud."

Steve laughed with his companion and turned his attention back to his notepad.

"Okay, Pete, we have everything we need here; let's head back into town before that thing hits. If what we are hearing from base is true, I don't want to be outside when it does."

Pete nodded in agreement and gathered his equipment, carefully placing it in the back of a battered old VW van before jumping into the driver's seat.

As the van made its way back towards town the first strikes of lightning could be seen smacking into the distant hills.

Beeping his horn, Pete manoeuvred his van around the tourists cars haphazardly left as their occupants stared into the night sky.

"Like bloody zombies!" Pete yelled as he smashed his fist into the horn once more.

Steve remained fixed on his notepad, flicking through the pages and recalculating equations full of letters rather than numbers. "Yeah. Zombies," he replied half-heartedly.

"Okay, what you seeing, Rainman?"

Steve hated that nickname; ever since school he was a mathematical genius, and by getting involved in weather patterns, he kinda had it coming, but it didn't mean he had to like it.

"Nothing, just that there is a strong chance of an EMP. No one has ever seen a solar flare this big. The outcomes are uncalculated, but it is all pointing towards a mass blackout."

"Blacker than this?" Pete nodded towards the blacked out town. A flurry of torches littered the streets as the crowds mingled joyfully.

"EMPs will affect more than lights. We will lose anything that is electrical, your van included, so let's just get back sharpish, okay?"

Pete looked at his dashboard, stroking at the plastic interior.

"Not Betty," he whispered to himself.

*

A large crowd was huddled on the beach, each lying in another's arms as they watched the spectacle before them. Young and old alike finding peace and solitude amongst the masses, everyone seemed happy and content despite being packed in like sardines.

Larry, a seasoned police officer, looked out at the sea of people and said a quiet prayer to himself. The storm was closing in. However smoothly things had been running up until now, add a little bit of rain and these crowds would be pushing and shoving for any shelter they could get. Plus, if this talk of an electrical cut off was right, he was going to have to deal with hundreds of stranded, pissed off motorists.

The cloud seeped across the sky, cutting into the edges of the light display. Knowing that it would soon be time, Larry moved towards the beach entrance, ready to guide people with his government-issued glow stick. Each tourist had been given one on arrival. The other police officers had joked that the whole thing was going to turn into a rave, an LSD-fuelled nightmare in Larry's eyes.

Larry felt something brushing down his neck. Reaching behind, he touched his skin and inspected the intruding article. A small amount of glitter had fallen on him. Looking around, he could see no one responsible for this new and somewhat bizarre accessory.

Again, another amount brushed down his arm and again across his cheek. Looking skyward, he could see small clumps falling from the clouds like rain. It mustn't have been glitter, it couldn't be, it must have been snow, weird warm snow.

Sticking out his tongue, he caught a small amount on the tip. An intense candyfloss flavour instantly filled his mouth.

Murmurings on the beach confirmed he was not alone. Others were standing now, mouths open, catching the glitter as it fell down on them. The crowd groaned with excitement, people so happy with the sky's gift they began to laugh and cheer.

The ever growing noise almost deafened out the sound of thunder ... almost.

*

"Holy fuck! You hear that?"

"Hear it! I bloody *felt* it!"

Steve was hanging from the van's window, gathering glitter in a Tupperware box.

"Just take this left and head in through the basement, I need to see what this stuff is"

Pete swung a left and headed into the belly of the observatory.

Heading down the ramp, they saw grown men in lab coats standing around the building, spinning and laughing under the shimmering shower. Pete recognised one as Dr Hans, a gruff, no nonsense man ... who was now lying on his back laughing like an infant as he picked bits of glitter from the grass before cramming them down his throat.

"Dude, I know I'm going to regret saying this but I'd rather an EMP than this bat shit crazy ... whatever this is." He drove onward, mouth open. As Dr Hans waved ecstatically at him, Pete couldn't help but wave back.

The moment the van was parked Steve leapt out and headed straight up the stairs towards the telescope. "Come on, we can't miss this, we have to see what's causing it!"

Steve disappeared up the stairwell as Pete stood alone in the car park. Another immense crack of thunder rumbled overhead. Only, this time, Pete could have sworn he heard whinnying horses accompanying the sky's roars.

*

Reeling as if the sky was about to fall on him Larry allowed his heart to settle after that enormous crash of thunder. In the distance he could hear horses braying.

"Poor bastards," he said aloud. As natural as thunder was, he always wondered about the animals at a time like this. Did they understand what was happening or were storms like this just pure fear for them?

His thought was cut short by a piercing scream; a young girl not too far from him had fallen to the ground clasping her eye. Jumping into action, Larry muscled his way through the crowd to aid the youth.

"MY FUCKING EYE! JESUS CHRIST MY FUCKING EYE"

The girl was no older than twelve, and even though he was not a stranger to foul-mouthed youths, her ferocity and venom took him by surprise.

"What's wrong, Hun?" he enquired, kneeling down to meet her.

Before he even touched her hand he could see blood seeping from between her fingers. Reaching for his first aid pouch, he pulled out an eyepatch and pressed it against the wound.

Her mother now stood over them clucking like a massive obese hen. "Who did this? Who the fuck did this? I'll break his fucking neck, glass my fucking daughter will you! Well then I'll shove a fucking bottle up your fucking arse!" She was indiscriminately aiming her verbal abuse at anyone who dared venture near to the action.

Larry knew that there was going to be trouble and knew help was going to be hard to get to. Pressing down on his radio he called for backup. It might not be needed yet, but with the amount of time it would take anyone to reach him, he opted for the instant panic option.

Trying to calm the mother, ask for witnesses, and tend to the girl, he failed to hear her next words.

"Glitter, the glitter did it."

Unfortunately, her mother's outbursts meant that her words went unheard by anyone and she slowly drifted into unconsciousness, her impending death to be labelled as tragic.

A lifeguard helicopter buzzed overhead, circling Larry and his predicament in an attempt to find a safe place to land. They needn't have bothered. Apart from the girl already being beyond saving, the whole town was swamped. No areas remained untouched, and as much as the crowds pushed and squeezed themselves together, they couldn't create enough space for the helicopter to land.

Failing, the pilot positioned himself close to the scene and a yellow clad paramedic was lowered down into the seething mass of fear and confusion.

Larry reached out and pulled the legs of the paramedic towards him, allowing her to land safely next to the patient. She faced Larry and shouted something at him; her words were trampled by the crowd's uproar. Larry did all he could by pointing at his eye and then at the girl.

The paramedic stared at Larry before shrugging in disgust and turning to tend to the wounded girl, freeing Larry to turn his attention to the wobbling mass of anger that had borne her.

A young woman stepped in to help aid Larry in his attempt to control the situation. Usually, he would turn a citizen away, but, feeling completely isolated, he welcomed the help. Besides, the woman was doing a fantastic job at redirecting the mother's hate solely on herself whilst simultaneously calming her foaming outbursts.

Another crack of thunder split the crowd, focusing everyone's attention.

"Please leave the area." A megaphone belted out the words over Larry's head. Looking for a source, he found none, but soon recognised the voice as his Sergeant. At last, the cavalry had arrived.

The paramedic had strapped the dying girl to a board and was shoving people aside as she attempted to attach the board to a rope hanging from the helicopter. Turning to Larry, she mouthed the words, *"I'm out!"* before majestically rising skywards.

Larry envied her escape route but had no time to feel bitter; he had to move this crowd on whilst trying to find out what actually happened.

Another explosion of thunder — only, as this one hit, the lights and music in the area stopped dead.

Larry shook his radio, batting it into his palm in an attempt to revive it. Cheers shot up as the limited light in the town was quickly extinguished, only to be replaced by hundreds of glow sticks.

A grinding mechanical noise quickly smothered the cheers, replacing them with screams of terror as the helicopter above started to surge and twist. Hurtling downwards, the spinning hunk of metal crashed, temporarily lighting the beach in a fiery glow.

Shards of metal flew through the crowd, slicing through anyone who stood in its path. A spinning propeller shard hurtled at breakneck speed, skewering three bystanders like a kebab.

Another explosion tore open the belly of the helicopter, showering the survivors in a blanket of liquid fire as it flowed mercilessly through the gathering.

The Sergeant watched in horror as flames washed over tortured faces. Helpless, he stood on the sea wall, megaphone in hand.

*

"Holy hell! That was a helicopter going down! I think it hit the cliff face!"

Steve was running around trying every switch he could find. "I told you! EMP! Jesus, everything's dead up here, we won't be able to see anything beyond that cloud!"

Pete pressed his forehead against the window, his breath steaming up his view. Tears slowly trickled down his face as he watched the flames lick the sky.

"What was that message you read before the screen went off?"

Steve was still checking every item, as if by miracle something would have survived

"Pete! I need you man, tell me about that message"

Pete rolled his head to face Steve. "It was bollocks, mate, some screwed up text from this EMP crap."

"Just humour me, tell me what it said again."

Pete sighed. "It said 'Glitter. Run. Unicorns.'"

Steve, satisfied that everything was dead, sat propping himself against a desk. "Right, well ... we have glitter. And that is followed with 'run,' which no one has done, so ... well we're in the shit, then."

     Unicornado!   27

"What about unicorns?" Pete managed to muster between growing sobs.

"I'm with you on that, Pete. Has to be some garbled transmission."

*

Larry picked himself off the ground, wiping a layer of glitter from his arms. His head spun as he tried to make sense of his surroundings.

Bodies littered the beach, pieces of metal entrenched into their victims. A steady crackle from the flames was the only sound in a surprisingly serene setting. Then the sound of rushing water filled his skull, before parting to permit the terrible screams that inhabited the seafront. The silence ended abruptly.

Everyone, literally everyone, was screaming and writhing on the ground like worms, their bodies coated in blood as they clawed at their flesh. Where his Sergeant was last seen, he could now see a grown man on all fours, screaming in agony as crimson blood poured from his face.

Desperate to help, Larry raised his arm, reaching uselessly in the sergeant's direction. Immediately, he regretted his decision. Pain tore down his arm as the glitter rain slashed through his uniform. Snatching his arm back, he pressed down on the wound.

It's the glitter! The fucking glitter!

Larry screamed for everyone to find shelter. Those who were still breathing crawled their way under cars and awnings, tugging on the lifeless remains of their loved ones, desperate to help them seek safety.

Larry saw the remains of a helicopter door to his side; grabbing it he raised it above his head as a makeshift shield and headed out amongst the survivors, pulling in those he could save.

THUMP

Something large and heavy landed behind him. Spinning on the spot, he whipped himself around.

THUMP

Another impact only feet from his side landed. Then another, and another. He kept turning, desperate to catch sight of what it was that was falling, but saw nothing.

Then it happened. A woman's scream erupted behind him. Facing the noise, he saw it.

Unable to function, he stood slack jawed and wide eyed. It wasn't possible! It couldn't be! How?

*

"Steve, you need to see this."

Stealing himself from a now dismantled computer, Steve walked towards Pete at the window. Steve was holding a collection of wires and electrical components, twiddling through them. Trying to fabricate something wonderful, no doubt. They looked out across the town. People were lying on the ground, completely immobile. Toward the observatories gardens, the blood soaked lab coats of co-workers protruded from the undergrowth, limbs racked at horrendous angles.

"My God! Are they ..."

"That's not the problem."

Pete gestured towards a large lump, slung over a balcony to their right. It looked like the arse end of a horse, a pure white steed with pink glittery hooves.

"How the Hell did that get up there?"

"It fell, Steve. It fell from the motherfucking sky."

Steve took a step back to assess his companion. Seeing that helicopter crash must have left him in a state of shock. Did he really believe horses were falling from the sky?

"The sky is raining unicorns," Pete continued. He was talking as if he was in a trance; wide eyed he remained transfixed on the horse's remains.

Steve opened his mouth, ready to question his friend, when an enormous crash destroyed part of the observatory roof.

Masonry crashed down in a far corner, amongst it lay the very noticeable figure of a horse and from its head emerged a very large, glittering, pink horn.

"Motherfucking unicorns," Pete muttered.

"Motherfucking unicorns," Steve replied.

*

Larry ran as fast as he could. The glitter rain, although subsiding, was still cutting into his skin. Blood flowed like tiny rivers down his arms.

A unicorn, a bloody unicorn, had impaled the woman next to him!

It had fallen from the sky like a bastard dart and run its horn straight through her.

His heart was racing, the pain burning a hole in his chest, yet still he kept running. There was a small cave just around the bend and he knew he had to make it; it would be the safest place in town.

Another unicorn smashed through a car, impaling a sheltering elderly man. The whole roof caved in as the pink spear tore through the metal like it was butter.

Tripping, Larry looked towards the near miss and caught a glimpse of the unicorn's face ... it was laughing! He would have put money on it! It had a ridiculous smile etched across its bastard face and was laughing.

The unicorn's eye caught sight of Larry, who was now scrambling to his feet. Pushing against the car, the unicorn pulled itself free, not a scratch on its body. It pointed its glittery spike of death at him. He didn't need to be told twice; Larry jumped to his feet and headed towards the nearby minimarket, an elderly lady holding the door for him. He landed heavily in a stack of asparagus, broccoli raining down from a shelf above. The old lady swung the door shut and pressed herself against it, ready for the impending collision.

The horn tore through her chest, spraying Larry with her blood. The old lady, unable to comprehend what had happened, quickly slumped in on herself.

Slowly retreating, the horn left the lifeless remains of the lady to drop to the floor. Larry slipped in the fresh blood as he got to his feet, causing him to fall sideways. As he did, the unicorn smashed through the door and barrelled full speed into the asparagus.

With his back up against the condiments, Larry began throwing anything to hand. Ketchup, mayonnaise, mustard ... all crashed against the snorting beast.

The unicorn raised up and roared in pain. A sizzling sound filled the air, and the smell of roast meat filled Larry's nostrils. The left eye of the unicorn was blistering and melting. Skin began to peel away, exposing the skull; the pure pristine white bone encased in glitter began to grow as more skin fell away.

Larry read the label on the jar: 'Horseradish.'

The one true weakness to unicorns.

Now it was up to him to spread the word.

Heading towards the display of kids beach toys, he gathered all the water pistols he could carry. Pouring horseradish into each gun, he was left woefully under prepared; only one and a half guns and then he would be out of ammo.

It was enough. It had to be enough. And he'd be dammed if he wouldn't at least try.

Making his way towards the back entrance, he steadied his breathing, ready to battle whatever lay before him. Rounding the final corner, he was faced with a gift from the heavens.

BUY 1 GET 1 FREE

A tower of horseradish taller than himself stood proudly before him.

"I'm gonna need more guns," Larry said to himself before hurrying off to load up a trolley.

*

Steve and Pete crept silently towards the equine horror. Its deep breaths echoed around the cavernous observatory.

"It's still alive!" Pete whispered. "What should we do? Is it hurt? Do we kill it? Can we get to a vet? Do you know a vet?"

Pete's rapid-fire questions fell on Steve's deaf ears as he inched cautiously towards the animal, his arm outstretched. Sweat was dripping down his forehead. He had always wanted a unicorn. He'd been mocked for believing in their existence but knew he was right. And here he was, mere feet from a real live unicorn.

So close he could feel the warmth from its skin.

"Do vets do unicorns? They are basically horses right? Horses with sticks on their heads — "

"Pete ... shut up."

Steve's hand rested on the unicorn's side. The moment he touched it, he felt the purity of this magnificent creature flow through his veins.

"Is it real?" Pete asked from behind him.

"Yeah, buddy, it's real." Steve's hand swept up towards the neck, his arm twitching with a pleasant vibration.

Shifting 'round, he positioned himself in front of the unicorn's head, cupping its beautiful cheeks. Looking deep into its eyes, he could see rainbows swirling, twisting within its iris.

Whispering gently, Steve told the unicorn all would be okay, everything was going to be okay.

The horse raised its head and laughed, a deep inhuman laugh that sent the perfect aura Steve was feeling crashing to the ground. Jumping backwards, Steve pushed his back hard against the wall.

The unicorn's laugh continued as it swung its head in ecstasy.

Pete looked at Steve as if Steve had the answer. It was the last thing Pete did.

The unicorn exploded in a fiery ball of glitter, leveling the observatory, reducing it to nothing more than smouldering chunks of concrete.

A delicate shower of glitter rained down on the corpses of Pete and Steve, the moonlight catching it, forming spiralling rainbows across the ruins.

Steve's body, contorted in a horrendous manner, lay motionless with a smile across his lips. The smile of a man who could say, 'I touched a unicorn.'

*

The earth shook beneath Larry's feet.

Whatever it was, it was big. Now or never. With a trolley loaded with plastic guns full of horseradish, he barrelled out the door. It wasn't long before he met his first target.

A pink, extra fluffy unicorn was repeatedly impaling a man against a wall. The man's body lifeless, still the unicorn continued in his torture.

Picking a slender yellow and red model, Larry pumped on the charge, the noise instantly drawing the attention of the masochistic fiend. The unicorn slung the battered corpse aside as it readied itself for a charge.

Larry raised his weapon and fired. An arc of cream-coloured goo emanated from the nozzle and landed square in the face of the unicorn.

The pink fluff began to burn, that now welcome smell of roast filling the air as the unicorn writhed in pain.

Not wanting to revel in his glory, Larry turned on his heels and pushed his trolley onto his next target.

He soon came across a small band of survivors held up in a doctor's surgery; they were fighting a losing battle against a small unicorn. *Jesus*, Larry thought, *even the little ones are lethal.*

Larry stormed forward, slamming his body hard against its taut body, sending it crashing to the ground. He braced his foot on the head of the snarling creature and rammed the gun's nozzle into its flaring nostril, squeezing the trigger. The unicorn's eyes rolled back as it began to convulse and foam at the mouth. Within seconds, it was dead.

The crowd, exhausted by their battle, managed a slight cheer as they gathered around the blistered corpse.

Handing out the guns from his trolley, Larry spread the word of his epic discovery. Soon, the survivors were armed and fighting back.

He headed deeper into town, jumping between car roofs as he assassinated unsuspecting unicorns. Entering a quiet cul-de-sac, he saw a family's garage being beaten in by two unicorns, each one taking it in turn to boot at the misshapen door. The screams of a family could be heard from inside, begging for someone to save them. Someone like Larry.

He checked his ammo situation. His gun was low on horseradish, and with two unicorns he was going to have to get uncomfortably close.

Looking around, he searched for anything that could aide him in his time of need. The garden was littered with an array of children's toys, plastic dinosaurs, roller skates, a tennis racket and a bucket of balls.

That was it! Tennis balls!

Pumping at his weapon, he sprayed the balls in a generous coating of horseradish. A test strike showed that, despite their coating, the balls bounced perfectly off the racket. Moving into position, he whistled at the monsters.

"Serve's up, bitches!"

The first ball smashed against the guttering, sending shards of blackened plastic raining down on the unicorns. An almighty roar came from them as they reared, their rainbow-coloured genitals piercing the night air.

Another shot, and this time the ball made a direct hit against its juddering phallus.

The unicorn's eyes opened wide. It exhaled a cloud of condensation. Saliva dribbled down its lips.

A shriek burst from its lungs, smouldering hair smoking from his groin as he ran down the street. As he collapsed in a heap, the deathly tremors soon dissipated.

Larry faced off with the remaining unicorn, who was now slowly backing off down the side of the house.

Raising his tennis racket, he prepared for another shot. But before he could toss the ball upwards, a gathering of Girl Guides dropped from an overhanging tree.

Each armed with plastic guns and smothered head to toe in horseradish, they made short work of the distraught unicorn.

It transpired that they had locked themselves in the local cricket club. A townsman had passed on the secrets of horseradish and help arm them with a small arsenal of guns.

My God, they were the most brutal in their vengeance. Tanya, the youngest, was seen that night parading through town with no less than seven horns in a necklace about her neck.

*

The unicorns were outgunned and outnumbered, their brute strength no match against the ingenuity of the Dawlish inhabitants. Justice was quick, and soon the bodies of humans and unicorns alike plagued the streets.

The survivors of the small Devon town stood proudly on the sea walls, triumphant in their battle against the unicorns.

The tide washed gently over the remains of those lost, its blood red froth lapping against the helicopter's burnt shell. Shops smouldered across town. Houses had been smashed beyond recognition. The smell of horseradish drifted in the early morning breeze.

The storm cloud was now wandering into the distance, leaving behind a wake of carnage and a small rainbow.

A roar erupted from the crowd; plastic guns held high they punched at the sky.

The only question on their lips: Is it over?

Is it over?

Nectar of God

S.L. Dixon

On the smooth stone floor, the old man sat in soiled white underwear, faded and yellowed with misfired streams and dribbles. On his back and shoulders, a long golden housecoat stained by time. Chunks of vomit rode his beard like ocean debris, bobbing along the surf.

There was a mess of small figurines scattered about the floor from a broken shelf. The old man opened his eyes and licked his lips, cracked and dry. His breath tasted of bile and gin. There was a sixty-ounce bottle on the floor next to him. He moaned; he had a hand in cause, but effect was natural and a hangover was a natural result of consuming too much Seagram's.

Shakily, the old man rose to his feet and peered onto his mess. He'd done worse before. He hoped he hadn't broken anything, as it was such a sad waste when the universe lost anything.

As a punishment for overindulging, the old man worked at picking up the strewn remnants of instability without giving his pain time to settle. It was a mess and it hurt to pick up, but he deserved it.

One shelf tossed of several thousand, not so bad, really.

While drinking, he liked to touch the glorious things that hadn't worked; those things extinct and impossible. There was nostalgia in fondling the species, mentally carved and fabricated things for the universe. He straightened the oak shelf on its oak pegs and bent to begin collecting strewn creation.

Every bend sent a rush to his brain, swirling pain, and then ease and then pain once again inside his wrinkled head. It wasn't a surprise that he spent the night where he had. The nearest picture frame window showed the most conscious of all his creations in recent time. He could watch and smile as the wonderful things grew beyond his initial designs.

There was no time to think about that now; he needed to finish cleaning and fill up on water and pain relieving tablets, tiny soluble advertisements for one pharmaceutical brand or another.

He thought he had Tylenol somewhere, but maybe it was Advil. He'd finish arranging the mess first.

"*Epidexipteryx*," he mumbled, stroking the tail feathers of the scaly bird. It was the last of the figurines on the floor and yet, two shelf spaces remained vacant. The old man rushed about the long stone hall of mounted picture frame windows, scanning the floor and corners for the missing object. His headache forgotten.

He returned to the space where he'd passed out and then awakened, he looked closely at the window.

He stretched a long bony finger to the open space and pressed. A ripple flowed from his touch like the surface of a puddle.

"Are you in there?" the old man asked, putting an ear against the soft invisible windowpane.

*

Stephen Dreger sat on his toilet, mid-morning routine; he'd already showered and dressed. He wanted to force movement before he went into work as he couldn't bring himself to use public toilets. There was a splash beneath him and yet he hadn't evacuated any waste. He leapt to his feet and looked back into the toilet water.

"Oh Jesus!" he said, tugging up his trousers.

The thing in the toilet continued to splash. It kicked its hooves and whinnied, reaching out a fat grey tongue. Its eyes were bulging and panicked and filth clumped its mane with several shades of bowel. There was flushed food stuck to its horn.

It was disgusting, and still, Stephen Dreger reached his manicured hand into the toilet and retrieved the impossibility.

"Incredible," he whispered as he put the creature into the sink. "A unicorn, a Christ'n unicorn."

The creature stood no more than ten inches hoof to horn. Its body was yellowed from its trip through the city's pipes. Its chest huffed and heaved and it swished its tail angrily. Stephen let go and the unicorn raced laps in the sink before zeroing on the drain. It dove, but couldn't fit beyond its head.

"Settle, settle," said Stephen.

At his feet, the cat meowed.

"Not now, Missus."

Stephen ran the water and reached for the cat shampoo from beneath the sink. It was a natural reaction; Missus often got into the garden outside and tracked dirt all over the condo. The unicorn slowed its fight under the soft touch. Once clean, Stephen dried it with a hand towel.

"There, now you're a clean ... oh my God," he said, the severity once again striking him.

He stared at the calmed eyes of the unicorn and the unicorn stared back at him. Missus had hopped onto the toilet seat, almost dropping into the unexpected opening, and stared at the unicorn from across the short counter space. Missus hissed and swatted. The unicorn turned and swung its horn around at the incoming paw. Missus yowled and jumped down from the toilet.

"Serves you right!" Stephen shouted nervously and then laughed. "Easy now," he said and reached out again, now aware that the horn was a weapon. The unicorn let him touch and then lift. "We have to call someone."

Missus watched, curious and jealous, but didn't mount an attack. Stephen placed the unicorn on the table and picked up his cellphone. Duty first.

He scrolled for a number from his contact list. It rang and a familiar voice answered, "Hey Janey," he coughed, "I think I'm dying here," he coughed again and listened, "Yeah, it's Stephen." He listened awhile and then waited, "Oh good, Ken is good, I'm sure I'll feel better by Thursday, if not tomorrow. Buh bye."

He hit end. He didn't like lying, but it seemed reasonable given the peculiar situation. He scrolled through his list for the next call. He needed someone smart, someone that knew about animals, someone ...

A knock hit on his door.

"Missus, be good," he said as he picked up the unicorn and put it inside his wooden roll-top breadbox on the counter next to the coffeemaker, "Just for a secy," he added, speaking to the imprisoned unicorn.

He rushed to the door and looked through the peephole. It was a woman in a business suit.

"Hello, my name is Layla Oates, can I come in and speak with you?" she asked, her voice sweet, yet powerful.

"It's not a good time, what's this about?"

"Sir, I'm with the Environmental Protection Agency and I just need a few words, please," Layla held up a laminate within a leather holder.

"Oh all right," Stephen opened the door, "What is it?"

"This will only take a minute, Mister..."

"Dreger, Stephen Dreger."

"This will only take a minute Stephen," said Layla. She pushed out her chest; the top button had popped to reveal pillowy mounds of motherly flesh. Her skirt was short and tight against firm thighs and she wore high heels.

An unreasonable outfit for an EPA agent out on foot, Stephen thought.

"Yes, all right, come in," he stepped aside and pointed to a chair next to a steel table of 50's diner fashion. Layla sat and Stephen fought his tendency to offer a beverage and waited.

"Your cat is certainly focussed on your breadbox," said Layla looking at the swirling tail and the lowered gaze.

"I keep her treats there," said Stephen, he closed the door and snatched his cat. He held Missus on his lap as he sat across from Layla, "Now, what can I do for the EPA?"

"Well, Mr. Dreger, Stephen, this is going to sound odd, but have you had any wildlife coming up through your drainage?"

The question struck like a stake. *How does she know?* He hadn't even called anybody yet.

"Nope," he said and felt his cheeks darken a shade.

"You wouldn't be lying, would you?" Layla pouted these words, leaning back on her chair.

"Nope, never lie. Friends call me Abraham, like Lincoln. Never lie," Stephen rambled, wishing he knew how to shut up when nervous.

"Oh come now," said Layla, she moved her fingers to the hem of her skirt. "Are you telling me, nothing came up your pipes today?"

"Nothing but the usual. Just H-two-oh and whatever they add in to keep it fresh and clean."

"I thought we could be friends."

"We're getting along fine," said Stephen as he squeezed Missus and the cat burst from his arms and raced to the breadbox. There was a scratching against wood, from within.

"I think I'll get your pussy a treat," Layla jumped to her feet as if she wore Nike and not Jimmy Choo.

"No!" Stephen shouted and reached an arm around Layla's waist. "She's had her treat for the day," he said. Leaning close, her hair smelled of apple shampoo and her neck smelled of something else, expensive and yet complimenting to the fruity scent.

"Pussy's had her treat? Every pussy's had her treat but mine," Layla whispered.

It all came together, her pouting, the fingering of cloth edges, the popped button, her word choice, everything. Stephen pulled Layla away from the breadbox, laughing.

"You got the wrong guy, sugar."

Layla dropped back onto her seat, "You think so?" There was a flicker in her eye as she adjusted to the circumstance.

Stephen fell into his own chair, smiling wide. *Beauty is a bitch when it works and beauty is a bigger bitch when it doesn't,* he thought.

"Yeah, I don't ..." Stephen started and watched Layla lean and slide forward, her skirt riding upwards against her upper thighs. A furry tail dropped behind her seat, swishing and swirling.

He gulped and let his eyes drink in the woman once again, all the same until he got to her chin. A fat pink tongue leapt from the bovid jaw. He looked into the dark wide-set eyes and every wet dream he'd ever had sat before him. A beast woman, the head of a satyr, body of a goddess. Her fingers roved about her collar, closing the button as fur sprouted, soft and inviting, beneath. She'd hid the prize below like a candy wrapper hiding a sweet.

"I mean ... I should be getting back to ..." Stephen shook his head. "You can't take it, I found it."

"No I can't, but you could give it to me, of your free will, you could," Layla's voice was still sweet, but it had a hardness about it. "How would you like to trade me?"

"Trade for what?" Stephen asked, unaware that his chin nodded slightly and his own pants had become tight around the groin.

"Trade a little something you found this morning, something hiding in your breadbox, for something so sticky and wonderful that you'll never forget it? Something of my dreams for something of your dreams?"

"You were a woman," Stephen mumbled. If Stephen had an unfulfilled fantasy, this creature, this Layla, had become it. Just seconds ago there was a pretty face riding atop the body hiding below fine silk underthings, a woman, beautiful, but just another woman ... besides, the creature, the glorious satyr is of myth, like a sasquatch, or a mermaid, or a ... unicorn. "How did you know?"

"Hush," said Layla and rose, guiding him upward with a strong hand. She led him through the only other open door in the condo.

Missus ignored them and jumped up to the breadbox, pawing at the hidden sound, as the bedroom door closed behind them.

*

  Unicornado! 

Layla Oates left Stephen Dreger's condominium with a unicorn in her pocket. The creature she'd worn melted from her face, the perfect beauty she worn upon arrival back in place. Until a meeting, one had to guess, but lust is complicated.

It was a comfort to feel so pretty, but there was only so much room in that silky flesh for the figure she'd worn the weeks leading up. She stroked the animal in her pocket, thinking she ought to celebrate. It was a fair trade, fantasy for fact, although Stephen would forever confuse which was which.

Layla walked along the clean streets toward the alleyway next to the Tico Variety. Pleasing Stephen had taken a lot of work and Layla entered the store, exiting minutes later with a bottle of Evian and a brown paper bag. She drank back the Evian and recycled the bottle in the alleyway bin. She twisted the cap on the bottle within the brown paper bag and inhaled the familiar scent. After a small sip, Layla pulled aside a flap of cardboard that leaned against the wall.

The corner of Tico Variety's shimmered and Layla stepped down through, crouching until she'd travelled clear of the structure. Layla snapped her fingers and the shimmery doorway behind her solidified. She continued along the stone hallway.

She tossed her jacket and blouse. She wiggled out of her skirt and continued, sipping from the heavy bottle of Seagram's gin as she strode past the various windows.

Visiting always took away some of the mysticism. Layla decided after she'd replaced the unicorn on the shelf she would visit a different creation and watch, maybe a fledgling, to see if any progress occurred in her absence.

She pulled the complacent unicorn from her pocket, "It's a shame you didn't work out, you should've grown like your brethren, maybe you'd still ... oh no bother," Layla kissed the unicorn and it hardened into a figurine. She placed it back on the shelf and moved on, wearing just her shoes and her silky undergarments.

She slugged back on the gin and stared at the last picture frame window of a never-ending hallway. The landscape was reddish under the close sun; a world full of hard decisions as life hadn't moved beyond flora.

Layla grew bored, put her lips to bottle and drowned her loneliness and uncertainty as she sat down with her back against the cool stone wall.

*

The beautiful woman awoke, her breasts hung below the unlatched bra, Victoria no longer keeping her secrets. Vomit covered the silk and the soft gently veined flesh. A bottle hiding within a brown paper bag lay on its side next to her. A small dribble of gin lay on the stone floor, but very little.

The beautiful woman massaged her scalp; the apple scent of her hair mingled with her hangover and induced a series of dry-heaves from deep in her gut. She'd forgotten to eat before drinking.

She looked at the shelving on the far wall. Several figures were missing, most didn't mix well, and worry fluttered alongside her hangover.

"Not good," she moaned, looking about the hall-way, hoping she hadn't tossed retired creatures back into existence, again.

Pushing her back against the wall for leverage, the beautiful woman got to her feet and looked through a window onto a young red world. There was chaos, elements and creatures fighting for their rights as figments of the greater imagination. There was blood and there would be more, a ruined thought.

The beautiful woman turned away; it could heal or fade. Two choices, she had the power to let it.

After all, it was only one world of many.

Don't Let It End

John Goodrich

Coleridge wrote that Kubla Khan created a great pleasure dome. Nickolaus Passionate wondered if the poet, in his drugged state, could have imagined anything as wonderful as the Garden of the Children of Ereshgikal.

Above him, ancient trees created a magnificent canopy of scintillating greens. In those mighty branches that had never known the axe, a village had sprouted.

Made of live, twisted branches, the small dwellings sprouted like fragile flowers. The Children of Ereshgikal swooped from branch to branch on their mighty, magnificent wings. How beautiful, to see those winged men and women diving from the great branches, opening their breathtaking pinions, swooping from place to place.

Below the trees were exquisite stone chairs, rubbed to an impeccably smooth finish, functional and irresistibly comfortable. Nick reclined one on, two of the beautiful Children running their warm, pleasing hands up and down his torso.

And Isaac was working some magic on Nick's cock.

Isaac's tongue twirled the sensitive underside of Nick's penis, bringing on a shudder of pleasure.

Ah, this is wonderful, the best part of the Garden. Nick had never felt so relaxed, had his needs so well attended to. Not even when he'd been a successful writer.

Isaac pushed forward and began a deep sucking action, and Nick's eyes rolled up in his head. It was almost too much. He was fast approaching the point of no return when Isaac withdrew. Nick counted the heartbeats until Isaac returned to finish him off. When it didn't happen, he opened his eyes. Isaac was gazing up at him.

Isaac slowly and deliberately turned Nick over, and buried his face between Nick's ass cheeks. His tongue action was hot and sloppy, and soon Nick was dripping.

"Time for something special," Isaac said.

"It's always special with you," Nickolaus said, turning back, his anus still dripping with Isaac's saliva.

"The Unicorn wants to make your acquaintance," Isaac said with a secret smile.

"Bahemuka," Nickolaus breathed.

A legend, even among the Children of Ereshgikal. Tall, dark as an old-fashioned telephone, Bahemuka was called the Unicorn because his cock was so large it resembled a horn.

The hands that had caressed Nick now held him, and he was lifted, face down, as if he was a crowd-surfer. Nick was confused, and a little afraid. But Isaac, hands keeping Nick's shoulders up, looked him in the eye.

"Have fun."

What was that supposed to mean? Nick was erect but nothing was around him but air. He wanted Isaac, he was nervous about the Unicorn. What was going to happen?

He heard the rush of mighty wings only the instant before they were on him. He was grasped by firm hands and pulled into the air. Nick gasped as the ground rushed past, and the wings beat to climb with the weight of two. The feeling of flight was glorious, liberating, terrifyingly erotic.

He felt a mighty presence pressing between his ass cheeks. He laughed. This was ridiculous. He was flying, and the pilot wanted to have him in mid-air?

"I have wanted you since I first saw you," Bahemuka's voice rumbled in Nick's ear, sending shivers down to his still-erect cock.

Nick regarded the perilous height at which they were soaring. How terrifying, and at the same time how arousing. This would be like no other experience.

"Yes!" He screamed it to the wind in their faces, wondered if the others could hear him, a hundred feet below. "Yes, I'm all yours!"

Those powerful arms shifted him, until the tip of the Unicorn's horn was poised right at Nick's anus. Nickolaus relaxed, spreading himself as best he could, welcoming that tremendous member.

It slid into him slowly. Oh God, he was stretched to the limit, filled gloriously to overflowing, stuffed in a way he never had been before.

The sensation was indescribable. The rhythmic beating of the Unicorn's wings made his body rise and fall, each beat moving his magnificent cock ever so slightly. It was delicious, made all the more wonderful by the sensation of flight, the safeness of the Unicorn's strong arms wrapping around him.

"This is the power of the Garden," the Unicorn said in Nick's ear. "The strength of love, the togetherness of souls of all kinds. If allowed, we could remake the world, in peace and harmony, compassion for all. Everyone."

Nick had once thought of himself as religious, but this was a greater, more spiritual happening that he had ever experienced. The dizzying height, the powerful words of love, the enormous phallus impaling him, each a tremendous experience, now made this all a greater, more loving experience than any he had experienced as a bigoted, small-minded so-called Christian.

He looked down at the green and beautiful Garden below him. How few had experienced its joys, its kindnesses, its love. Bahemuka was right. Together, they could drown the world in love and compassion, change it, stop wars, destroy greed and hate.

How few had soared with a magnificent, powerful lover, felt truly loved without reservation, so deeply.

Nick brought himself out of his own reverie by laughing at the pun. Deep love indeed.

The Unicorn's wing beats made a delicious frisson unlike thrusting. Nick's own cock was still stiff, even with the wind rushing past it, sticking out like a keel below them.

Ah, God, don't let this ever end!

Bahemuka began to grunt, and Nick could do nothing but gasp his own pleasure to the atmosphere. The wingbeats got more frequent, and Nick knew that the Unicorn, and he, were coming to their climax.

At the moment Nick felt the hot gush of semen deep inside him, the Unicorn folded his wings, and they plummeted, like two entangled stones, toward the treetops. Nick's stomach was left somewhere above them, at and the same time he was coming like mad, the fear and exhilaration combining to make his own orgasm incapacitatingly powerful.

The greens of the Garden rushed toward them, and Nick was all but out of his head. If he was going to die, he was deliriously happy.

At the last minute, the great pinions opened, and Bahemuka held him tight as their weight increased. They glided, less than six feet off the ground, fast as a speeding motorcycle, as Bahemuka's cock slowly deflated, then slipped out of Nick. He felt lonely, empty, wished that he could never lose that connection.

The unicorn slowed, lifted, then settled onto his feet. Nick wasn't sure his legs would support him, but strong, dark arms held him up until he was steady enough to walk on his own.

"How was it?" Isaac asked, when Nick finally tottered into his arms.

He was about to answer when the peace of the Garden was shattered by the stutter of gunfire.

People scattered, shrieking. Many took to the air, only to be battered down by a hail of bullets. Blood rained as the Children of Ereshgikal were punched out of the air, their feathers drifting delicately after their bodies slammed to the earth.

Everyone was screaming. Men with guns were pouring into the Garden. Hard-faced, men with automatic rifles.

"Abominations!" they shouted in their rage. "Consorters with abominations!"

Automatic gunfire rattled, people wailed.

Nick could do nothing but stare in horror. Isaac sprang into action, snapping his wings open and charging. He was greeted with bullets. Nick screamed in horror as four bullets punched through Isaac's torso, spraying Nick with hot blood. He stood and charged the advancing phalanx of men, but he was clubbed down with a casual strike of a buttstock.

*

He work to the smell of smoke, the sight of the glorious, ancient trees of the Garden burning. Aside from the crackle of fire, there was only eerie silence. He crawled over to Isaac's body, cradled his head in his lap.

Isaac coughed, opened his eyes. The bullet holes were the size of Nick's thumb. They still bled, weakly.

He stared down into Isaac's eyes, aware that he was utterly helpless. They had no medical facilities, and even if they did, he had no time. What would he do without Isaac?

Isaac opened his mouth, whispered something. Nickolaus bent his head to hear.

"Tell me a story." Isaac's voice was barely a whisper.

A story. His lover's last request. There was only one to tell.

"Once there was a man named Nickolaus, and Isaac, whose love saved his soul. And they loved each other very much, and they were not ashamed of who they were." The tears ran down his face. Isaac's breathing grew more erratic. "And they lived and they loved and they were happy for a very long time. And no one was cruel to them. They lived for a long time, happy and kind to everyone."

"Don't ..." Pink foam formed on Isaac's lips. He was too weak to wipe it off. "Don't let it end this way."

And then he was gone, his chest still, and Nickolaus was weeping his loneliness to the smoky and uncaring air.

Unicorn Prayers

Mary Pletsch

Will the unicorn be willing to serve thee, or abide by thy crib? — Job 39:9 (KJV)

𝕿he rec room door slammed open. Matthew squealed like a little girl before he could catch himself. A dagger-shaped wedge of light stabbed into the room, illuminating the three teenagers sitting in a chalk circle on the linoleum floor.

By candlelight, the objects in the middle of the circle had seemed exotic and dangerous: a smoking incense stick in a wooden holder, a shell filled with salt, and the Communion goblet from Saint Luke's United Church profaned with Jack Daniels. In the glow from the hallway, they looked like props from a low-budget movie. The salt had come from his own mother's salt shaker, lying abandoned on its side just outside the circle. Matthew had no idea how he was going to explain to his dad, who happened to be the minister at Saint Luke's, what the group was doing.

But the figure silhouetted in the doorway was too short to be his dad. Matthew let out a breath he hadn't realized he'd been holding. His parents were still out of the house, helping to host a relative's stag and doe party. The hosts had to clean the reception hall afterwards, so Matthew didn't expect them back until two or three in the morning.

Matthew had also expected his nine-year-old cousin to stay asleep in her bed all night. That was where his plans had gone haywire.

"Matty?" Lilly asked, staring at the other two teens in the circle. She looked so vulnerable in her pink princess pyjamas, particularly with her most recent bruise still yellow on her left arm. "You didn't tell me you were having friends over."

Friends was maybe a strong word to describe Kendra and Ricky. Matthew had only started talking to them a couple weeks ago. Or, rather, they had only just started talking to him. And the reason Kendra had deigned to speak to Matthew in the first place was because Ricky wanted real church stuff for this ritual. Ricky was already on probation for breaking into the community center, and Matthew was a minister's kid.

Matthew glanced warily at the other teens. Kendra was sneering. Ricky was scowling.

If Kendra had asked him to do this last year, Matthew would have said no.

Last year, Matthew and his best friend Tom had been inseparable. But over the summer, Tom had gone away to a camp run by his family's church, the Blood of Christ Christian Fellowship, and Lilly had come to stay with Matthew's family. When Tom came home from camp, he was no longer convinced that the United Church was Christian enough for God's liking. Tom said Matthew's dad was going to Hell, and Matthew too, if he didn't convert to the BOCCF and worship God as He wished to be worshipped.

Matthew had tried praying about it, but it seemed that God, like Tom, had stopped talking to him. Either that, or there was no God, and all his prayers just fell into the night like pebbles into a deep, dark well.

Meanwhile, Matthew had hoped that Lilly would just be with them for the summer. But by the time autumn came, Lilly's dad was in prison awaiting trial, and Lilly's mom was ... well, nobody knew. Her cell phone had been disconnected, and the last time Matthew had been over to her crummy apartment, the people inside said they'd never heard of her.

So the spare room in Matthew's house had morphed into a little girl's castle. The blue quilt on the bed had been replaced by a fluffy comforter covered in rainbows and unicorns. A brand-new toy box held more than forty grungy plastic ponies, some with Mohawk manes and bob tails, others sporting tattoos in blue ink and black marker. All Lilly had brought with her was a duffel bag containing a single change of clothing and those old ponies, most of them unicorns.

Matthew had expected Lilly to be difficult. Bratty. Loud. The typical offspring of a drug-addled mother and a father too quick to anger. Instead, he'd hardly noticed her except at mealtimes. She spent most of her time holed up in her room, doing God only knew what. Reading, probably. Matthew had seen her stuffing books from the public library into her backpack. Big, dusty things that weighed a ton.

School had started almost two months ago. Lilly hadn't made any friends as far as Matthew could tell.

She always came straight home after school, always alone, three times with bruises rising on her limbs. Matthew's parents had met with her teacher twice. Matthew had overheard the word *bullied* whispered between his mother and father when they thought he wasn't listening.

School was no treat for Matthew, but at least he wasn't getting beat up or anything. Tom had a new social circle, the kids from the BOCCF youth group, and Matthew was explicitly not invited. Matthew tried hanging out with different people, but he always felt like an unwanted intruder, right up until Kendra asked if he could get his hands on a Communion goblet, a pair of candlesticks, and maybe the big cross from the church altar.

Kendra was on her own, too, ever since she dumped her old friends: Tiffani Vanderhaydn, Theo Cazelar and Roger Chu. Last year, all four of them had been openly Wiccan, which repelled Tom and left Matthew feeling strangely fascinated when he saw them sitting in a circle on the front lawn of the school, holding hands, meditating or praying or whatever they did. Matthew felt guilty watching them, as though they could infect him with the Devil's will if he looked too long, and yet he was always so curious about them.

Kendra hadn't talked much about why she'd abandoned her former friends. All she'd say was that Tiffani, Theo and Roger were "fluffy-bunny white-lighters" who "couldn't hear the velvet sonatas of darkness." Matthew didn't know what that meant, but Kendra now called herself "a witch, not a Wiccan," and she'd started hanging out with Ricky Allard.

Ricky was new in school. He was a tall kid with stringy brown hair worn long and a battered leather jacket he never took off. Rumour had it that he'd been kicked out of his old school. Other rumours said he'd done time in Pine River, the juvenile detention facility. Kids said he'd sent a guy to hospital, stolen cars, ran a web site with naked pictures of girls from his classes. Matthew wasn't sure if any of those stories were true, and he didn't have the guts to ask.

Matthew had agreed to get Kendra and Ricky their stuff, on two conditions. He wanted to be part of whatever they wanted it for, and he wanted them to do it at his house. Since Matthew lived next door to Saint Luke's United Church, it was easy for him to take his dad's keys, go to the church, and take the stuff. He planned to return it again before his parents got home, before anyone even noticed it had been gone. Ricky, for all he acted tough, must really not have wanted to get caught stealing again, because he hadn't argued with Matthew's conditions.

Matthew was ninety-nine percent certain he already knew what was going to happen during tonight's summoning. Kendra was going to do her Wiccan stuff (though she'd call it "gothic witch ritual" and use a lot of adjectives like "shadow" and "negative"), Ricky would play the dark priest, and then they'd sit in the rec room with the lights off and wait. When Ricky got bored, he'd claim that the candles flickering or the incense going out was a sign of a demon's presence, and then he'd either pass around the whiskey-filled chalice or drink it all himself.

But the other one percent, the part that sometimes wondered if Tom was right, had pricked at his conscience when he'd taken the chalice and candlesticks from Saint Luke's. It had nudged him again when Ricky had pulled out a flask and filled the chalice with whiskey, giggling about perverting the Lord's tools to the service of Satan. It had given him a swift kick in the rear when Ricky announced that the purpose of tonight's ritual was to summon an infernal servant to do their bidding.

Matthew told himself that if they *did* summon an actual demon, he'd reaffirm his commitment to Christ on the spot. Given that God hadn't been paying much attention to Matthew's prayers lately, Matthew could totally be forgiven for doubting the reality of angels and demons. But when wondering whether God existed, well, proof of the Devil would be almost as convincing as proof of God.

Matthew forced a smile on his face. "Lilly, this is Ricky and Kendra, and you should be in bed. It's almost midnight."

"I thought you said we'd be undisturbed," Ricky hissed.

Matthew shivered. Ricky could beat the crap out of him, if he wanted to, and letting the summoning ritual get wrecked would probably make him want to.

Lilly shuffled right up to the edge of the circle and put her hand on Matthew's shoulder. "I want to play too."

Kendra rolled her eyes under their heavily made-up lids. "Are you *kidding* me?"

"Sorry," Matthew mumbled. It was hard for him to speak any louder. His stomach was churning so badly he felt as though he'd spew his dinner out onto the floor if he opened his mouth any wider. He couldn't bring himself to look Ricky in the eye. "I'll get rid of her."

"You do and I'll tell your dad what you guys were doing."

Lilly spoke in a tone so confident and calm that Matthew forgot all about his stomach. He goggled at his little cousin instead. She met his gaze and trapped it, pinning him in place while her words sank in.

He'd expected her to yell. He'd expected her to cry. He hadn't expected a little girl to threaten him like a grownup would.

Matthew thought fast. "I don't think you want to do this, Lilly. It might be scary."

Lilly didn't leave. She walked right through the chalk circle and plopped herself down between Matthew and Kendra.

"It's cool," Ricky said, much to Matthew's surprise. Matthew stared at Ricky, and Ricky leered at Lilly. "She can be our virgin sacrifice."

Kendra barked laughter. Matthew felt his stomach turn over again. He was pretty sure Ricky was joking, but he'd never been comfortable with the way Ricky talked about girls. He especially didn't like Ricky talking about his nine-year-old cousin like that.

It was almost enough to make Matthew volunteer to be the virgin sacrifice. He'd told Ricky and Kendra that he'd done it with a girl he'd met at summer camp, but that was a total lie. He just didn't want to sound like a loser next to Ricky's list of conquests and Kendra's story about performing "the Great Rite in fact" with Roger Chu.

In fact, right now Matthew wanted to tell Ricky that nobody was sacrificing anything, except that Ricky had just taken a butterfly knife out of his pocket. Kendra opened her purse and took out a box of bandages and a bottle of peroxide. Matthew tried to convince himself it would feel just like a paper cut — kiddie stuff, really — but his brain kept dwelling on what would be worse: being expected to cut his own flesh, or trusting Ricky or Kendra to do it for him.

Lilly met Ricky's gaze with that same unshakable calm. "If you want my blood, I want to summon a unicorn."

Kendra rolled her eyes. "Oh, for Hel's sake."

Ricky grinned unpleasantly. "I'll make you a deal ... what's your name again?"

"Lilly."

"Lilly," Ricky repeated. The name sounded different when he said it. It was as though his mouth were filled with slime, coating Lilly's name until it slid from his lips, all slick and filthy. "You can join us and we'll help you call whatever you wish. Then you help us call whatever *we* wish."

Lilly's brow furrowed.

All of a sudden Matthew was sure that everything he'd heard from Tom had been true. The Devil was real, lurking in the shadows of the rec room, waiting for good Christian boys and girls to do some wicked deed that would let him into their hearts. And Matthew was going to Hell for putting poor, vulnerable Lilly in the path of a guy like Ricky.

"Okay," Lilly said.

Matthew's heart stopped.

Ricky's grin broadened until it was a wonder the corners of his mouth didn't split and bleed. Matthew was reminded of those deep-ocean fish, the ones that were all jaws and teeth. "I mean it. You have to do *anything* we say." His eyes slid over to Matthew.

Matthew heard his pulse return with a vengeance, hammering furiously in his chest. He told himself this was all a game. Kids talked tough all the time. Ricky was just trying to scare Lilly. Or maybe Ricky was trying to scare *him*. Still, Matthew couldn't stop his brain from imagining just what kind of stuff Ricky might ask Lilly to do.

"But I get to summon first?" Lilly asked.

"Yeah." Ricky leaned forward and held out his hand across the circle. "What do you say? Do we have a deal?"

"Deal." Matthew shuddered to see Lilly's little hand, its fingernails painted with pale lavender polish, engulfed by Ricky's sweaty palm. They shook.

"Okay," Ricky said, releasing her at last. "Show us how to summon a unicorn."

Kendra rolled her eyes again.

Lilly reached out, grasped the whiskey-filled chalice, and climbed to her feet. With her long blonde hair and the silver cup in her hands, she looked to Matthew like one of the princesses in the fantasy stories that Tom had tried to make him feel guilty for reading.

We call, three to sing you, across the plains of time,
We call, three to bring you, across the years of space,
We call, three to wing you, across to where we wait,
The rhyme to fill this place, to break your gate.

Kendra stopped making goofy faces behind Lilly's back. "Where did she learn that?" she hissed.

Matthew thought Kendra was probably just jealous — her 'sonatas of darkness' always sounded more silly than spooky — but he was also a little freaked out that Lilly had learned such a creepy poem by heart.

Now answer three who need you, desert's wrath,
Now answer three who lead you, punish vice,
Now answer, three who feed you, eyeteeth bared,
Your path, your sacrifice, are now prepared!

Lilly chanted like a minister in church, except this was like no church service Matthew had ever attended. His dad never put this kind of enthusiasm into his Sunday chanting. Lilly's voice sped up in a relentless rhythm, but paradoxically it seemed to Matthew as though time itself were slowing down. He felt a floating sensation, like a little kid in a swimming pool buoyed up by water wings.

Matthew noticed that the smoke from the incense had stopped streaming straight up and started twisting in a distinctive corkscrew pattern.

The incense exploded. Matthew didn't know incense could do that, but there was no other explanation for the sudden flash of light, followed by thick, billowing clouds of grey smoke that smelled like sandalwood and tasted like bitter ash in his mouth. Matthew rubbed at his eyes. He could hear Kendra coughing and Ricky swearing.

"Lilly?" Matthew called, despite the way the smoke invaded his mouth, stinging his throat and clouding his lungs. He had a sudden terrible image of fiery embers searing Lilly's tender skin, or a demon reaching out to swallow her whole. He moved his arms through the smoke like a swimmer in water, as though he could shove the clouds behind him to clear his view.

Mercifully, a small figure became visible through the smoke in front of him. Lilly, looking back at him, smiling ...

... her small hand, with its lavender fingernails, reaching up to a glossy black shoulder.

Something else took shape out of the dimness. A neck reaching up far above Lilly's blonde curls. A coffin-shaped head moving down to rest on Lilly's shoulder. A huge black eye. A horn like a scimitar.

Matthew jumped to his feet, leaping backwards. He realized, too late, that he'd forgotten about the chalk circle. Kendra had said that it was supposed to contain whatever they summoned, which made no sense to Matthew when they were all inside the circle with the demon.

He had to back up a few steps more to get far enough away to take in the whole creature without turning his head. Matthew wasn't exactly sure what he was looking at, but it wasn't one of the happy white unicorns from Lilly's blanket.

It stood facing the same direction as Lilly, who was barely tall enough to reach the thing's stomach, and craned its head around to look at her. Its body occupied the diameter of the chalk circle. Its tail was long and slender and covered with short fur except for the tip, which was a charcoal tassel. When it lashed its tail, the tassel struck Ricky in the face. Ricky spluttered, spitting out wiry hairs.

Its feet — the front right of which had landed in the shell, cracking it and spilling a pool of salt onto the floor — were cloven like a goat's and decorated with the same long black hair as its tail-tip. Its mane was short and thick, standing upright on its neck like Lilly's old toy ponies with their haircuts and marker tattoos. It had jagged stripes under the fur of its shoulders, slashing its hide into brindled patterns of sable and sand.

Matthew had an uncomfortable realization that the ink marks on Lilly's ponies might not be a little kid's random scribbling after all. If he remembered right, they were remarkably accurate imitations of the patterns on the creature in front of him.

The unicorn had fangs, horrible ones, not like a cat's eyeteeth or even a dog's. White ivory longer than the blade on Ricky's butterfly knife. Longer, sharper, and serrated like his dad's saw.

It sidled, moving to face Lilly through the rapidly clearing smoke. The unicorn bowed its head and that wicked horn came to a stop over the little girl's heart. Matthew could see the divot in the front of her pink princess pyjamas where the sharp point pressed.

Matthew took an instant to pray to a God he still doubted. Then he lowered his shoulder, bodychecking Lilly out of the monster's way. She fell. He tumbled on top of her. Matthew rolled, keeping his own body between himself and his squirming cousin.

He stared upwards, transfixed, into the impossible black depths of the unicorn's eyes.

The creature drew up its head, as though startled. It snorted. Hot breath like a desert wind abraded his forehead, scoured his cheeks. It was like sticking his head in an oven. His face stung. He thought he could feel blood oozing to the surface of his raw flesh and seeping over his cheekbones. Distantly, Matthew felt Lilly squirming out from beneath him.

"No!" Lilly's voice came from a distance. "Not Matty." She was right behind him now, lifting his arm. "Man," Lilly insisted, squeezing Matthew's hand.

The creature's horn swung towards Kendra.

From the corner of his eye Matthew saw Lilly plaster her other hand over Kendra's hair. "Woman." He didn't know why Kendra let her get away with that until he recognized that Kendra sat in a spreading puddle of her own urine. Kendra's eyes bulged like those of a beached fish.

"And child," Lilly said, releasing Kendra to put her free hand over her heart.

Ricky's voice came from far away. "What the fuck," he was saying, over and over. "What the fuck *what the fuck* WHAT THE FU ..."

The unicorn glanced over its shoulder, whinnied, and looked back at Lilly.

Lilly smiled. "Sacrifice."

Lilly's monster flared its nostrils, showing brilliant red inner linings. It pivoted in place, delicately positioning its hooves, until it faced Ricky. Matthew ducked as its tail lashed over his head. The tassel slapped Kendra across the cheek, but she didn't respond.

Matthew didn't have time to worry about Kendra, or watch the red welt rising on her cheek. Lilly walked up to her monster's shoulder. The unicorn whuffled. The thing flared its nostrils and inhaled an inch above Lilly's head. Blonde bangs flew up into its nose as it lowered its head. The point of its horn came to a stop right between Ricky's eyes.

For a second, Matthew thought the unicorn was just trying to psyche Ricky out, which was pretty funny considering Ricky's usual sense of humour. Then a glimmer of red welled up at the tip of the horn. A single red tear tracked down the side of Ricky's nose.

"She knows your soul," Lilly said.

"This was supposed to be a game," Ricky moaned. "You were supposed to do what I said. You, Matthew, Kendra, you were all supposed to do what I said."

Matthew didn't know what Ricky had been planning to say. He wasn't sure if he wanted to know. Ricky

had been very good at playing with power and fear. Lilly had been better.

"You wanted to scare Matty and screw Kendra." Lilly put her hands on his hips.

Ricky's mouth trembled, but he didn't deny it. Matthew expected Kendra to be outraged, but she didn't seem capable of expressing outrage or anything else. She sat behind the unicorn's hindquarters like a discarded doll, and Matthew wondered where her mind had gone. It didn't seem to be present any longer.

"Tell Matty," Lilly said, her voice a low whisper. "Tell Matty what went through your mind when you saw me."

Matthew didn't know, and didn't want to know. Ricky never managed to say. The unicorn took a step back from Ricky, and the bigger boy promptly jumped to his feet, screaming swear words, kicking over the incense stick in its burner. The smoke went out, but Matthew could still feel that spiraling wind, here in what should be an enclosed basement room. The candles flickered.

The monster's tail lashed, slapping Kendra's catatonic form. Its ears flattened against its skull. Its eyes narrowed.

Ricky's eyes darted between the small window behind him and the hallway door. The unicorn stood between Ricky and the portal. Matthew imagined Ricky trying to decide if he could climb out the window faster than he could reach the stairs. Ricky inched towards the window, probably in an attempt to see how it opened.

The unicorn's head darted forward.

Logic deserted Ricky. He shrieked and bolted for the door, arms flailing. Matthew realized the creature's feet had not moved. It was playing with Ricky. Herding him.

Ricky ran left, around the outside of the circle. Had he been smart, he could have run right, keeping Lilly and Matthew between him and the monster. His cunning had abandoned him, burned away by fear.

The unicorn's hindquarters bunched, and under the guard hairs, the markings on its hide curved and twisted themselves into patterns that seemed to Matthew like ancient cuneiform. What kind of poem might be inscribed on such a creature?

An answer jumped unbidden into his mind.

The hymns of retribution.

The unicorn leapt, vaulting towards Ricky.

Matthew's father had been a New Testament kind of minister, the sort who encouraged his congregation to turn the other cheek. Tom's church had gone in for the fire and brimstone preaching. Matthew remembered sitting in a pew next to Tom after a sleepover at his best friend's house, listening to a sermon detailing the wrath of God.

He had never understood the wrath of God until tonight.

Ricky fell, and Ricky screamed, and as Ricky flipped onto his back, hands slapping ineffectually at the unicorn's face, Ricky begged for his life in a language not made of words. Ricky pleaded in *nos* and whimpering noises and the occasional strangled *please* gargled up through snot and tears and a mouthful of blood.

The unicorn watched him, and then it looked to Lilly, and Lilly moved her hand and her will was done.

"Help," Ricky gurgled as the unicorn hoisted him aloft, skewered through the chest by its scimitar horn.

Kendra did not help. Her paralysis broke, as though a witch had snapped her fingers and released Kendra from her spell. Kendra lurched to her feet and ran out the door, leaving droplets of what Matthew was pretty sure was pee in her wake. Matthew heard her steps growing fainter and fainter, then a slamming noise that he guessed was the screen door on the back porch. He wished he could run, too. But he was already home, and he had Lilly to think of.

"It's okay," Lilly said, squeezing Matthew's hand. "He had it coming."

Matthew wanted to say that judgment was the Lord's, but he still felt uncertain about the existence of God. *Vengeance is mine, saith Lilly*, Matthew thought and laughed hysterically.

Matthew watched the unicorn fling its head once, twice. Ricky's body slid off its horn on the second attempt and landed at Lilly's feet. Matthew had thought he'd see the corpse fly across the room, maybe shattering the mirror above the couch. The truth was nothing so dramatic. Ricky's body crumpled into a lumpy heap, like the burlap potato sacks in his grandmother's basement. The only difference was the slow, sticky red tint that began to turn Kendra's pool of pee from lemonade to blood orange.

Now we defile this sacred vessel. That's what Ricky had said when he filled the chalice with whiskey.

Matthew looked at Ricky's corpse facedown in pee and wondered if you could get any more defiled than that.

He wasn't sure how long he stared at the body. How was he going to explain that to his parents? Matthew puzzled on that question for a long time before he realized that maybe he should be asking what sharing the rec room with a corpse would do to an already traumatized little girl.

When he looked up, though, he didn't see Lilly any more. Matthew ran to the hallway door, searching frantically up and down the corridor. He saw only the unicorn's tail disappearing into the stairwell.

Matthew should be relieved that the monster was going away, but all he could think was that he shouldn't let it get *out*, and where was Lilly? He chased after the unicorn instinctively, hoping he could come up with a solution before he caught up to it. Instead, he almost skidded right past the stairs, and by the time he caught his balance the unicorn was already at the top of the stairs, its forelegs in the living room, its hindquarters standing on the top step.

Lilly sat upon its back.

"Lilly!" Matthew shouted.

She turned around, waved to him, and smiled.

Matthew ran up the stairs. He could hear the thud of the unicorn's hooves as it picked its way across the living room floor. Each hoofbeat sounded like a judge's gavel slamming down.

"Lilly, wait!" Matthew panted. He staggered into the living room, staring in horror at the unicorn standing on its hind legs before the front door, ready to beat it down with its forelegs.

And, surprisingly, Lilly waited. She tugged at its mane; the unicorn went back down on all fours. It craned its neck to stare at Matthew and whuffled.

Through the windows of the living room, Matthew could see a storm raging. Sheets of rain cascaded down the panes, blurring the distant flash of lightning. Streetlights barely illuminated the low, heavy clouds. Matthew hadn't noticed anything more than a few clouds when Kendra and Ricky had arrived, two hours and a lifetime ago.

"You can't go out in that," Matthew stammered. He gestured helplessly at the unicorn. Lilly summoned it; Lilly was supposed to be able to command it. "Can't you make it go away?"

Lilly shrugged. "Maybe. When I'm done."

She gestured. The front door flew open. The interior doorknob rammed into the living room wall so hard that it broke a hole in the plaster and stuck there. Matthew threw up his hands, shielding his eyes from the driving rain, as Lilly rode her unicorn out into the storm-lashed street, where funnel clouds were forming on the horizon.

Matthew had the distinct impression that Lilly's dad was going to go to trial a lot sooner than he thought, and it wasn't going to be the kind of trial held before a jury of his peers. It was going to be a trial of a distinctly Old Testament variety, Matthew thought.

He wondered if Lilly would stop there. Somehow, he doubted it.

The Modern Equus

Amelia Gorman

Silken carcasses from the steeds of sunnier days
are sewn together with a leg-to-torso running stitch,
again, and twice more in the back. They're saved
from sticky factories, from sucking swamps.
We weld a metal spire square between the eyes.
That's the trick that makes it work when before
two legged experiments with flat foreheads failed
to reach for the sky, lightning rod atop your head.
When we call down the thunder with your horn,

we're bringing back the dead.

Distant clouds are forming on the moors,
lonely clouds, keen to touch our science.
Storming screams pour down from heaven
and sheets of rain to guide us.

Currents gallop through the horse-body
gross assemblage though it is,
and crackling St. Elmo's fire
spirals on the golden prong.

Somewhere else, a plague of fear is growing,
gathering in swarms. Locust people,
starving, come to eat our progress
the succulent species from shiny future and mythic
past.

The deluge can quench all fires.
Flash muddy floods and walls of dirt
take down a hundred torches but the
thousand-legged worm made of terror keeps coming
and when the storm breaks the only horn
still sticking skyward is on a pitchfork

from the center of a newly birthed bog.

Birthday Boy

Nikki Guerlain

I was lying in bed, busy spit-shining my pecker, while I waited for dinner to come on a tray.

My mind drifted, eyes spaced out into the darkness of the night outside my window. Attempting to refocus, I gave it a couple more good pulls, but it continued to just rest there like something good for nothing, waiting to be brushed away. Old. Useless. Largely already dead.

What was the use? I was all dried up. I couldn't even come right anymore. The whole debacle came out looking like a sick animal coughing up phlegm.

I was getting all down on myself when a small ruckus erupted outside. I tucked my pecker back beneath my gown, and hobbled over to the window to spy what all the trouble was about.

That's when I saw it with my own two eyes. *The Flaming Unicorn of Death of Gravesend's Way.*

Largely thought to be an urban legend perpetuated by retirement community staff to keep old people with little grip on reality from wandering outdoors after dark. But, there it was, and it had Grandma Jenny pinned against a tree.

A ball of blue flames encased each hoof. Its horn was two feet long and inky black. Jenny was wailing a storm, feebly beating at the beast with a hair dryer. Seeing as the beast was faced away from me I was privy mostly to its rear end, which appeared to glow white like the moon. Its tail fell in a cascade of tiny black cornrow braids. It arched its tail up and to the side revealing what could only be described as a blushing pecan of flesh nestled below its arsehole.

"Dinner's ready, Mr. Mann. Well, well, well. Good to see you're feeling better."

I turned around quickly. "What're you talking about?"

The nurse cleared her throat and made a general gesture towards me with the tray carrying my dinner. Then she gave me a strange smile, cocking her left eyebrow. I reddened when I realized my pecker was hard and making a pup tent out of my gown.

Goddamn.

"Could you just leave my food on the table? I'm busy," I told her.

"Uh-hmm," she said, placing the tray on my bedside table. "We've got peas and carrots in butter sauce tonight. Your favorite."

"Nice."

I turned my attention back to the battle between Jenny and the unicorn. The unicorn's tail braids began spinning around its arsehole like little fan blades.

The nurse cleared her throat again.

Annoyed, I turned back to her, "What is it? Leave already."

She pulled a small box out of the pocket of her lab coat.

It couldn't be.

"That there wouldn't be a large jar of Pond's Cold Cream, would it?" I asked her.

"Uh-hmm," she said. "Happy Birthday, Mr. Mann."

Oh boy. A brand new jar of Pond's Cold Cream. She placed it on the table next to the food and left. So I was a Birthday Boy? Hmmm. I'd totally forgotten.

I looked down proudly at my stiff pecker, to my new jar of cold cream, to the peas and carrots in butter sauce. Then, Jenny nearly ripped my eyes out of their sockets with a horrendous scream.

I peeled my eyes away from my bedside booty and pasted them firmly to the window. The unicorn had crammed its horn into Jenny's abdomen!

With a jolt, the beast threw its head back. Jenny's impaled body slid all the way down its horn to the base of its skull. Her blood, black from the night, ran over the unicorn's eyes, giving it the appearance it was crying oil. The unicorn's arsehole opened up like a spiral space door and its blushing pecan burst into flames. The braided tail, already whipping, spun faster and faster, fanning the flames, making them burn brighter and brighter. Until at last, the arsehole couldn't get any bigger, the flames any brighter.

Then a phosphorescent beam of light shot out of its ass which, combined with the fan-like movement of its whipping tail, created a strobe-like effect upon my vision. And for the first time in years I actually felt blood coursing through my entire body. I throbbed with life.

I thought just then about how good it felt to be alive. How nice it'd be to have that jar of cold cream.

But I couldn't leave the window. And I couldn't reach the jar from where I was standing. And if this wasn't bad enough, the smell of those sweet buttered peas and carrots was making my stomach growl.

A heavy confliction had set itself upon me. One I couldn't have been happier to have. Flaming unicorn cooch, Pond's Cold Cream, buttered peas and carrots. Oh my.

Before I could choose, the unicorn jerked its head up and back, flinging Jenny's body into the tracking beam of its ass. Jenny's body froze mid air.

Oh Mary.

Cooch. Cream. Sauce.

"I brought you a cupcake, Forrest," Gracie said.

Gracie's room neighbored mine. She carried a large metal cross with a crucified Jesus on it wherever she went. Whenever you asked her a question, she asked you back: what would Jesus do? She's real nice and before she went crazy we fooled around a bit. I generally don't take advantage of crazy people, so at this point we were just friends.

"Gracie, you see this?" I asked her. I heard her shuffle towards me.

"I brought you a cupcake, Forrest," she repeated.

Crazy Gracie.

I peeled my eyes from the window to take a cupcake from her. She'd used her metal cross as a serving tray, impaling a cupcake on each one of the spikes pinning Jesus to the cross.

"Stigmata frosting, my favorite," I told her. I tore a cupcake from the cross and shoved it into my mouth greedily. Just then, a little voice in my head told me to look back to the light. Jenny's body was spinning in the light.

"What's that, Forrest?" Gracie asked.

"That's the Flaming Unicorn of Death," I told her, "and what's left of Grandma Jenny."

Preparing to explain everything I'd seen thus far, I gathered my thoughts excitedly. I had news to tell. Important happenings only I could convey. And I had an audience. To boot, my pecker was still stiff. Life was finally looking up for this Birthday Boy.

"What're you talking about, Forrest?" She took her cross and tried to smack my pecker, but missed, sending cupcakes flying to the floor. Her attempt had made my arsehole shut up so tight I felt it behind my belly button. Which, oddly, I found arousing.

"Friends remember?" I shook my head then looked out the window. Jenny's body was spinning so fast I couldn't hardly make out her features. I hopped from one foot to the other in excitement and felt about ready to spill, not at all like some near dead thing. I couldn't take it; the spinning was too much to bear.

"Crazy crazy crazy crazy!" Gracie started chanting.

"Oh Gracie! I can't take this anymore," I told her.

"Can't take this anymore. Can't take this anymore. No. No. No. Can't take this anymore," she said.

Then I thought, fuck it.

"Gracie, Gracie ... go over there and hand me that cold cream, will you?" I asked her.

"What would Jesus do, Forrest?"

"Now stop that. You just go over there and get me that cold cream," I pushed her.

"No. I know what you're going to do. And you're not going to ignore me no more." With this, she hiked up her gown, exposing her piss-soaked adult diaper.

"Focus, Gracie. Cold cream. Hurry," I pressed, "before Jenny's sucked into the light!"

"No. No. No!" Gracie shook her head.

"Fine, fucking *carpe diem* then," I said.

Then I ripped the diaper clean off Crazy Gracie and mounted her.

"Yes! Crazy. Crazy. Crazy. Gracie. Good!" she screamed.

And I barely made it, but I came before Jenny's body was sucked completely inside the unicorn's arsehole.

Then I turned my attention to Gracie, stroked her gray neck hair, and told her, "It's all good now, Gracie. I just needed to get a little crazy too."

"Happy Birthday. Happy Birthday. I brought you a cupcake, Forrest," she said, then smacked her lips loud to give me an air kiss.

Such a lucky boy.

Birthday Boy.

The Fucking Blobfish

Kerry G.S. Lipp

The day the Noah's Ark story happened, whenever the fuck that was:

Thunder cracked overhead as lightning split the darkened sky. Hard rain started to fall.

"C'mon, man, let us in," Buella the lesbian unicorn said, gesturing to her mate with her large, wet horn.

"I'm sorry," Noah said, holding his palms up flat. "But you're late. And you're lesbians. I gave your spot to the blobfish."

"You what?!"

"Look, ladies, we only have room for one male and one female."

"That's discrimination, you fucking bigot!" Buella bellowed, stamping hooves in the moist dirt below.

"Look, this is what God told me, okay? My hands are tied here. I'm sorry, but this is about reproduction. We'd have better luck mating a horse and a rhinoceros than scooping a babe from one of you two colorful lesbian unicorns, and since neither of you showed up with a male, I gave your spot to the blobfish."

"The fucking blobfish? Someday people are going to look at that and say it's the ugliest animal in the world."

"Keep your voice down, they can probably hear you," Noah said.

"Fish? Seriously, the world's about to *flood* and we lost our spot to a *fish*?"

"It wasn't an easy decision." Noah shrugged, "I gave you five extra minutes. And even so, we can't have two of the same sex on the ark."

Buella the lesbian unicorn spat in Noah's face. The gooey mucus soaked into his beard.

"Okay, now it's an easy decision; looks like we're done here," Noah said and started pulling up the door to the ark, his white beard flinging wet wads of sputum in all directions. "You two enjoy your extinction."

He pumped his sweaty muscular arms, jerking the rope until the door slammed shut, leaving the two lesbian unicorns stranded as the water rose past their hooves.

Buella snorted and tensed her muscles, ready to dash into the boat.

"What in the name of Peggy Suss are you doing?"

"I'm gonna poke a hole in the side. And then I'm gonna poke another, and another until either that boat sinks or my horn breaks off."

Buella ran at the ark, full gallop and lowered her head, and snapped her fucking neck. She died.

"Oh dear," Blinky, her lesbian lover turned widow, exclaimed, her four hooves now stuck in the mud as the water continued to rise.

The falling rain now completely covered Buella's corpse and began to lift the ark. The fat drops splashed in Blinky's eyes as the level rose to her nose. The cold water slowly warmed up. At first Blinky thought it was nothing more than urine from all of the doomed animals collectively pissing themselves as they fell to the wrath of a dickhead god who chose to flood the world to prove his divine power to Job or something.

But then she saw the Devil, all hooves and horns and black eyes and red skin.

"Fucking asshole wouldn't let me on either," the Devil said as the water crept higher.

"Why not?" Blinky asked.

"There's no female devil," the Devil said. "I told him all women are the devil, but he still wouldn't let me on."

"I'm sorry," Blinky said.

"So am I," said the Devil. "Hey, since you're about to die, you wanna make a deal?"

Blinky looked around her as the world drowned and decided she had nothing to lose.

"What kind of a deal?" she asked.

"You give me your horn, and I'll make sure that people remember your species forever, even though you won't survive the flood."

"My horn?" She sobbed.

"I can do magic," the Devil said. "Give me your horn, and some day, way off in the distant future, I can make them all horny. Just like you and Buella."

"She was always horny." Blinky smiled.

"I meant literally horny, like the horn on your head, but you've made a good idea even better," the Devil said. "May I have it?"

"Yes," Blinky said,leaning her head close to the Devil.

He reached out and snapped it off.

"Thank you," he said, and put two hands on Blinky the lesbian unicorn's head, drowning her, and laying her next to Buella at the bottom of the rainfall.

Then he studied the massive horn for several minutes, before he said "2016." He slowly slid it up his ass, before disappearing through the rising water and the ground beneath, straight into the heat of Hell at the center of the earth.

He waited.

*

The day the Devil brought the horns, some time in 2016 or whenever the fuck you're reading this:

In Hollywood, California a make-up artist leans in close to put the finishing touches on Dwayne "The Rock" Johnson's costume. She bends lower, giving him a shot of her cleavage. With her face flushed, hands shaking, and underwear wet, she fantasizes about him throwing her up against the wall and taking whatever he wanted. She giggles.

"You all right, sweetheart?" he asks in his deep voice, smiling, flashing those white teeth.

She nods, finishes and steps back to look at her work.

"How do I look?" he asks, making his eyebrows dance up and down.

She almost faints. She studies him, realizes she's missed a small spot on his forehead. She picks up her brush and leans in. She's inches from his face now. She can smell him, the recent shower and the workout just before. She takes a deep breath, blinks her eyes and leans in to apply the last bit of make-up.

But she never gets her chance.

The Brahma Bull becomes the Brahma unicorn as a single, large, sharp horn springs from his forehead like a switchblade and jabs squarely into her wide, sur-prised mouth. It pokes all the way through, out the other side.

The Rock jumps up and jerks his head to the side just in time to dodge the horn coming from *her* head. It scratches him, but he'll be okay.

From other parts of the set he hears the terror and runs to see if he can help. At a full sprint and not ac-counting for the new two-foot protrusion from his head, it catches on the doorframe and launches him flat on his candy ass. His head thunks against the floor and he doesn't even get the opportunity to rescue him-self.

*

In Sacramento, California Todd Timmons is on his knees, nervous as he takes his first communion in front of the whole church. The priest is standing over him, saying some prayers.

Todd feels some heat at the center of his forehead, then pain as he feels something shoot straight out his head. Whatever it is punches through the priest's robe and right into his crotch. The priest screams and Todd screams and the whole congregation screams.

Jerking his head as hard as he can, Todd still can't free himself, but his youthful strength topples the priest as they both tumble down the pulpit. Todd gasps as he sees a massive single horn sprouted from the priest's head. It spikes Todd's friend Caleb, kneeling next to him at communion.

Craning his neck, Todd scours the church and sees that everyone has sprouted a horn, and at least half of them caused damage to someone else when it happened. A mother's tit skewered by a newborn's horn. Hands impaled, stuck to foreheads from scratching at the worst possible moment. And on and on.

The shocked screams bellowed by the congregation are enough to nearly tear the roof off of St. Peter's Catholic Church.

*

In Cleveland, Ohio the Browns are playing the Pittsburgh Steelers. Tiny quarterback Johnny Manziel squats down about to call for the snap.

"Green 69," he says.

All the players' muscles tense in anticipation, ready to run and block and kill each other to either take the ball or protect the ball.

"Hut," Johnny says. The center snaps the ball.

Johnny's unicorn horn bursts straight through his helmet and deflates the ball. The horn shoots right up the center of the center's ass. Amid the confusion, Johnny thinks he hears the 350-pound player giggle a little bit.

But then all hell breaks loose. Johnny's not the only one with a horn. Everyone's got one and amazingly they are all still trying to get the football. Helmets crack and shoulder pads clack as the defensive line storms the offensive line. A linebacker rips Johnny's horn free from the center's ass, tears the ball off, and without a second thought to the horn on his own head or the pandemonium surrounding him, runs it in for a touchdown.

All around him fans have sprouted their own horns and are slaughtering each other in either celebration or shame.

The noise is enough to shake the sky.

*

In Illinois, thousands of longhaired, basement-dwelling, stinky hipsters have gathered to attempt the Guinness World Record for largest game of naked leapfrog.

About three thousand of them are jumping at the same time when the unicorn horns come. They don't even have a chance to check out the craft breweries and food trucks nearby.

*

All around the world, consequences are the same. Newly sprouted horns shoot through windshields and cause grotesque multi-car pileups. Couples making out end up killing each other. Couples fucking usually have a survivor, but it greatly depends on what position they are using. People in close proximity, like at concerts or theme parks are usually dead before they know what happened, at least the majority of them.

The survivors don't know what to do. Paramedics and doctors continue carrying on their jobs despite the weight and terror of their new horn, but they often forget it's there and end up doing more damage than they repair, or worse, cause new damage as they put a nurse's eye out while asking for 50ccs of whatever they need or shove a horn through an assistant's ears reaching for a scalpel.

As hope fades and the gravity of the situation takes hold, despair grips humanity. The collective screams and terror of the world cause the winds to rise. The heat from the force of 8 billion people yelling at once melts the glaciers and raises the tides. Mother Nature tries to control the wrath as everything slips from her natural grasp and the earth goes to war with itself. When the tsunamis crash and the hurricane winds gust, the twisters form.

Giant tornadoes the size of skyscrapers composed of breath and screams sprout all over the globe, wreaking havoc and sucking up survivors like a line of coke. As they swirl at 300-miles-an-hour, horns stab and slice and impale the people of earth while they fly helplessly through bodies and debris. The twisters grow in size as they all move toward a central point.

The strength of their winds and gravitational pull pushes the continental landmasses back together causing earthquakes and fissures as Pangaea reassembles itself. When the winds finally wear themselves out, the human debris gathered in the dervish rains down over the remnants of the world that was.

*

Buella, Blinky and the Devil have their revenge at a god who refused to be diverse and inclusive.

Or that's at least what Noah, one of his followers, said was God's word.

If people were still around to remember this day, they damn sure would never forget the unicorn. Perhaps the Devil underestimated his own power and ruined it all, but in the last moments of all those human beings, the final thoughts were all the same: *am I turning into a unicorn?*

The aftermath is nothing but the destruction of places and cities and structures, the collective body of work of thousands of years ripped apart like a library by an angry toddler. No human survives and nearly all of the animals are dead as well and the weather beats the barren planet for another thousand years or so.

*

Long after the dust settles and the fires burn themselves out, the ocean, seemingly the only constant, continues to lap at the barren beaches with its warm waves.

And one day a big wave crashes and leaves a pair of little creatures behind.

They are blobfish, but they've got little arms and legs and lungs that will continue to develop. They crawl up the beach, exhausted after their long journey.

Then they fuck.

But they won't begin to populate the earth, because they are gay.

And God is either happy or pissed off.

But no one will ever know for sure.

I Love My Job

J.M. Northwood

"A lot of people think cerebrospinal fluid is opaque, or a very faint gold."

I continued prepping the table.

"As anyone who's ever had a spinal tap can tell you, though, if you're healthy, it's clear."

After fifteen years of practice, my hands were on autopilot: I peeled instruments out of sterile packaging, checked IV fluids, and verified the surgical area was properly prepped.

"The most important thing to remember is to check spinal pressure before you inject or draw near the spinal cord or base of the brain. Too much pressure, and *boop,* the brain can actually drop from its position in the skull."

My patient's eyes widened, then scrunched shut in denial. He was obviously trying to shake his head, but he couldn't do much with the restraints in place.

"Hey, hey ... calm down." I stripped off my glove and grabbed his hand, letting him feel the warmth of human contact. "It'll be okay. Trust me. You're going to come through this just fine, and you'll feel so much better afterward."

I took a tissue and blotted the tears leaking from his eyes, squeezed his hand once more, then pulled back, heading over to the scrub sink to clean up and re-glove.

Returning to the bed, I started the Propofol into the line — a Diprivan drip, as it were — and talked him through the process of letting go.

"That's it, count backward. Slowly. A number each second. And you'll be awake and back up in no time." I watched his vitals, making sure the oxygen mask was seated, and prepped the equipment for emergency intubation, just in case.

As he drifted off into a twilight sleep, and then fell more deeply into Morpheus' arms, I slipped my mask up and started to work.

Shaving the front and sides of his head, I applied an ointment that would prevent the hair's regrowth; then, clamping veins as I went, I carefully split the skin on his forehead and separated a silver-dollar-sized section of muscle, clearing the way to the skull beneath.

Using a half-millimeter bit, I drilled a small hole to start, screwed a threaded post in place, and then performed the craniotomy: slightly smaller than the hole in the muscle tissue, I removed a circular section of bone, then placed it into the pasteurization basin: after a bath in sixty-five c saline for thirty minutes, it was time to drop it into the automatic mortar grinder.

Listening to the crunching whirr, I once again checked vitals, verified that the surgical site wasn't drying out, and took a few minutes to call my wife to let her know I'd be home in time for supper. I hung up

once the grinder beeped, and verified there was nothing but a smooth powder in the catch basin.

I mixed the powder with abalone and a near-micro-
scopic amount of Osmium, folded it all together with a
surgical resin, and embedded the tiniest whorl of horn
I had, and then began patching the skull.

I built the bone into place, building it up toward a
bulge in the center, and then set a UV light to shine on
the area to help cure the resin. While the light was active, I began to clean the surgical station.

Once everything was clear and the timer on the
light had gone off, I began the process of returning the
muscle to its previous position and sealing the wound
with surgical glue. When I was done — aside from the
angry wound, of course — the only sign of the surgery
was the small knob of bone shining just under his skin.

I stopped the Propofol and moved him to the re-
covery area, loosening the restraints and moving a
bucket into place should he be ill once he awoke.

Perhaps ten minutes later he began to stir, and a
minute past that he used the bucket. It's a hazard of
the trade, and I brought him a glass of water to rinse
out his mouth.

"It's done?"

I smiled, reassuring him. "It's done. I've a script for
pain pills waiting for you, and a note for you to take in
to work releasing you for the next week while you
heal."

He smiled, and — with a little help — stood up. He
wavered a bit, which was only to be expected, and then
I helped him back out to the waiting room where he
met his daughter, who would be driving him home.

As they drove off, I couldn't help but smile, thinking of how much joy he'd have once the horn really
started to come in, and once the rest of his mane grew
out. I knew he'd be back eventually for a hoof trans-
plant, or — depending on how well he was built — a
rather discreet graft.

One way or another, though, one conversion at a
time, I was bringing unicorns back into this world.

I love my job.

The RoboCorn 6001

Logan Noble

Though Steven wasn't much of a patriot, General Nash's speech made him want to stand up and salute. The audience, seated in the auditorium, were enthralled. They hung on the General's words. *Why shouldn't they?* Steven thought. *The man is a juggernaut.*

"The world we live in," General Nash said, his coarse baritone echoing through the auditorium, "is a dangerous place. In 2024, a terrorist group executed an attack on Chicago that left hundreds dead. It left our nation feeling weak. Feeble. The American people demanded that we *do* something.

"The Commander in Chief, his cabinet, and the Secretary of Defense can feel the eyes of America's enemies upon us. ISIS. The Red Knife. The New Socialist Extremist. All dangers to national security. Ladies and gentleman of our esteemed nation, today is a time for new beginnings.

"Today," Nash grinned and motioned toward the stage, "Lady Liberty strikes back."

From the speakers, the national anthem blared. From above Steven, the stage lights spun, dizzying mixes of red, white and blue washing over everyone.

The stage gave a metallic grind. From under it, a plat-form began to rise.

"Our president initiated Operation Myth. We creat-ed a series of weapons, colossal war machines that are personifications of the most powerful creatures of pop-ular fiction."

As the lift rose, a long, spear like object rose into view. *The horn,* Steven thought, his heart pounding. It was his machine. He'd worked with the general to cre-ate them. Weapons of incredible power. *It's happen-ing. America will be safe. And, more importantly, you're rich. Behold —*

"The Titans of Myth!

"The Minotaur. A creature made of arcanism met-al, over twenty feet tall, equipped with .50m cannons and laser horns. Located in Los Angeles.

"The Dragon. An aerial threat that can level a city with its flamethrower capability, and crush nearly any-thing with its powerful mechanical jaws. With a wing-span longer than three football fields, no threat in God's blue sky can compete. It's being held by our as-sociates in New York City.

"The Unicorn."

Nash paused for dramatic effect. The audience dangled from his words.

The lift finished its ascension, the metal gears set-tling with a loud *click*. The audience gasped. Steven teared up. His favorite.

"The Titan you will be glimpsing today. I introduce to you! The RoboCorn 6001!"

The applause was rapturous.

Steven ran the specs through his head. Over fifteen feet tall at the tip of the horn, the RoboCorn was the most terrifying land weapon ever created. The horn fired a concentrated Aepac Plasma beam, enough to pierce tank plating. Arcanism armor, created by the military, was impenetrable. It could run at speeds of over 200 miles per hour. And, last but not least ...

"... a weather modification matrix. The combat science team remotely controlling this Titan can activate a unique device that sends energy rings into our atmosphere, which will literally change the weather conditions. RoboCorn can create a tornado. RoboCorn can create hurricane-like conditions. RoboCorn can make a tsunami. The possibilities are endless. Our enemies, faced with a combat drone with *this* level of offensive capabilities, will be driven into the dirt. Crushed under the unified fist of America. The next time our enemies show their cowardly faces. RoboCorn will strike!"

The audience continued to cheer, their eyes glued on the metallic mass of RoboCorn. The head and neck were painted red. The LED screens that served as its 'eyes' glowed a bright red. The rest was blue and covered in stars. *This level of gaudy patriotism makes me sick. Just remember who signs your paychecks now.*

After the applause died down, Nash switched gears. Steven had heard this speech a dozen times in rehearsal. He smiled. He knew what came next.

"Without our talented team of combat scientists, the Titans of Myth would have never became a reality. I would like you to give a huge round of applause for the creator and project lead, Doctor Steven Darling!"

The audience went crazy. Steven stood and gave them a quick wave. *I'm a genius. And they love you.* Steven scanned the faces. He caught the general's eyes. Nash gave him a wink.

The lab was quiet. Steven took another sip of his coffee, swiping through the status reports on his tablet. The rest of the staff had left hours ago. *It went well. Very well.* The military was pleased. RoboCorn had been tested extensively, and, in a matter of weeks, would be ready for field combat. *My little Titan. All grown up.*

From behind him, the lab door opened with a *whoosh*. General Nash entered, his dress uniform tidy and pressed. Up close, he was a massive man, his bald head gleaming under the harsh lights.

"Great job, General. I think the media loved it."

Steven shook Nash's hand, his grip like iron.

"Of course they did, Doctor. The civilian fools are practically sheep. They have no idea of the military significance of what we've unveiled today. How are systems working?"

Business. He's always about business.

Steven pressed a few buttons and his tablet cast up a hologram. They looked into it. In the hologram, numbers and graphs showed the various power levels and system strengths of the RoboCorn.

"All systems nominal. Fuel lines and tanks full and intact. Weapon systems charged and ready for action."

The RoboCorn was stored in the lowest level of the Washington DC Science and Weapon Development Compound. The ground floor, the lobby, was filled with Army commandos on a 24 hour guard. The facility went underground from there. The next floor down was the research and construction area. Whatever Steven and his team dreamt up, the engineers constructed. B3 was the lab, the floor that Nash and Steven currently stood on. The final floor, B4, was where RoboCorn was stored. Also there was what they called the Control Nexus. A portable device that controlled RoboCorn's every move. With no one at the controls, the enormous machine was useless.

"The Control Nexus was checked by Corporal White about an hour ago. It's in place."

Nash nodded, pleased. "Corporal White is a good man. One of our best. How's security?"

Steven reached down, ready to swipe over to the security menu.

Then the alarm sounded.

"Jesus." Nash said, reaching for his pistol. *Oh no,* Steven thought. He swiped and the security menu appeared. Everything blinked red.

"Attention in the facility," The artificial voice spoke through the PA system. "Initiate Security Level Delta. Ground floor has been compromised."

Nash pointed with his pistol toward the screen, his face turning red. "Navigate to ground floor cameras. I need eyes. Now!"

Steven did, a stone of dread dropping in his stomach. The lobby was a bloodbath. The commandos were long dead, bodies riddled with bullets. Blood covered everything. Steven knew these men. Had seen them every morning when he came to work for the last five years.

"Who did this!?" Nash's voice shook with rage. As they watched, a figure wearing goggles moved into frame. Dressed in a red jumpsuit, a machine gun clenched in hand. The man grinned. The muzzle flashed. The camera went black.

"The Red Knife." Nash's voice was quiet. "Filthy neo-Soviets. They're after our Titan." He turned to Steven. "Lock the facility down. If you and I can get to the Control Nexus, we can activate the RoboCorn. We can-"

The lab door opened with a *whoosh*. Time crawled. Steven turned and saw two men. Red jumpsuits. Armed. Muzzles came up. Time was elastic. Nash screamed beside Steven, his howl stretching into eternity. He pulled the trigger. Everything ... was ...

Chaos.

Bullets tore through everything. Steven felt one crash into his shoulder, the pain and force spinning him down onto the floor. One Red Knife commando went down under Nash's gun. The other riddled Nash with bullets. He sprayed in a line, from neck to groin. The General gargled as he hit the ground, his throat blood pooling.

I'm in shock ...

The commando advanced to Steven, his boots squeaking on the floor.

"You!" The commando's voice was heavy with a Russian accent. "Come vith me!" The commando pulled him from the floor roughly, his gloved grip crushing the muscles in Steven's good arm.

They were moving, out the lab doors and into the hallway. *We never saw them coming.* The commando dragged Steven toward the elevator, the pain in his right shoulder pulsing painfully with each step. Steven caught sight of himself in the silver reflection of the elevator doors. He looked like hell. Covered in Nash's blood.

The Red Knife soldier threw him into the wall. Steven went down hard, hissing through his teeth from the pain.

"Enter your code. Now."

"I can't! I — "

The gun rattled in the commando's hand as he raised it. "For each no you give, I take a joint. Knee caps. Then your elbows. Code. Now!"

Steven used the wall to stand. He looked at the keypad. 12 numbers, a new code randomized and shared with the RoboCorn team daily. Down one floor, before they could reach their machine, he would need to use the fingerprint scanner. Two incorrect inputs on either security measure, a security team would be dispatched. *Too bad security is dead.*

He entered his code, slowly hitting each button, four years of long codes running through his head. *He couldn't get it wrong. He couldn't —*

The keypad blinked red. He'd entered the wrong numbers.

The commando moved quickly. A back-handed blow across Steven's teeth. It sent him reeling back into the wall, a flash of white pain pin-balling through his eyes and into his skull.

"Enter code! Now!" The commando glanced back toward the way he'd come nervously.

Steven entered the code shakily, his fingers quaking. This time, the keypad blinked green. The elevator door slid open.

The door closed and the elevator descended. Beside him, the commando spoke into an earpiece. "Vadim here!" He finished his message in rapid Russian. A voice answered him, the message curt.

At the end of the ride, the door slid open. Vadim dragged Steven down the hall. Steven ran the outline of the floor through his mind. One last checkpoint. Fingerprint scanner. Beyond that, the Control Nexus. And an exit out through an interior stairwell. If the Red Knife got the Nexus, then RoboCorn could be risen on its platform straight through a hatch into Washington D.C. *If that happens, everything will be over.*

When they reached the fingerprint scanner, Vadim shoved Steven forward again.

"Open."

Steven did, his mind trying to find a way to stop this. He could attack the commando. But that was foolish. Vadim was undoubtedly highly trained, and would kill him. *As soon as he's done with you, he's going to kill you anyway.*

They moved through the door. Steven could see, through the bullet-proof viewing glass, the RoboCorn 6001. *Attack! Do it!*

"It's beautiful." Vadim said, his yellow teeth pushing through his wet lips. "I may leave you alive long enough for you to see me use it on the people you love. I plan to-"

Steven swung a fist as hard as he could. It hit Vadim in his lips, the blow solid.

Vadim barely seemed to notice. He turned his gaze back to Steven, blinking. Blood ran from his lip. Vadim raised his gun. And fired. Steven's foot exploded in pain. He went down, his world a glaring, agitated beehive of soaring agony.

"You hit like girl." Vadim chuckled and went back to the Control Nexus.

Steven watched, his eyes filled with tears. Vadim opened the device, the screen blinking to life. Steven recognized the RoboCorn controls. The lift, on the other side of the wall, began to rise. Darkness edged in on his vision. Vadim was laughing, head thrown back.

I'm sorry ... my unicorn ... it will kill everyone. He blacked out.

*

Steven awoke to a familiar voice. He opened his eyes, a face doubling in his vision.

" — late! The RoboCorn! We need to stop it!"

Corporal White. He's a good man.

He was being pulled from the floor. Steven's vision stabilized. Corporal White, his head of security for the fourth floor. The man, young, his beard long, was coated in blood, his eyes filled with fear.

"The Red Knife has the Nexus. They are currently leveling D.C. to the ground. How do we stop it?"

Distantly, muffled, Steven heard something explode. "We ... we need the Control Nexus back."

White furrowed his brow. "Okay. The Red Knife insurgents have been reduced in number. As far as we know, only three remain. And they have the Nexus. If I can get you to it, can you stop it? Can you turn it off?"

Steven's mind was still in a frenzy. He saw his opportunity. *Any deaths. They're your fault.* His chance for redemption. "Yes. Yes I can."

They took the stairs. Every step was Everest. The pain had subsided some, but Steven could feel his blood leaking from the hole in his foot. White was impatient. As soon as they reached the hatch, he began cranking the wheel. *Get ready.* With a grunt, White pushed into the hatch and into Washington D.C.

The air smelled of fire. They stood on the street, Steven's mouth agape.

Carnage.

The city park outside their building was charred. Trees gone. A car had been crushed. Buildings, all along the street and in the distance, burned and crumpled. Explosions and screams of agony riddled the air. Black smoke traveled the wind. In the distance, the Washington Monument had been cut in half. The base, jagged and broken, stood tiny in the grey sky.

"We must move, Doctor." White was crouched, moving quickly for cover behind what cars remained on the street.

Bodies littered the ground. Limbs, burnt and bloodied, peppered the earth. Several helicopters roared overhead as Steven and White moved down the street. In White's hand, he held a tracker. It beeped. *He's tracking the three remaining commandos.*

As they rounded the street corner, something exploded. The sound split and superheated the air. The shockwave rattled Steven's bones. *This place is a war-*

zone now. Up ahead, miles away, he could see the RoboCorn.

It was locked in combat with a tank and a battalion of soldiers. The enormous machine moved agilely, legs propelling itself quickly, stump-sized hooves crushing bodies as it pranced. Its hind quarters struck a tank, flipping the heavily armored vehicle into the air. Robo-Corn leapt, two hooves crushing the machine. Soldiers scattered, guns forgotten. A helicopter buzzed overhead. The .50mm machine gun rattled from the side. The cement below splintered, the bullets ricocheting harmlessly off the RoboCorn's hide.

The air hummed.

Get back! Get back!

The tip of the horn glowed blue. The helicopter veered. It was too late. The beam fired, the helicopter exploding as it struck, sending the copter blades wheeling into the nearest fleeing soldiers, slicing them to ribbons as they ran.

White grabbed Steven, pulling him from the horrifying spectacle.

"I know!" White's eyes bugged in his head. "I know how horrible it is! But only we can stop it! Only us! Are you with me!?"

Steven could feel his head nodding.

White dragged Steven along just as the RoboCorn threw its body into the nearest building. The earth shook. The street rippled and cracked. The building went down. Crowds of people ran past them screaming, dirty faces turning back to witness the destruction.

Then, from around the corner, the three Red Knife commandos emerged. Steven spotted Goggles, the first man that he and Nash had seen. Behind him was Vadim, his eyes glued to the Nexus screen. White growled and raised his weapon.

The first couple shots took out Goggles. His skull exploded, splattering Vadim and his companion in brain matter. Vadim turned to run as White gunned the third soldier down. The soldiers gun went wild as White's bullets put him down, sending them whizzing through the air past Steven like angry hornets. White pivoted, squeezing the trigger. With a howl, the fleeing Vadim went down.

They went to him, the Control Nexus on the ground beside him. Vadim was dying. His chest was filled with holes.

"Stop the machine Doctor. I've got this scumbag." Steven crouched, reaching for the keyboard. When he saw the screen, he paused, fear turning his blood icy in his veins. In red letters, the screen read: CAUTION: ARTIFICAL TORNADO INCOMING. WEATHER MA-TRIX ACTIVATED.

Steven couldn't even speak.

Vadim spit out a mouthful of blood. "Say ... good-bye to ... everything. The Red Knife ..." He began to laugh, his great whooping sounds gargling as he choked to death on his own blood. He went quiet as his eyes went blank.

Steven mashed the keyboard, his fingers roaming across the keys desperately seeking a way to end it. Every path. Every program. ERROR.

Above them, the sky had awoken. Black clouds spun, thunder rumbling. They spun centrally over where the RoboCorn was located. The air felt still. Pregnant with violence.

Steven turned west, toward the RoboCorn. He could see it now. It stood on the ruins of a building, enormous metal wire taut off its sides, anchoring it to the earth. *So the tornado doesn't take it away ...*

Its horn blinked black, the light a beacon of destruction. A funnel descended from the clouds, the shape thick and flickering with silent lightning. The wind had suddenly picked up. Debris tumbled across the street.

"What can we do, Doctor?"

Steven thought. His brain hurt. Every path, every option felt wrong. They'd played God and created something indestructible. Something that would level this city. His creation was beyond even his control. *It's over.*

"Corporal. We can't do anything."

The clouds split. Beyond. The funnel was about to touch. Steven could feel the twister pulling at him.

A shape was forming in the sky. *What? It can't be! New York sent its-*

A metal dragon tore through the black clouds, godlike, its wingspan devouring the horizon. Claws opened. *The RoboDragon 4105.* It soared. Pure power. It opened its maw.

The RoboDragon struck the RoboCorn hard, claws tearing into the metal torso, lifting it from the ground. The sound of the metal grinding was apocalyptic. The air rippled with the force.

The funnel faltered, the process interrupted. After a moment, with a great sucking sound, it shrunk and vanished. The RoboDragon slammed the RoboCorn down hard into the earth, metallic tails and limbs flailing together in a immense orgy of violence. Great sheets of metal and earth smashed into bits. All around Steven, cracks sprung into the street. Buildings fell from the impact.

With no one to control the RoboCorn, the dragon had no problem. Its jaw unhinged. With a mighty bite, the RoboCorn lost its head. The dragon held the severed head, the horn nearly scraping the cement below. The RoboDragon dropped it. Then it roared.

Corporal White saluted. The RoboDragon pushed off the earth, enormous wings beating the sky into flight. Two wings. Both red. Stars littered its blue torso.

"God bless America." White whispered. The dragon vanished into the clouds, the darkness fading away as it flew.

Steven couldn't help but agree.

Double Rainbow

Michael Shimek

"Everyone, run! A rainbow is coming!"

The word has become synonymous with destruction.

I remember a time before the fear, before the gratuitous killings. Rainbows used to be a beautiful display of nature, where children once imagined leprechauns dancing a jig around an overflowing pot of glittering gold. The arched colors were a sign that the dark clouds were receding and a fresh start was on the way. They brought smiles to faces and happiness to all.

Not anymore. Now people run when they see them. Now they bring unicorns.

I hear the scream from a woman, someone running down the street. People stop what they are doing when they hear her. I do, too.

From the second floor, my fellow coworkers and I step away from our cubicles and rush to the open window. She's frantic; her arms wave around like a lunatic, and her legs wobble as they try to balance on business heels. I've never seen anyone more terrified.

I look down the street, the direction the woman was fleeing, and I see the familiar red, orange, yellow, green, blue, indigo, and violet rays shooting through the sky of parting grey clouds. It is just like the images and videos dominating the television and internet as of lately — an alluring evil. My heart races faster and faster. Before the rainbow can touch ground, I pull away from the window and run deeper into the building.

"Joel!" I yell toward his open office door, hoping he isn't holed up in some stupid meeting and can hear the fear in my voice. "Joel! We have to get out of here!"

I round the corner and find him yapping away on the phone. Hairy legs are up on his desk, a growing belly rests on his lap, and one hand holds the phone to his ear while the other strokes a thick and brown beard. My sudden entrance surprises him, and he puts the person on hold.

"Jeremy, I'm a bit busy." He only uses my full name when he's upset or angry. "Whatever it is, it can wait —"

I blurt it out: "There's a rainbow landing in the city!"

Mahogany eyes widen, and his mouth drops open, revealing a pink cavern of silver cavities. He stammers something, but he can't form complete words or sentences.

We talked about it just last night in bed, how crazy it all sounded. But we'd seen the photos; we'd witnessed the live destruction of Los Angeles and London within the past few days. We never thought it would happen in Minneapolis. Sure, it's a decent sized city, but it's nothing compared to the big ones like New York City or Chicago. So, we brushed it off.

We were ignorant.

He slams the phone into its cradle and hurries over. Our lips meet and he gives me a big bear hug; I can feel him physically shaking. I've never seen him more afraid in the past three years of knowing him.

"What do we do?" he says.

"We leave," I say.

He fidgets with unsure eyebrows. "Don't you think it would be safer to stay inside?"

"No," I say with a shake of my head. "You've seen what those things can do to a city. We need to get the fuck out of here." I grab his hand for support.

He nods and pumps my hand to reciprocate his love. Hand in hand, we race for the first floor.

Our coworkers have the same idea, running for the stairwell or screaming on their phones to loved ones. I follow those dashing for the exit; Joel does both. There is no need to guess who he is calling. I can already hear him yelling at her to take the car and drive north, away from the city. I want to rip the device away and tell him that his own safety is more important than hers, but I know that will only cause another heated argument we've had numerous times before about his mother.

Thankfully, Bob from Accounting appears and takes my mind off the touchy subject. The bald and older man blocks our path, wagging an accusing finger in my face. "It's here! One of them is here, and it's all because of people like — "

I punch him in the mouth and say, "Shut up, Bob! If it's because of anyone, it's because of *bigots* like you." I've always hated Bob and his sneering looks of disgust. I finish by spitting at the cowering man's feet.

Joel chuckles as we continue to flee. "I've always wanted to do that."

"Me too," I say, shaking off the pain in my most likely now bruised hand.

We push forward.

The stairs are packed with recognizable frightened faces. People shove, and people kick. Friendships are thrown out the window as it becomes an every person for themselves situation. Joel and I are heaving, him more so. We are active individuals, but we are both bigger guys and he's carrying at least an extra seventy-five pounds on me; so I'm ahead, pulling him along. I will never let go, not until we are safe and sound.

We reach the bottom of the stairs and head for the main entrance. We should head toward a back exit, away from the direction of the hysterical woman in the street, but I'm scared; I am one with the flock, guided by confusion. I'm not sure where we'll go when we reach the freedom of outside. He doesn't own a vehicle and I can't drive, opting for the buses and light-rail instead.

We make it out into the bright sun and damp air, but I stop Joel from running any farther.

"Wait," I say, trying to catch my breath.

"What? We need to get out of here!"

His chubby face is red, and his large chest and belly heave for air. Honestly, it turns me on, and I make a mental note to jump him once we are out of harm's way. I return to the task at hand: staying alive.

"Yes," I say, "but to where and how?"

His shoulders slump in defeat. I can tell he hasn't thought about it either. People kick and elbow through.

I move us to the side just as everyone freezes and looks down the street. I follow the mass gaze and tremble in terror.

The rainbow strikes the ground in an earthshaking tremor. The street shatters, sending chunks of pavement flying through the air. Several people are struck and fall to the ground with various injuries. I want to help them, but I dare not move any closer to the danger. I feel sorry for them, and that's all I can do.

Then, I see it. Another rainbow. Soaring high and parallel to the other one still staining the sky.

It slips from my mouth: "A double rainbow."

Joel hears my stuttered whisper and follows my eyes upward. His bearded mouth drops open, and his hand squeezes mine even harder.

The colored arch lands with just as much force as its twin.

I want to run, but neither of us can move.

Then we are further hypnotized by the queerest thing to ever pass through our vision.

Unicorns are majestic beasts, their white hides shimmering with a shade of pink. They are more than twice the size of any normal horse. Their manes are thick tendrils of sparkling smoke, and they have wings made of silver feathers as sharp as knives. They are as beautiful as they are deadly.

These two are no different, huffing and snorting in the middle of 1ˢᵗ Ave., grinding their spiral horns together. Their actions create a fine white dust, falling as magical snow into their flaring nostrils — the stuff is the most expensive drug in the world.

They stop, rear up on their hind legs, and release thunderous neighs into the sky. Only when one starts spearing the closest people and the other starts shitting diamonds do we finally find our legs and run.

Safety. It's all I can think about.

An explosion rocks behind us. I turn, braving a glance behind my sweating cutie, and I witness my favorite music venue explode in a brilliant and colorful display of destruction. One unicorn dumps out another shit-covered diamond and kicks it at the Target Center, blowing a hole the size of a small restaurant at the base of the giant building.

My legs keep running.

I remember laughing it off when I'd first heard about unicorns destroying the world. The devastation was terrible, sure, but come on.

Unicorns? Who would have thought the world would end at the hands of magical creatures usually found in stories involving princesses?

I'd laughed even harder when I heard they arrived at the ends of rainbows. I'd almost pissed my pants when I heard they poop diamonds the size of softballs that explode with the combination of vaporizing mini rainbow rays, toxic glitter, and fire.

Joel is right at my heels. "Where are we going?" he yells.

"I have no idea," I yell back. It's hard to think straight with death and destruction taking up your surroundings. Then, an idea hits me. "Follow me!"

I dislodge from the running horde of screaming people and head down a different street. A good chunk of them follow, and I pray to the universe they don't have the same idea as me.

We are going to make it, I think, slowing my burning legs.

A shadow glides overhead. The sound of metal hitting pavement and other metal clanks loudly behind us. So do the shrieks and wails of people. I realize what is happening — there are many videos of it on the internet — and rush into a side alley.

Joel and I hug the building wall, waiting for the silver rain of death to pass by. It provides us shelter, but not enough.

Pain sears through my left shoulder. "Fuck!"

"Oh, shit," Joel says. "Don't move. You have one of those feathers stuck in you. Hold still, and I'll yank it out."

Before I can object, the immense pain returns before dying to an aching throb. He pulls out on of his many handkerchiefs and applies pressure to my wound.

"Here, hold this." Joel hands me a weighty feather made of solid silver. Its edges are sharper than any blade, and a good portion of the end is smeared and dripping with blood.

My blood. The world spins, and I feel like I might throw up.

I do when I see the aftermath of severed limbs and glinting metal in the street. My vomit joins the blood running into the nearest gutter.

"Come on." Joel helps me balance on my wobbly legs. He turns me from the gory scene and looks me straight in the eyes. "Babe. Jerbear. Where are we going?"

The nickname snaps me back to reality. "Bikes," I say. "We need to find a bike station."

He nods, and then this time he's in the lead.

There are plenty of areas to rent bikes in the city. We've done it many times in the past, sometimes playing hooky from work and riding into nearby parks for the afternoon. Both of us are members; both of us have keys to unlock a bike. Joel pulls me along, knowing that the closest bike station is only a block away. My shoulder hurts, but I bear through the pain.

The police have finally shown up, but the steady *pop-pop-pop* of gunfire in the background will do nothing. Regular bullets don't work on magical beings. In fact, only one unicorn has been found dead since this all began, stabbed on accident by its companion during the slaughter last week in Tokyo. The unicorns will eventually disappear with their rainbow, but only after releasing their gorgeous fury.

We make it to the bike station. My mind fills with hope when I see a handful of bikes, but at least one woman has the same idea and struggles with her credit card at the pay station. Seconds tick by; it feels like forever. I'm about to shove the bitch out of the way when she finally finishes, zipping off as fast as she can. We each use our keys and take out a bike. More explosions rock the area, but I can't see the whereabouts of the unicorns.

I get on my bike, and I'm off. My only worry now is making sure Joel is by my side. Buildings, SWAT teams, and screaming people pass by in a blur. We weave through it all, pedaling south on Hennepin Ave. until my legs can't take it anymore.

I collapse in front of the Walker Art Center, where a crowd has gathered, their horrified eyes locked onto the glittering rainbows and plumes of fire taking up downtown. Joel falls next to me. We huff and puff, joining the onlookers watch the city we all love so much perish under fantastical elements. My shoulder is a mess of blood and pain, but I don't care.

Joel is alive and well next to me, and it brings the biggest smile to my face. I grab his hand, and he leans his head against my shoulder.

Some older lady comes up to us with what appear to be two crying grandchildren at her side. "Sweet Jesus, what's happening over there?" She must have noticed us riding from that direction.

I open my mouth to answer, but Joel beats me to it.

"Fucking unicorns, man. Fucking unicorns."

The Unicorn Graveyard

Rodello Santos

She waited in the unicorn graveyard, in a cabin of bone she had built amidst the scattered helix horns and lily-fragrant carcasses.

At noon, beneath the merciless sun, the skeletons blazed a blinding, restless white. At night, beneath the spectral moon, the bones glowed like ghosts, though Yvonne knew their spirits had long departed, that the only shades haunting this valley were her and her need for vengeance.

In the graveyard, the wind never stirred and no grass grew. No birdsong graced the air. All was still, the disquieting pause between dying breaths.

Yvonne often wondered if time passed here, but she had only to look at the long snarled white of her hair, the purple rivermap of veins, the knobs of bones salient against her sagging skin, and she knew time had not forgotten her.

Nor had pain. It wracked her body, stole more of her strength each day. It *grew*.

She caught the muffled clop of hooves, and shivered with hope. *Finally. Can it be?*

Years had passed since the last unicorn had come, seeking the final sleep, but finding her.

She waddled out of her cabin, leaning heavily on the long, bleached leg bone that served as her walking stick.

An early morning fog had fallen, blanketing the world in gossamer grays. It muted sight and sound, curled like beckoning fingers, made the graveyard seem more than ever a passageway to the world beyond.

The unicorn approached, a silhouette growing in the fog, gingerly stepping over bones. He broke out of the pearly mists, shaking his head with a husky neigh. Yvonne could not tell where his mane ended and the wisps of fog began.

He studied her, his eyes like dying stars challenging the night. "Human," he said. "You trespass on sacred soil."

When Yvonne heard the deep voice, saw its azure eyes, her soul died a little more. *It is **not** him.* She wailed with the anguish of wasted years, and fell hard to her knees upon the cold dirt.

"Why are you here?" the unicorn asked.

When Yvonne replied, her voice came so weakly a passing breeze might have borne it away. Memory clouded her eyes.

*

A lifetime ago, there lived a naïve little girl who grew to be a naïve young woman. She always strove to stay kind and pure.

Yet her body was stunted and squat, her skin pocked darkly as if diseased. Children jested she was a witch ... such was her ugliness. As she grew older, she came to see that no man could ever love her, and she would never wed.

So, one day, she decided to wait by the forest near her home, an ancient sweep of pines where a unicorn had once been seen. She prayed purity would be enough, that the unicorn would come, steal her away as the legends promised, to its home that she might be loved all the years of her life.

She waited. Empty days became empty months. For that first year, she rose, waited from dawn to noon, full of hope. The second year, she lingered through dusk, full of fear. The third, fourth, fifth desperate years saw her languish into the deep hours of night, full of anger. Was her devotion not pure? Had she not suffered enough?

On the day that she vowed she would wait no more, a miracle happened. As twilight came, the sweet perfume of lilies anointed the air. A unicorn with eyes of golden fire galloped toward her, hoofbeats drumming as he wended around the pines. When he came to the woman, she wept and knelt before him.

And do you know what he said?

*

"Do you know?" With a grimace and sharp inhalation, Yvonne stabbed her walking stick into the earth and thrust herself to her feet. She tasted blood between her rotting teeth.

The unicorn in the graveyard shied away, nickering beneath her gaze.

"His voice boomed as merciless as thunder! He told me I was pure in body, yes, but that my spirit was stained. Of course it was! All those long, lonely years! How can one live that way? And without one word more, he left, *he left*. Back into the dark wilds. Even *he* had abandoned me, my last hope, fleeing from my hideousness, making me feel soiled. *Worthless*."

Yvonne's eyes glazed over again, and she swayed on her feet.

The unicorn came closer, his movement stirring eddies in the mist. "And you wait for him still?"

"Yes! For when I learned of the unicorn graveyard, my mind was bent to finding it, that I might see him once more before he dies, that he might know his sin. And pay."

Yvonne bowed her head, tears falling to her feet. A strange noise bit through her despair, and she looked up to find the unicorn laughing.

"You mock my pain?" she screamed. From her mildewed robes, she pulled a dagger, its blade crafted from a splintered, spiral horn. It was stained and crusted with old blood.

"No, not your pain, but your ignorance. I sense death growing within you, blooming like black flowers. Your time is short, as is mine. If you so desire, I would show you the fate you longed for long ago."

His words surprised her, made her suspicion rise. The unicorns who had come before had been meek without exception, wishing only to lay down and depart in peace. Of the dozens she had slain, none had ever made an offer.

"Are you bartering?" she asked.

"I am teaching. You judge us by what you know. Before I die, I would give one last gift of comfort."

"Why?"

"Because you suffer needlessly, and it is in my power to help. Do you think you are the first ever to feel abandoned thus? In my youth, many threw themselves before me, lamenting. Do you think I did not feel guilt? The final days approach us both. We can live them with some measure of peace."

The unicorn turned away, then paused for one inviting glance.

Though his skin was a pale silver-white, his body thin and frail compared to the golden-eyed unicorn from Yvonne's youth, his beauty still stole her breath.

She sensed no duplicity. She never did with unicorns; they seemed incapable of lying. *Though no lie cuts more deeply than truth,* she thought, the taunts of children still echoing in her mind. And that was what this unicorn offered. More truth.

The unicorn snorted at her hesitance. "You humans pretend to desire knowledge. But if you wish to die wed to falsehood, then I grant that final wish ... the benediction of ignorance."

Falsehood? Ignorance? Yvonne's leg spasmed, a stab of pain from thigh to calf. It subsided to a tight ache that lingered like a cloud of flies upon carrion.

He cannot hurt me, no more than I already hurt. It was pathetic she could find comfort in the thought. "What falsehood do you speak of?"

"Follow and see." He entered into thicker mist, and Yvonne was left, alone. Apart from her ragged breathing, all was silent, and the silence smothered her. A too familiar pain made her swallow.

Tucking the dagger away, she hurried into the mist.

For long moments, she traveled blind. Fear gripped her at the thought of being lost in gloom forever.

When she glimpsed a sheen of starglow, her aching legs struggled to chase it. Several times she lost her way; several times the flick of a silver tail or the clatter of unseen hooves guided her forward.

And then the mist vanished, the change so sudden that Yvonne lurched.

Around her stretched a glen of idyllic splendor — a green, vibrant world lush with birth and life. A vast, glorious lake commanded her view, its waters pure and diamond-clear. Lilies with the colors of the sunrise grew wild around its periphery, and birdsong brightened the air.

Yvonne's mind reeled at the beauty. At her age, she had thought herself immune to wonder. But here, before the lake ... she felt small, a naïve young girl once more, able to believe in things greater than herself.

"Impossible," she cried. "I have walked the length and breadth of the graveyard, and I have never seen this place."

"Because you never sought it. Like the graveyard, this glen is not a place to be measured in footsteps."

All along, she had lived near such pristine grandeur. *To be so close and never know.* A peace settled upon her, light as a breeze, alongside the memory of a wish — *she is waiting by the forest, a unicorn with eyes of gold fire approaches, he speaks, he speaks ...*

Her face darkened, and a premonition crippled her. Movement in the water caught her eye, and she staggered closer to the lake ... closer ...

The blood emptied from her face. In the watery depths were thousands of skeletons. The bones — *human* bones — swayed in unison at the bottom, undulating in some unseen current, their arms and skulls raised, imploring. Their eye sockets were empty, but Yvonne felt their dead gazes, pleading from beyond.

"Do not enter," the unicorn warned her, his voice taut.

"Why do you show me this? Who are they?"

"You must already know."

Yvonne could only gape. The unicorn kept his distance.

"No." Her whisper sliced through the silence.

"This would have been your fate had that unicorn taken you years ago. Forever has this lake been linked to my kind. As the lake is clear, so too our spirits and bodies. Its waters are our lifeblood and that purity must be maintained."

"By drowning innocence?"

"By preserving it," the unicorn said, "in the lake, and thus, in ourselves."

A jumble of emotions shot through Yvonne's heart. Shock, at how distorted the legends had become. Relief, that she had not been chosen only to be betrayed. Rage, that these women, these naïve young women, had died with their hopes in this watery grave. All to feed the beautiful monsters.

She looked at the unicorn through half-lidded eyes. Perhaps it was the horror that inspired her to ask, "If a crone, bitter and dying, should step into these waters and drown ... ?"

The unicorn stood still as a tombstone, his azure eyes fixed upon Yvonne. The air grew chill, and his terror was pungent in the air.

"Human, I brought you here as a kindness. If you drown in this lake you will destroy not me alone, but all unicorns everywhere."

"And you wish to live on, to lure more maidens to their deaths?"

"All that live must feed," the unicorn said. "We do not kill without purpose as men do. As you no doubt have done."

"Vengeance *is* a purpose. And my need for it is greater than your hunger."

"I thought you would be grateful to learn what you had been spared. I thought this would bring you peace."

Yvonne brandished the horn dagger once more, turned her focus back to the lake. Part of her *was* grateful. And yet ... *Better to have died young and innocent than to live a lifetime of misery. Wasted. Lost.*

A few steps forward, and her life would have purpose at last. She would be the savior of all those maidens yet to be chosen. *Poetic.* They would never know, of course. They would never thank her. Perhaps they deserved their fate, pining in the forest like moon-touched fools, their egos drunk with selfish, senseless dreams of redemptive love.

She imagined her own bones in the water, thick and heavy amidst the graceful sway of the dead maidens. Bitterness welled in her heart. Even in death, they would be more beautiful than she. Even in death, she would be ugly.

She released a breath pent with despair. The smile she gave the unicorn deepened her every wrinkle. "You are beyond my understanding, you with your unearthly majesty and inhuman need. I am not qualified to judge you. But I wish you to know the pain you all have caused." Though she said 'all,' in truth she meant one.

With the tip of her dagger, she slit a shallow line across her palm, held it at the lake's edge.

The unicorn whinnied in panic, his breath expelled in labored snorts. "You will taint us! Our purity cannot be regained. Why —?"

"*Why?*" she shouted. "Because *I* am teaching *you*; teaching the sting of unrequited need, of dreams dreamt alone and caresses never shared; I teach you of tears that scald, of a heart, cracked and terrified; I teach you the lesson of vengeance, the only lover to return my embrace; of an empty bed, like a coffin; of the trampled garden of my life where the only blossoms grown were poisoned, black, and thorned."

"Wait!"

"I am *done* waiting!" Her clenched fist wept red tears, drop by falling drop, corrupting the lake with her bitterness.

She flashed a look of triumph at the unicorn. It was not her imagination that the unicorn's hide grew ashen, the silken skin pebbling, the lifeglow dimming, fading, fainter, fainter. Purple veins, so much like her own, crept like ivy beneath his skin. His spiral horn darkened and tiny cracks wormed down its length. His eyes bled thick, black tears.

She imagined the golden-eyed unicorn — *her* unicorn — out there, suffering as he found himself now afflicted with her pain. *Let him know what ugliness feels like.*

"Look at me," said the unicorn before her. "Look and remember till your dying day. Whatever sins you accuse us of, we have committed only to survive. *You* have caused harm for harm's sake. That is your legacy, human."

Behind him, a bank of mist congealed from empty air, and he turned and fled into it. He vanished, his departure so profound it was as if he had never existed. Her heart sped, as restless as an animal too long caged.

"Don't leave, coward!" she said. "See your precious lake desecrated. Stay, behold my victory!"

The lilies around the lake were withering.

"Don't leave," she cried again.

Don't leave me.

Pete the Pirate's Strange Sea Story

Berti Walker

Pete the Pirate obnoxiously banged his mug upon the bar, because pirates arc obnoxious, and Pete was the most obnoxious of all.

Barbara the Barmaid shook her bountiful bosom as she waggled her finger at him, because barmaids' bosoms are meant to be large and jiggly. "Now, Pete," she said with a scowl."You know there are other patrons waiting patiently for their refills."

"Pirates don't have patience, wench!" He spat on the floor and clanged his hook on the side of his mug, the sound ringing out above the din of frat boys drinking PBR and playing beer pong. "Am-I-right-mate?" he slurred at the man seated next to him.

The man wrinkled his nose as Pete the Pirate's rancid beer breath washed over him. He wiped spittle from his suit jacket and moved down a seat.

Pete took a mighty gulp from his newly-filled mug, slopping the contents onto his pantaloons, giving the impression that he pissed himself.

He strained to focus his one good eye at the mess, his stool lurching as he wavered in his seat. Stabbing his hook through the dirty bar towel, he dabbed at the liquid, managing to make it look even worse. He tried to toss the towel aside with a few choice curses but it clung to his hook.

He downed the rest of his mug in one breath, taking noisy gulps of air in when he was done, beer glistening in his beard and moustache. He looked around for Barbara but she was all the way at the other end of the bar ignoring his calls.

He swiveled in his seat to harass the man who was sitting beside him and found he had moved, so Pete picked up his mug and occupied the empty seat between them.

"You were wonderin' how I got this hook, patch, and peg-leg." He waved his hook in the air, towel flapping like a black flag. "Well, you're in luck. You pay for me ale, and I'll tell ya me tale."

The man rolled his eyes. "I don't know if you're homeless or hitting on me, so let me just stop you right there, man. I'm not interested." He tried to move down a seat again, but the seat was taken, so he just tried his best to look otherwise occupied, pulling out his phone to play Candy Crush or Angry Birds or some shit.

Pete pulled out his crooked, chipped, and crusty dagger and used it to pick his teeth. One popped out and landed on the bar, spinning to a stop beside the man's hand. The guy looked at the tooth, then at Pete, who smiled a rotted-tooth smile while twirling the tip of the dagger into the wooden bar.

"You were going to tell me how you got that eyepatch, hook, and peg-leg, and I was going to buy you an ale," the man said, trying not to defecate himself.

"Yar, that's a fine idea, matey. They call me Pete the Pirate, because that be my name. What do they call ye?"

"M-Mark."

"Alrighty, Muhmark. Have ye ever heard the story of the sea-uniponies?"

"Sure, of course," Mark lied, looking around for someone to notice the crazed dagger-wielding pirate. But no one did. Because crazy shit happens in bars and nobody cares.

Pete the Pirate nodded, eyeing Mark's full mug. Mark slid the mug to Pete who took a slurp, leaving behind pube-looking beard hairs, and then passed it back to Mark before beginning his story.

*

"Yo ho ho and a bottle of rum," the little feathered asshole on Pete the Pirate's shoulder squawks.

It used to be a parrot, but it met with an unfortunate accident. A drunk shipmate, a cannon, and an annoying parrot that only speaks in cliches are a dangerous combination. All that remains is a little feathered asshole that squeaks and a beak that squawks.

"Yar, that be a good boy, Polly." Pete the Pirate gives it a little pat.

"Polly want a cracker."

"Alas, me matey, no more crackers for Polly. They just go right through ye."

"Land-ho!" One-Eyed Eddie shouts from the bird's nest.

"Are ye sure this time?" Pete the Pirate shouts back.

"Land-ho!" Polly repeats.

Holding a telescope to his eye, Pete mutters some choice pirate curses and vows to get someone with two eyes on look-out. Sure enough, ol' One-Eye has spotted land.

But before Pete the Pirate could get too excited, storm clouds roll across the sky, gang up on the sun, and put its lights out. Tumultuous waves form, but instead of moving towards land, they're moving away, right for Neptune's Rage.

Pete starts shouting out commands, but all eyes are on the wave looming ahead. As it breaks, creatures shoot on-board like torpedoes and they skewer everything in sight. They're half-unipony, half-fish, and all attitude.

Men scream as they're impaled by horns being tossed from the wave like darts at a dart board. The ship and the men alike become riddled with holes. Guts and blood and piss and shit spill onto the deck and into the sea. For every sea-unipony they take down, two more take its place.

As the ship begins to sink, Pete the Pirate pulls himself free from the unipony who has him pinned by the leg to the deck. He slits its throat and tosses it aside.

"Polly! Polly where are ya?"

He hears a squawk and whirls around, diving for his pet. Just as his hand closes around It, a unipony spears him through the hand and right through poor Polly.

"Nooooo!" Pete the Pirate wails, slashing at the unipony in a blind fury. The unipony's last flails land a hoof in Pete's eye.

He looks around the churning bloody waters for any signs of his crew, but they've been slaughtered to a man.

Clambering inside a floating barrel, he hides in safety from the sea-uniponies, riding the current until he arrives at Pickle Port, surviving off of his own urine and the meager remains of Polly.

*

Pete the Pirate wiped a salty tear from his only eye. "And that's how it happened."

"That was ... disgusting ..." Mark said. He dropped a twenty on the bar. "For your ale ..."

Pete's eye was still glazed over as the memory lingered. "I be the only scallywag to have seen the beasts and lived to tell the tale. They be out there. Aye, and they be waitin' for ol' Pete to return to the sea. But they'll never catch me here!"

Barbara the Barmaid snapped him out of his reverie. "Goddamn it, Pete! How many times have I told you not to bring that in here?"

Pete sheepishly looked down at the dagger in his hand. "A good few too many, I reckon."

She yanked the towel off of his hook. "And I've been looking for this all over the place! I think it's time to call it a night."

The bar broke out into a drunken rendition of Journey's "Don't Stop Believing." Pete the Pirate winced. "Yar, perhaps you're right." Beneath his breath he muttered, "Every night with that bloody song."

"I'll be seein' ye, Muhmark." Pete the Pirate gave him a hearty pat on the back, remembering just in time to use his good hand. Mark flinched and mumbled something about watching out for sea-uniponies.

Pete the Pirate wobbled out into the street. He paused by the Pickle Port sign to light his pipe, which he was deftly good at doing with only one hand. His eye swam with tears, making it even more difficult to focus.

"T'aint right, a pirate becoming a landlubber. T'aint right at all."

He pivoted on his peg-leg, teetering for a moment before walking down the street, every other step echoing into the night.

"Hey, Pete! See any unicorns today?" A douche-bag teen in baggy pants and too much jewelry yelled.

"Ain't it past yer bedtime? Teenagers have no respect for pirates these days." If he weren't without a ship to flee, Pete the Pirate would strike them all down just for fun.

His legs began to vibrate, and then wobble, and then shake.

No, it wasn't his legs, it was the ground. The teen stared behind Pete the Pirate, his mouth agape, eyes bugging. It gave Pete a flash of satisfaction before the roar began.

He turned ever so slowly, to see the wave looming high above the town, seeming to linger there as if waiting for him to notice it. The horns of the sea-uniponies stuck out from it like spikes on a puffer fish.

Pete the Pirate let out a hearty laugh. "See! What did I tell ye?"

He turned back to gloat, but the teenager was halfway down the street, holding his pants up as he ran to make better time.

"Run all you want! They're gonna get ya! They're gonna get you all!"

Heads poked out of the bar he had just left in time for Pete to make an obscene gesture. "Polly, my pet, I'll be seein' ya soon."

And the uni-tsunami dropped down from the sky, swallowing Pete the Pirate and taking Pickle Port with it.

Horns of Silver and Gold

Stanley Webb

The unicorn Silver flirted her tail at the rutting bucks, then ran away down the lakeshore. The bucks pursued.

Gold outraced them all, coming up alongside her. They rounded a point, and paused beside a cove.

On the far bank, Behemoth raised his towering neck, said, *"GOOD AFTERNOON,"* then returned to his grazing.

Silver aimed her horn at the water. "Let's hide there."

Gold replied, "I fear to."

"Behemoth will not harm us."

"I fear Leviathan."

"Silly! He lives in the salt sea, not the sweet lake."

She waded in. Gold's pride, as well as his lust, required him to follow. They went out until the water covered their backs.

The other bucks rounded the point.

She said, "Duck your head under."

He did not like being under water, and was happy that the experience was brief. When they surfaced, the other bucks' rumps were flying out of sight.

She said, "You've won me!"

Gold forgot his discomfort. He pranced behind Silver, reared from the water, and mounted her.

"Oh my," said Silver. "It *is* Leviathan!"

Behemoth averted his gaze.

A pair of kangaroos passed on the beach, followed by two anteaters, then two swans. The parade continued with pairs of snow leopards, peccaries, and —

"What are those?" Gold asked while dismounting. "Giant moa birds?"

Pair after pair of diverse creatures passed along the beach, and disappeared over the horizon. Curious, the unicorns waded ashore, and accosted a couple of reticulated pythons.

One of the serpents explained, *"Yahweh hasss decided to dessstroy thisss world, and ssso sssummonsss a pair of every kind of animal to be pressserved, and repopulate the next world."*

"You lie!" Silver cried. "Are the unicorns not Yahweh's favorites? Has he not given us indomitable horns, shining beauty, and wisdom beyond all other beings? And, among all the unicorns, are not Gold and I superior? *We* would have been the first called!"

She lowered her horn. The pythons hurried away, to be followed by countless other pairs, the last of which were zebras.

"The serpents might lie," Gold said uneasily. "But *something* is happening."

"That is true; we shall investigate."

They followed the zebras to a vast plain of tree stumps. In the middle of the plain, dwarfing the hovel beside it, there stood a colossal wooden box. The paired animals paraded up a wooden ramp, and entered the box via a huge, square doorway.

Gold asked, "Is it a barn?"

The zebras entered the box. A bearded, old man emerged in the doorway, and peered down at the unicorns.

He called, "Are you coming?"

"I should think not!" Silver scoffed. "This explains everything: it's some foolishness of the humans."

The old man retreated with a shrug. The ramp rose without any apparent motivation, became a door, and closed with a suction sound. Gold approached the box, and found no crack around the door. All of the box's planks fit together as if they were of one piece.

"Silver, I'm worried."

"Stop worrying; it's — Yikes!" She leaped as if stung.

"What's wrong?" Suddenly, something splashed on his back. "Yikes!"

Then, uncountable drops of liquid plummeted from the clouds, and beat the earth into mud. The unicorns bolted, but there was no place to hide. They cowered against the side of the box.

Silver's nose wiggled. "It's only water!"

"Falling from the sky?"

She stepped into the open.

"This is nice! Come play with me."

She looked so beautiful, prancing through veils of mist, with curtains of water drops exploding against her back, that Gold overcame his fear, and chased her through the phenomenon.

He had just caught her, and was about to mount her again, when a rabble of angry and terrified humans rushed toward them, carrying axes and other dangerous tools. The unicorns bolted faster than any other animal could run. They paused at a safe distance to gauge the pursuit.

"They aren't chasing us," Silver exclaimed. "They're attacking the box."

The rabble's tools rose and fell, the thunderous clamor rising above the drumming of the water, but no wooden chips flew from the planks. The humans' feet sank in liquid mud.

Gold looked down, and saw that his hooves were also submerged.

"Silver ..."

"Don't worry; it's only water."

"What if this doesn't stop?"

She was silent for a while. Then she said, "Mount Ararat is near. We'll climb the foothills."

They gazed down upon the plain. The rabble of humans was gone under the flood. The box was half submerged.

"All of those poor animals," murmured Gold. "Trapped to drown."

"It's moving!" Silver cried.

The box rocked, then floated. A breeze urged it toward the far horizon.

"They're saved," said Gold. "The pythons spoke the truth."

"No! God would not have forsaken us!"

The water crested the hill, and lapped around their hooves. The unicorns retreated toward the mountain,

but a channel of swiftly flowing water blocked their path. They waded in up to their necks. A human carcass floated past.

"I can't do this," said Gold.

"Stay beside me. We'll swim as hard as we can, angling into the current."

Gold held his nose above the waves as his hooves clawed in the depths. He was downstream from Silver, and the current pushed her against him. He could not see Ararat's slope through the curtains of falling water.

A tangled shape loomed up out of the flood, and swept down upon them; it was a tree, which the flood had ripped from the earth. He urged Silver to hurry. The tree rolled, and the roots surged up like huge, wooden talons. Then, he felt the muddy slope under his hoof.

He and Silver staggered up to shallow water, as the tree rushed downstream behind them.

Gold cried, "We've made it!"

Suddenly, a panicked lion appeared in the flood, its roaring struggles beating the water to foam. The lion collided with Silver, and clutched her with all four of its paws. They both went under.

For a moment, Gold was numb with loss. Then, the water roiled, and the battle resurfaced. Gold lunged, and stabbed his horn through the lion's heart. The impact killed the beast instantly, and flung its body into the spate. Silver regained her feet, bleeding from numerous lacerations. Gold let her lean against him as they climbed out of the water. She then stood shivering, her head held low.

She said, "The water is salt."

He looked out across an endless expanse of waves. The foothills were submerged, and the horizon was obscured behind densely falling water.

"The Earth has become a sea," he said. "We must achieve the summit."

"Why bother? Yahweh *has* forsaken us."

He could not move her. After much futile urging, he turned his back, and walked away. Gold hated to do so, but shortly he heard Silver's hooves sucking through the mud, and she appeared beside him.

The landscape was treacherous. The gathering water formed new rivers, which cut channels into the softening mountainside. Silver and Gold were not the only beings who sought refuge on Ararat: a family of naked humans struggled upward against the mire, until a sudden river swept them all away; an elephant wept in mortal despair as it sank into a boggy hole; and, at the limit of Gold's vision, a massive figure plodded inexorably toward the summit.

The unicorns eyed the figure warily as all three achieved the rocky mountaintop. Most of the soil had washed downhill, except for a sodden hollow where a small olive tree drowned. The stranger was humanoid, but twice as tall as any man. His skull rose in a tufted ridge, his eyes were beetled, his nose flat, and coarse, odiferous hair covered his powerful body.

He said, "Greetings, unicorns."

"Greetings," said Gold. "What are you?"

"The last of the Giants, driven from our caverns by the flood."

Silver said, "Yahweh has forsaken you, also."

The Giant shook his head sadly. "I forsook Him, through overt pride in the strength of the body which He had created for me. Unicorns, I hear, take similar pride in their horns."

The unicorns exchanged a glance.

"If we are prideful," said Silver. "It is because He has made us to be so."

The Giant shrugged. "Perhaps we are a part of His plan; perhaps the rain will stop before we drown."

"Rain," said Gold. "I do not know that word."

"It means, 'Water dripping from the cave's roof.'"

Night sneaked in behind the rain.

"It will not stop," said Silver.

A bellow came out of the darkness; it was somewhat like the bugle of an elephant, and also similar to the bleat of a calf. The voice was as large as thunder, though its words were unclear.

Said Gold, "It's Yahweh himself!"

The cry repeated nearer.

"HELP ME!"

Behemoth's tall, swaying neck seemed to materialize in the rain. The creature's tremendous body churned up waves that rolled across the mountaintop. Clumsy in the water, he lost stability, and rolled. His feet kicked in the air, then his neck rose again, draining off sheets of dirty water. Behemoth gave a squeal of panic loud enough to drive the survivors to their knees.

"He's coming here," Silver said, regaining her feet. "He'll push us into the flood!"

They retreated to the opposite side of Ararat's summit as Behemoth planted his front feet on the underwater slope. The entire mountain quaked. He struggled to climb out of the flood, but sank halfway into the mud.

Gold saw a rapid movement in the darkness. A gargantuan, triangular fin sliced across the sea, throwing tails of water to either side.

"What is that?"

The Giant said, "I have seen him before: Leviathan."

Leviathan rose to strike. Gold glimpsed a conical snout, flat eyes as big as ponds, and multiple rows of serrated teeth. Then, Leviathan plunged, and closed his teeth on Behemoth's tail. Behemoth screamed in agony, as his thick blood turned the muddy sea to crimson. Leviathan dragged the great beast down. The water whipped into a frenzy. Huge masses of flesh breached the surface, to fall with titanic splashes.

After some time had passed, the waves quieted. Leviathan's head rose from the water, one eye blankly regarding the survivors, who now stood knee-deep in the rising flood.

He spoke, his voice thrumming from deep inside his body.

"The last terrestrial life. One final taste of hot blood!"

His snout turned toward them. His chasmal jaws opened.

"Mighty Leviathan," cried Silver. "We are not the last!"

Leviathan paused. *"What else dares to survive?"*

"A great, wooden box, full of two of every kind of animal, and humans! We saw them drift away, and if you spare us, we will guide you after them."

"It shall be so."

Leviathan closed his jaws, and nudged his snout against the mountain. Silver climbed aboard. Gold hesitated in distaste at his mate's bargain.

"Don't be a fool," she hissed.

He could not bear to die without her. Gold boarded the monster, then turned to the Giant.

"Are you coming?"

The Giant turned his back. "I will have no part in this."

"As you wish," Leviathan said. *"I will return later, and swim over your bones."*

Leviathan departed, traveling awash in consideration for his passengers. Gold braced his hooves among the monster's toothed scales, and looked back at the Giant, until all that he could see was rain.

"Name which heading to the blood."

Gold leaned close to her, and whispered, "Please, let's not do this."

Silver's voice trembled in reply, "If we are not Yahweh's favorites, then none else shall be. Head east-southeast, Mighty Leviathan!"

The monster came about, waves rolling across his back. The unicorns retreated to the lee side of his dorsal fin. Far astern, his mighty, hooked tail lashed the sea.

The unicorns grew weary, but they could not recline, for Leviathan's side curved too steeply down from his fin. The salt spray burned their eyes. They became dehydrated.

"Leviathan," called Gold. "We need water!"

"There is plenty all around you. Your gills will fil-ter the salt."

"We have no gills."

Leviathan chuckled.

The sun rose, unseen behind the overcast. Gold's eyes were swollen from the sea spray. He lifted his nose toward Heaven, so the rain could rinse away the salt, and opened his mouth to wet his tongue. Silver's belly rumbled.

"I'm starving! I should not have forsaken Yahweh for Leviathan. We cannot live like this. I miss the earth!"

"What say you?"

Gold called, "We are hungry!"

"Hunger is a wonderful abyss; always demand-ing, and never full."

Leviathan altered his course, toward a lighter patch on the sea. As they neared, Gold saw a school of huge, silver fish, basking in the rain. Leviathan charged. The fish scattered, but his wide jaws caught two of them, and his teeth gnashed as he ate.

"Pick your meal from my wake."

A severed fish head drifted astern, its gills still throbbing. Gold turned away, nauseated.

Leviathan resumed his heading. The day pro-gressed into another night.

"Where is this box?" he demanded.

"We do not know, exactly — "

"Then, I'll wash you from my back, and have you in my belly!"

Gold scanned desperately, wishing that they had remained on Ararat to drown in peace. Just as

Leviathan began to arch for diving, Gold spotted a meager shine through the rain: the flame of a distant oil lamp.

"There!"

Leviathan raised his snout.

"Yes, I see it! I smell the wood, and feel the heartbeats of those aboard. Great Yahweh, Thank You for this delicious gift; thank You for making me supreme on the Earth!"

Silver wept.

"Their blood is upon my heart! God was right to forsake me."

"Perhaps we can stop Leviathan."

"How?"

"With our horns."

But then, Leviathan launched himself at the box, and the waves tossed the unicorns off his back. They struggled toward each other in his wake.

"I cannot swim," said Silver. "I am too weak."

"Ask Yahweh for strength."

"I'm unworthy!"

"Then, lay your head across my back; I will hold you up."

Leviathan rammed the box broadside. There was a powerful *thump*, and the box shuddered sideways. The monster circled, and rammed the other side. Then, he dove deep, and rammed from below. When that attack also failed, Leviathan breached high, fell atop the box, and drove it under. But, the box rose beneath him, and shrugged him back into the sea.

Leviathan ranted, *"Why do You deny me my gift? I am Your favorite!"*

Lightning struck a distant wave. Minutes passed before the thunder came.

"You dare to mock Leviathan? I shall laugh last!"

The monster came about, and rushed back toward the unicorns.

Gold said, "Close your eyes."

He waited for Leviathan's toothy cavern to engulf them, but instead the monster rose from below, lifting them upon his snout.

"Your horns are indomitable; stand forward, and serve as my rams!"

Gold looked Silver in the eye, then glanced at Leviathan's broad skull. Silver nodded.

Gold said, "We are ready, monster."

Leviathan accelerated, his tail thrashing the sea to foam. The unicorns braced themselves into the wind and the waves. Leviathan made a great circle, and aimed them at the box.

Gold cried, "Now, use the horns which God gave us!"

The unicorns turned and leaped, dropping point-first between the monster's eyes. Their horns penetrated to the hilts, and split Leviathan's skull.

Leviathan's back arched so sharply that he sprang above the waves, dislodging the unicorns into the sea.

The impact knocked Gold's wind out, and his involuntary gasp filled his throat with seawater. Gold struggled for breath, but he could not keep his head above the violent waves. He saw Leviathan roll belly-up, but he could not see his mate.

"Silver!"

She did not reply.

Leviathan sank, leaving a slick of oil and blood. As the resulting suction took Gold down, he glimpsed the box, full of Yahweh's chosen, drifting peaceably on its way to salvation.

He awoke beneath the water. Gold felt no surprise or panic, although he knew at once that something profound had occurred. He swam to the surface, and exchanged his stale breath for fresh. The rain had stopped, and the overcast thinned.

A blunt, gray creature emerged nearby, and sprayed from the top of its head. A long, shining spiral horn extended from the creature's nose. The being saw him, and shied away, but Gold recognized her horn.

"Silver?"

"Gold? Is that you? What are we?"

A name appeared in his mind. "Narwhales. Yahweh has changed us."

"As a punishment, or a reward?"

"I do not know, but I don't *feel* punished."

A white dove flew overhead.

"Let's follow; it may be a message."

The narwhales pumped their tails, and pursued the dove. By the time they caught up to it, the dove had reached an island, and rested in a small olive tree. The Giant sat nearby.

"You have survived!" Gold cried in delight.

The Giant squinted at him. "Unicorn? The wonders know no end. Yes, I survived; the water rose as high as my nose, then began to recede." He patted the tree affectionately. "I lifted this above my head, to save it from drowning. What became of Leviathan?"

"We killed him."

"That is as well. All of the old things are gone, except for me, and when the water recedes completely, I will hide myself in the wilderness. The new world should belong to the new."

Then, the clouds parted before the sun, and a rainbow spanned the world.

The dove picked an olive leaf, and flew away.

What'd You Wish For?

Shenoa Carroll-Bradd

Carla opened the rectangular box and peered inside as the clamor of restless children carried through from the other room. "What the hell is this?"

"Stacey's birthday cake. Like you asked for."

"No, what I asked for was a vanilla sheet cake with a unicorn drawn on the frosting. You know how obsessed she's been. This is ... what, a gay pride cake?"

"It's just a rainbow. Gays don't own all the colors."

She pinched the bridge of her nose. "You just had to go pick up my order. That's it. I don't understand how you could have gotten it so wrong." She sighed. "Where is the real cake?"

He shrugged. "Ask the wrong address you gave me. When I got there, it was a laundromat. I had to stop at this weird mom and pop bakery instead."

She rolled her eyes. "Well, it's too late now. I guess we'll have to make the best of it." She plopped the cake on the counter and held out her hand. "Give me the candles."

He pulled an object from his pocket and laid it in her palm.

She looked at it for a second, and then slowly turned, eyes narrowed. "You only got one candle? Jesus, Dan. I don't understand how you could have screwed things up this badly."

"It's all they had at the store, and I thought it kinda looked like a horn, so-"

"Fine! It's fine, I'm sure Stacey's not going to care." She stuck the tapered cylinder into the frosting and lit the wick. "She's going to be too upset by the cake to notice this one weird candle." Carla lifted the cake out of its box and turned toward the living room. "At least get the lights, would you?"

Dan leaned through the door to flick the lights off.

The dozen children crowded around their dining room table immediately and reverently hushed, awaiting cake.

They began to sing as Carla brought it in and set it in front of her daughter, who looked puzzled.

"But I wanted —"

She's more like her mother every year. "Just blow the candle out and make a wish, honey," Dan called from the doorway.

Stacey looked around the room as the song ended, her gaze registering each unicorn paper plate, each pink napkin, down to the glittery tablecloth. She took a deep breath, then puffed out her cheeks and blew.

The room plunged into darkness, and everyone cheered.

Dan hit the lights again so Carla could see what she was doing as she cut the cake.

"What'd you wish for, darlin'?" he called.

"Don't tell him," one of the other kids piped up.

Stacey grinned, showing the gap from her latest lost tooth. "I wished for more unicorns!"

𝔘𝔫𝔦𝔠𝔬𝔯𝔫𝔞𝔡𝔬!   153

Of course she did.

Carla glared at him over her shoulder as she finished portioning out the cake.

"You shouldn't have said that," that kid continued. "Now it'll never come true."

Yeah, because that's what stopped a unicorn from manifesting.

His wife came to stand with him in the doorway. "That rainbow goes all the way through," she groused. "You know how I hate giving Stacey artificial colors. Think of all the chemicals they're ingesting …"

She might have said more, but Dan wasn't listening. He watched Stacey as she inhaled her piece and lifted the plate to lick it clean. "They seem to like it just fine."

It was true. All the children had devoured their serving in under a minute. He felt a touch of satisfaction. Clearly he hadn't screwed things up as badly as Carla pretended.

Suddenly, Stacey clutched her stomach. "Ow!"

All around the table, the children reacted the same, grabbing at their heads and stomachs.

"Shit!" Carla smacked his arm. "Are you kidding me? Not only are you late, with the wrong cake, but now you've given a dozen children food poisoning."

"Mama," Stacey groaned. "My heeeaad …" As she whined, the skin of her forehead bulged, like her skull was trying to blow a flesh bubble.

Carla shrieked.

A blood-streaked horn burst from the center of Stacey's head, the skin around it peeling back in a sticky flower.

The children's hair fell out *en masse* as they writhed, strands of every length and color drifting down into piles on the table as everything not in a straight line down their scalps abandoned ship. Their shrill cries turned into whinnies, and smooth golden hooves burst from their palms like fossils emerging from ancient bedrock.

"What is happening?" Carla screamed.

Dan could only stare.

The children's skins sloughed off into the puddling lakes of blood beneath the dining table, revealing the damp, red coats of a dozen miniature unicorns. The little monsters looked at each other and screamed, flailing their new hooves and slashing their horns through the air in horror.

Dan grabbed Carla's hand and dragged her down the hall to the bathroom. He locked the door behind them and pulled her into the tub, where they cowered together, listening to the awful din.

Carla wept and shuddered against his chest.

The unicorn sounds rose to a fierce, warlike cacophony, and then there was a wooden splintering, either of the table or the front door, followed by the fading thunder of departing hooves.

Alone in the now-silent house, Dan finally voiced his fear.

"I'm never going to hear the end of this, am I?"

My Lil Poem

Joel Kaplan

My little
my little
my little bony white flank
raise your rainbow tail
take me to pony land
lost in your big bright eyes
your long bright face
the melody of your long pink mane
resounds in charnel temple of my flesh
we vibrate in a rainbow of ecstasy
my fingers lock in your curly pink hair
her voice squeaky and hoarse
but she's not a horse, she's a pony
make me yours she begs
her now purple flank quivering in the starlight
I thrust deep and now she's my pony
we fall through the floor
and fuck on the ceiling
her pony aperture is a spaceship
we fly through the cosmos

The Last Unicorn

Sydel Brown

"Check her out!" said Bruce, nudging Ricardo's arm and pointing his chin at the blonde taking a seat to their left.

"Nice!" said Ricardo, knowing he would never make it with the blonde. His tastes were more refined. He kept scanning the room as the women took their seats all around the basement room of the local rec center, wondering if any of them had that something special, the *je ne sais quoi* he'd been looking for so long.

"What about the redhead? She has nice — "

"You know I'm not into that superficial stuff, Bruce, c'mon!" replied Ricardo.

He kept scanning the crowd, starting to dread having to go through even five-minute awkward flirts with all of these women who were obviously not his type.

As he began to wonder if he'd wasted the $50 speed dating fee, *she* sauntered in and positioned herself at the table nearest to the door. She looked as nervous as he felt, stepping forward and back, which endeared her all the more to him. From that moment on, he only had eyes for her.

"Yeah, yeah, you go for the brains, not the brawn, I know!" Bruce made sure to say loudly, so the women at the tables closest to them overheard and giggled.

As long as *she* didn't think he was an asshat like his friend, Ricardo didn't care. He was trying not to stare, but she was so beautiful, he couldn't help it.

After leering at the bottoms of a couple of the stragglers, Bruce noticed that Ricardo was focused on someone near the door. "Oh no, man! Not the fucking unicorn! You always go for the strangest one in the room."

"Someone has to, right? Why not me? And really, she's, as you say, a fucking *UNICORN!* Who wouldn't want to hit that?"

"Any human in their right mind! She's a horse with a horn that could impale you as you hit it. And she probably farts rainbows or glitters in the sunlight or something equally disturbing. It's just not right."

"She's not a vampire, you idiot. And you're the one who dragged me here! You go for the cute girl with the high heels and bangs in her eyes. I'll go for the most beautiful magical creature I've ever seen!"

"You're so messed up, Rico, man. I thought you were past all that Brony shit. But I guess at least you know what you like. More power to you."

The men drew numbers which told them which table to start at in the room and move clockwise until they'd had their five-minute flirt with each woman. Ricardo's number started at the table next to the mare of his dreams.

It took all of his willpower to not stare at her instead of pay attention to the woman at the table in front of him. As she asked him questions about himself, he kept sneaking glances next to him. He tried to overhear the conversation beside him, but there didn't seem to be a lot going on, other than *her* shifting back and forth.

He was so relieved when the bell went off to move to the next table/flirt, he bolted up and nearly pushed the guy out of the way to sit across from *her*. He sat down, taking her all in. She brayed slightly, flipping her mane to the side. He smiled shyly.

"Ahem," said the swarthy man beside him. "We're going *clockwise,* moron!"

Ricardo looked around and realized he was the only one who'd gone the wrong way. Blushing madly, he apologized to the floor and scooted two tables over to face the redhead he was sure would hook up with Bruce by night's end. She was definitely Bruce's type.

Too embarrassed to look at *her* again, he threw himself into the flirt. The redhead was quite funny, and he hoped Bruce would date her instead of only sleep with her, even though he knew that's all Bruce was interested in. He talked Bruce up, and then the bell went off, so he moved to the next table, *clockwise,* and fell into a pattern of flirting outrageously with each of the women, and ending with talking Bruce up. If nothing else, he was an excellent wingman.

After just over an hour of intense flirts with women he had zero interest in, he was two tables away from *her*. He toned down his flirting and had to make a concentrated effort not to look over at *her*. She probably thought he was a complete moron for the mistake he made right at the beginning and wouldn't want anything to do with him. It was devastating to think the woman of his dreams was so close yet so far because he'd screwed up. Damnit!

The bell rang and he moved to the table next to her, sweat forming on his brow. The poor woman in front of him, Carrie or Cara or maybe it was Carly, had trouble keeping his attention with even the simplest of questions. He apologized to her: "This wasn't my idea. My friend Bruce wanted to try this speed dating thing out, so here I am."

She smiled and said, "I know. Meeting so many people at once is nerve-wracking. We can just sit here quietly until the bell goes, get our wits about us before the last of our trial-by-flirting-with-strangers."

Ricardo thanked her and was left with two minutes of silence with his current flirt to contemplate what to say to *her*. He noticed that it was uncomfortably silent at *her* table, as well, and was beginning to wonder why when the bell went off. He smiled at Kate? and moved over to the table with *her*.

He looked at his hands on his lap, refusing to make eye contact. He was aware that his pits were darkened from the sweat now pouring from every place he had glands. He intended to sit there staring at his hands for the next four minutes and thirty-four seconds, when the bell would release him from this uncomfortable hell.

"Hello, handsome!" said a tender voice in his head.

He looked up to see *her* looking intently at him.

"How did you do that?" he asked.

She snorted. *"I'm a fucking UNICORN! Of course I can talk to you in your head."*

He nodded his head, drinking her in. She was even more incredible up close. Her coat was pure white with a light blue shimmer every time she moved. Her eyes were large, crystalline, and he saw all of the past and all of the future as he gazed into them. Her horn glistened like morning dew on the daisy petals in his childhood garden. She was utterly perfect.

"I've never met anyone like you before," he said.

"I'm the last of my kind," she told him. *"I want a baby. Will you help me have a baby?"*

He nodded. "I want to be with you," he said. "Forever."

Her equine smile beamed at him with all the force of nature, nearly knocking him off his chair. She leaned towards him. Her horn was mere inches from his forehead. He breathed faster, realizing he had a hard-on. He blushed and crossed his legs so she wouldn't see.

Her glistening horn touched him ever-so-lightly between his eyes, which he had closed as waves of magical bliss pulled him under. He no longer felt like himself, but like he was everything and nothing at once. When he opened his eyes, she was there, smiling at him with that full force of nature, and he smiled back.

"Holy shit, man! What the fuck?" said Bruce, standing beside him.

Ricardo noticed he was much taller than Bruce now. His horn tingled as Bruce's thoughts rippled into his head.

"Leave it to Ricardo to turn into a fucking unicorn!"

"I'm a fucking unicorn, Bruce!" Ricardo shouted into Bruce's head as he clomped his front hooves. Bruce took a few steps back.

"This is too weird, man. I'm outta here!" Bruce said and took off out of the room.

Ricardo didn't care. He turned to *her*. *"Thank you! You've given me such a gift and I don't even know your name!"*

"Isidore, my darling. Now I'm no longer the last of my kind. Let's go make some babies!"

Even though this was the first time, he never thought of himself as one to turn down unicorn sex, especially now that he was a unicorn himself. Ricardo followed her out the door, oblivious to the disgust on the faces of the men in the room and all the women scrambling to change the name Bruce to Ricardo on their flirt cards.

All he saw was the swish of Isidore's tail which reminded him he still had a hard-on from before his transformation, except now it was horse-sized and he was no longer crossing his legs to hide it but ready to use it in full force on his new mate.

They barely made it through the magical portal she'd opened up to her place beside Creation Lake, the place that started all life in the universe, before he was mounting her in ecstasy.

*

The first month was a tangled blur of unicorn sex, the likes of which he'd never begun to imagine. Orgasms with Isidore felt like explosions of purity mixed with darkness. They were like no orgasm he'd ever had, filled with life, death, and every possible experience in between. He never wanted to stop copulating. Ever.

*

The second month, Ricardo started to miss his friends. On a rare afternoon with no unicorn sex because Isidore was chasing rainbows or, as she called it, "Paying the goddamned rent!" Ricardo realized he could read Bruce's mind, even from this distance.

"I can't believe Ricardo ran off with that fucking unicorn! I'm left with that dweeb Felipe as my wingman. He sucks as a wingman! All he does is talk about himself, which doesn't help me land chicks in the least. Bastard Rico!"

Ricardo felt bad for Bruce momentarily, until his thoughts rambled into this: *"And how is it that every single woman, including that hot redhead, chose a fucking unicorn in speed dating over someone who actually stuck around in this dimension! So unfair. Fuck you, Rico, fuck you in your fat unicorn ass!"*

What? The speed-dating women all chose him? Even the funny redhead? Hmmm ...

He soon forgot about all that when Isidore returned and they blissed out on orgasms for the rest of the week.

*

The third month, Isidore started getting pissy. She wasn't pregnant, even though they'd spent most of

their waking moments the last couple of months doing each other every which way. She questioned Ricardo's commitment to her, even though he spent all of his energy on trying to make her happy.

But she wasn't happy. Even chasing rainbows and impaling those damned happy leprechauns at each end so she could take their gold to pay their exorbitant rent for their shack beside the over-hyped Creation Lake had lost its charm. She wanted a baby, and wondered if maybe a turkey baster might be a better baby daddy than this sad sack in front of her.

Now, whenever he tried to mount her, she groaned and claimed an earth-shattering headache, which meant she had to expend magical energy to make the ground move. At least earthquakes took less energy than she'd expended in the first couple of months when she was making Ricardo think orgasms were life, death, and everything in between.

Ricardo was beginning to be thankful when Isidore made the ground quake. Orgasms had lost their lustre. Sex was a chore, and it wasn't getting them any closer to having a baby. He suspected he was shooting blanks because there was no way he'd missed the mark that many times for two months. No way.

*

The fourth month, Ricardo started going on long walks by himself. He told Isidore it was to try to find himself, but he was actually returning to his hometown to see if he could pick up where he left off.

He spent a lot of time hanging out with Bruce, drinking beer and reading his mind about the many lays he'd had. It was quite sexy. Bruce's mind retained all the sordid details of a decade's worth of casual sex.

Ricardo would return to Isidore after these long "walks" and dutifully giv'er a good mount, but it always ended with another earthquake.

*

The fifth month, Ricardo's walks lasted several days at a time. Isidore didn't mind. She was bored of him. Bored of earthquakes. Bored of not being a mother.

*

The sixth month, Ricardo went for a walk. She didn't see him for a few weeks. She wouldn't have minded so much, but he'd promised to bring her back some apples from her favorite orchard, and she was peckish.

She opened her mind to him and found him staring at the rump of a redheaded horse just as he was about to mount her. *"Get your ass back here, you ass!"* she said to him. He sprinted back to her, head hung in shame. At least he remembered to bring her apples. She didn't let him have any.

*

The seventh month, Ricardo went for a walk. When Isidore tried to find him with her mind to ask him to pick up a bale of hay on his way back, she couldn't see him. He'd blocked her! It wasn't something she'd taught him how to do.

She showed up in his hometown, ready to spit fire, something she hadn't done in millennia. She galloped to Bruce's house and broke down the door with her hooves. Inside was something she never expected to see again: at least twenty unicorns all going at it like the house was on fire. Unicorn orgies were common back in the day, but this, this was unnatural.

"WHO ARE ALL OF YOU? I'M THE LAST OF MY KIND!"

Ricardo dismounted from a redheaded unicorn and trotted up to Isidore.

"You should be happy, darling. I learned how to transform more humans into unicorns, just like you transformed me!"

Isidore glared at Ricardo. *"You WHAT?"*

Bruce, who was also now a unicorn, dismounted from a threesome with two blonde unicorns, to join Ricardo. *"Rico is a saint! Chicks really dig unicorns and were totally down with getting down with one, especially when they found out they could become unicorns themselves. I've never had orgasms like this! It's like life, death, and everything in between. Amazing!"*

Isidore used her horn to slash Bruce's shimmering horn off his head, and he fell to the ground. Ricardo neighed, pushing at his friend with his front hoof. He tried talking to him with his mind. *"Bruce? Talk to me, Bruce!"* but Bruce was already dead.

Ricardo turned on Isidore. *"Why did you kill him? He didn't do anything wrong!"*

Isidore ignored Ricardo and turned her attention to the rest of the stunned group of oversexed unicorns. *"Follow me, lovelies,"* she said in her most alluring internal voice. *"I want to blow your minds with a new trick!"*

Oversexed unicorns are not the brightest of animals, magical or otherwise. They followed her out of the house to the middle of the street. *"Run with me!"* she said and all of the unicorns ran with her. Ricardo followed them outside but kept his distance, still upset about losing his best friend to this — fucking unicorn!

The unicorns ran towards the end of the street, then circled back, around and around like they were running track.

"Faster, my lovelies!" Isidore called out, and the oversexed unicorns ran faster. As they gained speed, they also started to gain air. Ricardo watched as each unicorn blurred into the next, a cornucopia of hard muscle and horns and speed, a thought that started to make him horny. *"Faster!"* she sang, and Ricardo could feel the wind of unicorn's breath trying to suck him in.

"Faster! Harder! Faster!" she called out, reminding him of the first time they copulated, so many months ago.

Now he could feel the force of their efforts, hooves on air, a massive force of magic and muscle. The air crackled with energy. He could hear the rumbling of thunder, see the bolts of lightning forming in the middle of their tunnel. Ricardo snapped out of his horny reverie and started to run away from this unnatural force of power.

"FASTER!" she called out, directing the unicornado towards her one-time lover.

There was no way to outrun them. Ricardo was pulled up into the eye of the unicornado. He whinnied and tried to go up or go down, any way except where the hooves and horns blurred around him.

"Slower, my lovelies!" Isidore said, and the unicorns slowed.

"Turn inward, my lovelies!" she said, and they all turned inward.

"Move closer, my lovelies!" she said, and they moved closer.

"That's it, my lovelies!" she said, as their horns tore at Ricardo's equine flesh.

"NOOO!" said the redheaded unicorn right after her horn struck the final blow that removed Ricardo's horn. The light went out from his crystalline eyes and he fell to the ground, dead.

The oversexed unicorns, in a frenzy of motion directed by Isidore, had killed their creator, their friend. They knelt next to Ricardo, poor Rico, and wept pools of tears.

The only one not crying was Isidore. She looked with pity upon these weak carbon copies of unicorns. And once she thought that, she realized it was the reason why she could never become pregnant with Ricardo — he wasn't a real unicorn, he was just a carbon copy of one, a fabrication made from a potent combination of lust and magic, but not born of unicorn blood.

"ARGH!!!" she said and de-horned the rest of the unicorns.

And once again, or even still, she was the last of her kind.

GEUs

Sheryl Normandeau

I've got my hand on the gearshift and I'm backing the truck out of the lot when the call comes in. Buzz is requesting backup. I don't hear any urgency or panic in his voice, just his regular slow delivery, like he's on the delicious and fragile cusp of one too many beer.

I frown. I'm on my way home to fit my tired ass into the comfort crevasse in my couch, pop open a few cold ones, and watch this week's episode of "Dancing with Dogs." I've waited seven days to see if pop darling Leah Infinity and her shih tzu Popper were eliminated last round. Buzz has got shit for brains if he thinks I'm going in to help him kill a few bedbugs.

Except ... Buzz never, ever, ever calls for backup.

I might be the well-muscled mind of this operation, but Buzz is an exterminator extraordinaire. There isn't a pest alive that makes him flinch — and trust me, we've been in some pretty interesting situations. You don't want to know what some people harbor in their cracks, and I mean that in every possible way you can imagine.

"What's up?" I ask.

"We've got a situation," he says.

"'bugs grow cruise missiles for balls? Buzz, you know I gotta get home. My show is on soon."

"Well, now," Buzz continues, "that might be a problem. I think you'd better get down here pronto."

I'm both so pissed and intrigued by Buzz' unprecedented request that I burn rubber to the apartment on 107 Street.

It doesn't look like much from the outside, a concrete five-storey artifact slapped together in the early Seventies. The exterior has seen a few coats of paint, and is currently sporting a dull yellowish-brown that I hope the owners got a good deal on.

I park illegally and step outside, just as the double front doors of the building explode.

I don't have time to duck or bolt, but somehow the flying glass doesn't reach me. I stand there, agog, as two women run screaming past me, their white lab coats Rorschached with blood.

They are followed by a unicorn.

No, make that two unicorns, and both of them are breathing fire. Off the boulevard, two azaleas and a small walnut tree burst into flames as the animals give chase.

I had clearly inhaled too many esfenvalerate fumes that afternoon.

I watch as the unicorns easily overtake the women in the coats and scorch them right there on the sidewalk, gaily stomping on the charred remains with cloven hooves. Their silky white manes and tails are something straight out of a shampoo ad. I am transfixed by the bright purple horn each one sports in the centre of its forehead — they remind me of something.

Buzz appears at the busted doors and yanks me inside just as I grasp a hazy recollection of a long ago night of strippers and pills and a colossal amount of vodka.

I hear the sound of an alarm coming from below us, somewhere in the basement. I stumble over shards of glass and a severed arm and what looks to be someone's intestines or spleen or maybe brain — I never was any good with anatomy.

He's tugged off his mask, but Buzz is still in full spraying regalia, suited up from neck to toe, sprayer harnessed to his back. Bedbugs are serious business. So are unicorns, apparently.

"Of course, you know I'm missing 'Dancing with Dogs,'" I say.

Buzz looks pained. "I've told you a million times, Jack, you need to buy a DVR."

I feel my blood pressure rising. "A DVR! No way, Buzz, it's not going to happen. You get one of those things and then you are in constant panic mode, wondering if you have enough space to record six seasons of the latest megashow on HD. Which of your precious recordings will the machine sacrifice when it uses up that last gigabyte on its hard drive? I won't do it, Buzz, I will not be enslaved."

Buzz slaps a gloved palm to his forehead, but wisely changes the subject. "So, I'm up on the third floor fumigating Mrs. O'Grady's place, like we're booked to do, when I hear this noise outside in the hall. It sounds like horse's hooves, which is pretty weird, so I stop what I'm doing and go out to take a look."

"Let me guess," I say. It's nice to know the pesticides have finally gotten to both of us.

"I got one eyeballful and locked myself back up inside O'Grady's suite. That's when I called you." For the first time since I've known him, Buzz actually appears rattled. Then again, it could just be the vindaloo we had for lunch. "I waited until I couldn't hear them anymore, then took the elevator down to the ground floor. This is some pretty weird shit, Jack."

There is a loud rumble outside, followed by repeated blasts of gunfire. I drift to the doorway and am nearly mowed down by a dozen gentlemen in camo flak jackets. Their guns are pointed at Buzz and me.

"Yo, wait a minute!" I shout defensively, but they are already moving on past us, stepping over the body parts to head down into the basement.

"What the hell's in the basement?" I ask Buzz.

"That's classified," booms a loud voice ahead of an equally loud presence.

The guy fills the entire double doorway — I can't figure out how the military can afford to pick up the tab for the miles and miles of fabric needed for his suit. He's like something out of a comic book, but I'm not laughing because, well, I'm standing in a puddle of someone's blood and assorted gooey bits.

"We've seen the unicorns, sir," I say. "So has half the neighborhood, and by the looks of it, some of the tenants of this building have already bought the farm. So maybe you should come clean with us."

The gigantic man looks apoplectic. "That's 'General Boler, sir' to you," he bellows. "The basement of this building houses a government research facility. That's all I'm going to tell you, citizen."

"This research facility wouldn't happen to be genetically engineering unicorns for use as weapons?"

My query is lost in the crackle of Boler's radio. Apparently the soldiers outside have been unsuccessful in gunning down the escaped unicorns. Bullets don't seem to be harming them, and six military personnel are dead. Most of the shrubbery in the hellstrips is up in flames and the beasts are heading towards Midtown Mall, several blocks away.

There is gunfire in the basement and a whole lot of screaming. Unicorns are coming at us from all angles. Two erupt through the closed door marked "Stairs" — presumably they're finished with their upper floor walkabouts. Three more gallop up from the basement, their eyes wild with the thrill of destruction.

We are caught in the crossfire, and General Boler is blocking the door.

Buzz violates many of our safety protocols by failing to put his mask on, and by spraying in an enclosed area containing unprotected subjects. I'll write him up later, but for now, the dude's a hero. He lets loose a blast of bedbug-killing soup (my very own recipe), his wand aiming for the beautifully-lashed eyes of the GEUs.

We all split once General Boler has the presence of mind to heave his massive bulk out of the way. We stand on the pavement, every mucous membrane stinging, as Buzz comes tearing out of the building, unicorns at his heels. But the creatures seem sluggish, and they're not breathing fire. They appear to be in flight — not fight — mode, and that gives me a brilliant idea.

"General Boler," I say, "I think I know a way to destroy your GEUs."

The big man looks at me. "You do that, and I'll make sure you're properly compensated by the government of this fine nation," he says.

That's good enough for me. I barrel down to my truck and go back to the shop.

*

I may not have a PhD in chemistry, but I'm a whiz at skirting national pesticide safety regulations. I'm not bragging when I say I have no equal when it comes to filling out government paperwork.

That particular skill combined with my superior home brews are the reason we're number one in the extermination business in this town, and now that I've finally convinced the local police that I'm not running a meth lab on company property, we've been more popular than ever.

It helps that my network of suppliers is next to none. There isn't an exterminator in the country who has access to the resources I have. It's too bad I don't have time to call on anyone for an express delivery — I got a guy in Chicago who has some new stuff I've been wanting to test. What I have in storage will have to suffice.

Colonel Sanders' eleven herbs and spices ain't got nothing on me: my secret unicorn-destroying formula is a drop of this, a drizzle of that, a hand-shakingly terrifying moment when I splash in too much azinphos-methyl. It doesn't immediately dissolve the sprayer when I pour it in, but I'm missing my eyebrows and part of my moustache.

General Boler's voice is so loud on the radio, the truck is shaking. I don't have to open the door to hear what he's hollering. He's at Midtown Mall. "I need you here yesterday at 0800 hours!"

"Yeah, yeah," I mumble as I carefully maneuver the industrial-sized sprayer into the front seat of the truck. I can see the contents swirling and shifting inside the translucent cylinder, and I'm fearful of the condensation that is clinging to the interior walls. The stability of my formula is highly questionable. If she blows, I blow, too. I strap it in with a combination of bungee cords and the seatbelt and think about Leah Infinity and adorable Popper.

There are news choppers in the air over the scene of the mall, and firetrucks and ambulances are careening around me to reach the prime parking spots in the fire lanes. The southwest side of the building is burning, a mob of screaming shoppers clinging like flies to the place, presumably sticking around to see if there will be Black Friday-comparable discounts when this is all over. I see Buzz and Boler and his men standing outside the northeast exit.

I freak out as the truck lumbers over the speed bumps, but my Unicorn Blaster doesn't spill, combust, or implode. Not yet, anyway.

Boler instructs his remaining men to round up the GEUs and herd them our way. Buzz fills his sprayer with Unicorn Blaster while I put on a hazmat suit. I

 Fossil Lake 3

barely get my helmet on when the unicorns bust out of the mall.

I am staggered by their otherworldliness — well, except for the one that has a ladies' polka dot panty set hanging off his horn. That one's just funny.

"Now!" I holler at Buzz, and the two of us spray like we've never sprayed before in our lives.

I feel sweat dripping from every pore, and my nose suddenly starts bleeding. But this is our moment: Buzz and I are the exterminator versions of rock stars. We are infallible. We are more than likely seriously high off of the Unicorn Blaster. But we keep on keeping on, despite the spasmodic gut-clenching moment when I fear my recipe has failed, that I have not measured properly, that I forgot that to add the chlorpyrifos.

The unicorns are going to kill us all. They bare their teeth, they blaze their eyes, they fling that gorgeous swirling hair. They stoke whatever interior blazing fur-naces furnish their fiery breath. My life should be flashing before me, but instead I'm catching a rerun of the musical number at the start of the last episode of "Dancing with Dogs."

"Streaming video!" Stoic Buzz is screaming, spittle coating the lower half of his mask. I am in awe of his complete dedication to the job. We are the greatest team in the history of pest control.

"What?"

"On the Internet! You can watch your show when-ever you want!"

I think about my comfort crevasse, and give the unicorns hell.

The Unicorns of Rainbow Lake

Frank Sawielijew

Lisa wasn't sure whether spending her vacation at Rainbow Lake had been the best or the worst decision of her life.

Before this fateful trip, her personality had been defined by an amalgamation of horrible hipster stereotypes. Rainbow Lake was the perfect antidote. The naïve little girl she had been had wanted nothing more than to frolic in the company of gaily galloping unicorns. The disillusioned woman she was now couldn't stand the things.

A few days in the company of unicorns had been enough to cure her of her idiotic hipster sensibilities. They were like horses on LSD, constantly jumping and dancing and singing and getting high from inhaling their own rainbow-scented farts.

And they were so fucking arrogant about it. Their obnoxious nature made her reconsider her veganism — she had tried unicorn steak and liked it. The taste of their meat was the only reason not to drive the entire species to extinction.

They also made her temporarily give up the only hipsterish habit she didn't want to give up. She loved going barefoot, and even in winter she put nothing more substantial on her feet than sandals, but the piles of unicorn shit littering the ground made her wear closed shoes for the first time in years.

The shit sparkled and smelled like flowers and cinnamon. It was absolutely revolting.

"Hooo there, my human friend! How are you on this fine day?" a passing unicorn asked in a voice that made her want to punch it. Prolonged contact with unicorns made Lisa realize that pacifism was, after all, not her thing.

"Not too bad, until you came along."

"Hoo, why so hostile, young one? I merely came to bring you merriment!"

Lisa sighed. "I don't want your merriment. I just want peace and quiet."

The unicorn whinnied. "But it *is* peaceful here! Look around you, there is love and peace and joy and fun and song and dance and party everywhere!"

"Fuck off," she said, barely able to resist the urge to turn the annoying creature into a burger with her bare hands. "I just want some time alone, okay? I want to relax. I want to take those damn shoes off and dangle my feet in the water ..."

As she said it, she realized she actually didn't. She didn't want to dip a single toe into the water of Rainbow Lake. Not even with shoes on. The lake owed its colorful appearance to decades of unicorn bathing orgies, permanently staining it with the sweat, cum, and vaginal fluids of these glittering creatures. Everything that came out of their bodies was more garishly colored than the flagship of a gay pride parade.

"Yes, come into the water, dear human friend! We're having a party there soon!"

"If by party you mean orgy, I'm not interested."

"Oh, you'd be missing out! You don't know what our horns can do to your human anatomy, whooya!"

She turned her head and stared the unicorn right in the face. She really wished looks could kill. "Would you please fuck off and leave me alone?"

"Nooooohohohooo!" the unicorn whinnied, ac-comp-anied by a fart. "You cannot be alone and sad here at Rainbow Lake! You should have fun and play games and dance and party and have fun! Stop being so grumpy and cheer up!"

That did it. Lisa had always been a peaceful and re-laxed person, but this was too much. From the moment she had stepped off the bus, she hadn't been able to catch a moment of rest. Even in the hotel she couldn't find peace, as her room was located on the ground floor — and every couple of minutes, a unicorn would pass by the window and scream something cheerful.

She yanked her shoes from her feet and shoved them down the surprised animal's throat. The soles were covered in mud and glittering poop. "Fuck the fuck off, you fucking fuck!"

As she wasn't experienced at swearing, her choice of insults wasn't very creative, but it probably got the point across. She hammered it home with a few punch-es to the abdominal area. With two dirty shoes clog-ging up its throat and a pair of fists pummeling its bel-ly, the unicorn couldn't help but barf. A sticky, sug-ary-sweet substance erupted from its muzzle, drenching the world around it in pink. There were bits of candy in the liquid.

"Oh, for fuck's sake, you puked on me."

The unicorn hacked and coughed in a desperate attempt to dislodge the shoes stuck in its windpipe. "Human ... friend ... why?"

She grabbed the creature's horn and, bracing one foot on its collapsed body, pulled with all her might. "It's the only way to *shut you the fuck up!*"

The horn tore from the unicorn's skull with the sound a plunger made unclogging a toilet. The only sound of pain that managed to escape through its blocked windpipe was a pathetic whimper. Its cute round eyes teared up at the sight of its majestic horn dripping with sugary unicorn blood, severed from the head it had adorned just a moment ago.

Lisa noticed the sadness in the unicorn's eyes. "Want your horn back? Fine, here it is!"

She rammed the horn into the unicorn's eye socket, driving it deep into its brain.

It was dead.

She had peace.

It felt wonderful.

A few days ago, she had been a vegetarian. Now she considered becoming a butcher.

She sat down and relaxed. Her eyes drank in the beauty of her surroundings. It was a landscape made for being printed on a postcard. Lush green forests covering the hills, grey mountains touching the clouds above, a sky as blue as the jeans she wore, and at the center of it all — the reflection of sunlight on the sickly pink waters of Rainbow Lake.

The unicorns ruined everything. They polluted this beautiful place with their noise, their shit and their sex. Lisa had always imagined unicorns as serene and majestic creatures living in harmony with nature. In truth, they acted like nymphomaniac drug-addicted children.

Her world was shattered. All the stories she had loved as a kid were a lie. It made her question everything she had ever believed. All that bullshit about love and peace and happiness. What if it was *all* a lie?

Lost in thought, she stared into the horizon and wiggled her bare toes in the dew-kissed grass. She loved the feeling of wet grass on her bare feet ...

"Ah, shit!" she yelled when she noticed that what had kissed the grass wasn't, in fact, dew. Dew didn't have bits of candy in it.

She regretted having shoved her shoes down the unicorn's throat. Now, she had to be extra careful not to step into piles of unicorn poo on the way back to the hotel.

She sighed. It was a deep sigh filled with sadness. "This could be such a beautiful place without these disgusting creatures ..."

"I didn't expect to find anyone here," said a voice behind her. "What the heck happened to that unicorn?"

A handsome young man sat down next to her, careful to avoid the pool of puke. He carried a big suitcase. It had the word *merchandise* written on it in big, colorful letters.

"Who are you?" Lisa asked him.

"Just call me Ben," he answered. "I sell stuff to tourists. You know, like, souvenirs. Things to remind them of this place. I came here to have some peace. This is one of the few spots around Rainbow Lake that doesn't have a party going on for twenty-four hours every day, every week."

"Yeah. That's why I'm here, too," she replied, turning her head to face him. His reddish beard shone like bronze in the sun. "Can I see what you're selling?"

"Oh, yes, sure." He opened his suitcase and a big purple cardboard castle popped up. The things inside were the most garish things Lisa had ever laid eyes on. "See anything you like?"

"Not really, no," she said honestly. She was so sick of the unicorns and their flamboyance she couldn't even pretend to not hate this shit.

"But maybe I got something you need?" he asked, throwing a glance at her bare feet.

"Oh, you mean because I shoved my shoes down this unicorn's throat to suffocate it, and now I have to walk barefoot through this unicorn-shit-decorated landscape?"

"Yes," he said, taking a pair of socks from his suitcase and holding them up for her to see.

The socks were striped and rainbow-colored. She despised them at first glance.

"Okay, two things," she said. "First, I hate wearing socks. I don't even wear them in boots. And second, I'm sick of everything cute and colorful and the mere sight of these things makes me wanna puke."

"Would you rather get unicorn shit on your bare feet?"

She thought about it for half a second before coming to a conclusion. "You got a point. What do I have to pay you?"

He handed her the socks and smiled. "Nothing. Consider it a gift."

"How generous of you." She wiped her feet on a clean patch of grass before putting the disgustingly colorful socks on. "This supposed to be an attempt at flirting?"

"Maybe," he replied with a shrug. "Around here, it's almost impossible to meet a woman alone at a romantic place. So when I get the chance ..."

She grinned. "... you have to take it."

Lisa liked the guy. He was refreshingly sweet, a rarity at Rainbow Lake. Most of the tourists were just as bad as the unicorns.

She placed her hand on his. This was truly a romantic place. The calming song of birds, the whisper of the wind among the leaves, the faint rumbling of ... wait, rumbling?

"Did you hear that?" she asked.

"Hear what?"

The rumbling grew louder. And suddenly, a panicked unicorn galloped past them.

"HELPHELPHELPHELPFUCKINGSHITHELP!" it yelled.

"Something's wrong."

"Yes," said Ben. "Look over there!"

He pointed to Unicorn Mountain, where the unicorns of Rainbow Lake had their home. From afar, it looked like a fountain of mud erupted from its face, as if a mountain-pimple had been popped and this was the pus oozing from it.

Another unicorn zipped past.

"OHMYGODNOFUCKNOSHITFUCKNOOOOO!"

Lisa threw a rock at it before it could vanish among the trees. The rock hit one of its legs with full force, fracturing it and causing the creature to fall to the ground.

"OWSHITWHYI'MGOINGTODIE!"

"Shut the fuck up you little shit," she told the unicorn, kicking it in the side. It hurt. She reminded herself not to kick anything when she had no shoes on her feet. "Tell me what's going on or I'm going to hurt you."

"I'MGOINGTODIEOHGODPLEASEHELPME!"

This time, Lisa stomped on the unicorn's fractured leg with her heel. This didn't hurt her foot, but it hurt the unicorn. A lot, judging from its screams. "Stop talking like your mouth's a machine gun, I don't understand half the words you say. And tell me what the fuck is going on, or I'm going to hurt you again."

The unicorn forced itself to calm down. It didn't like pain. It wasn't really able to calm down, either. But it tried, because not calming down would make the woman hurt it again.

That sent it into a panic, which made calming down even more difficult.

"I ... oh god ... please don't hurt me! It's OHGOD IT DOESN'TMATTERWE'REALLGOINGTODIE!"

Another stomp broke the leg with a sickening crunch, causing bone to tear through flesh. "I told you to stop talking like a machine gun. Why are we going to die? What's going on?"

"Shit! It's shit!" the unicorn cried. "Our sewers are exploding! All the shit is coming out!"

"You mean... the stuff spurting from Unicorn Mountain is shit?"

"Yes! Yes! We're going to be BURIEDINSHIT OH MYGOD!"

Lisa stomped down on the broken leg again, then added a kick for good measure, this time being extra careful not to stub her toes. Now the leg was so deformed it looked like a work of modern art.

"We have to get back to the hotel," she said to Ben. "Fast."

"I agree. Let's go."

They ran through the woods as fast as they could. Neither of them had any idea how much unicorn poop the sewers within Unicorn Mountain contained, but if it sent the unicorns into a panic, it had to be enough to flood the area.

"You know, if anyone had asked me what I'm going to do on my holiday trip," Lisa said, "running away from an avalanche of unicorn shit would've been the last thing I'd imagined."

"I hope they drown in it," said Ben. "I hate these creatures."

For some reason, Lisa liked him even more now.

After a short jog through the woods, on which they encountered surprisingly few piles of unicorn poop, they reached the hotel. Lisa's new socks had a few holes and tears from running over rough ground, but at least she hadn't stepped in equine waste.

People sat outside, calmly sipping their drinks, oblivious to the looming apocraplypse. "Quickly, get inside! An avalanche of shit is coming this way! It's going to bury you all!" Ben shouted.

Someone laughed. Apparently, the tourists thought this was a joke. Most of them didn't laugh. It wasn't a particularly good one.

Lisa jumped in front of a unicorn server carrying a tray on its back and yelled at it. "Don't just stand around, you dumb creatures, do something! Your toilets have exploded! Go to your dumb mountain and fix it!"

The unicorn grinned like the retard it was. "Heh. Toilet humor. I like it."

She snatched a bottle of wine from the tray on the unicorn's back, hit it over the head and stabbed it in the face with the broken glass. "This is not a joke! We're all gonna get buried in shit!"

Instead of taking her warning seriously, the unicorn merely cried out in pain.

"It's no use. They don't believe us," Ben said, shaking his head. "To be honest, I wouldn't believe us either. Screw these people. Let's find shelter."

Lisa nodded and ran into the hotel. The safest place, she thought, would be on top of the roof. Even if the sewers within Unicorn Mountain contained decades worth of unicorn shit, she didn't believe it to be enough to reach the top of the hotel.

"Top floor?" Ben asked when he noticed which elevator button she had pressed. "You wanna go to the roof? Don't you think we should stay inside?"

"Nah. If we stay inside, we might end up trapped. It's much safer up there."

When it had reached its destination, they got off the elevator and climbed up a flight of stairs to the rooftop. From there, they could observe the imminent apoopcalypse. A glittering brown mass, like chocolate cake dough with sprinkles in it, rolled over the forest, burying the trees and everything else beneath it. The sweet, cinnamony smell of unicorn poop filled the air.

"Do you smell that, my dear?" said one of the tourists below. "Seems like the cook is preparing cake for us!"

"Yes, smells like candy! Oh, I do love this place. We really get spoiled with sweets here."

Not long after they had uttered these words, the avalanche hit them. Screams and cries could be heard as the tourists were served way more sweets than they'd bargained for.

"I don't know about you, but I think the sweet smell makes this shit even more disgusting," Lisa said.

"Not disgusting, but disturbing. Everything about these creatures is disturbing," Ben replied. "Unicorn poo smells like candy, unicorn puke smells like candy, unicorn blood smells like candy ... that's just wrong. It's unnatural. Makes me uneasy, you know."

"Yeah, I know what you mean. If at least their personality was as sweet as their bodily fluids, I might even enjoy their company. But they're all dicks."

As if they had been summoned, two unicorns with jetpacks appeared on the roof to prove just how dickish they could be.

"Hey, you! Get out of here!" one of them yelled.

"Yeah! Away with you!"

"What? We're here to seek shelter from the avalanche! Get lost!" Lisa said, giving them the finger.

"No, this roof is for us unicorns!"

"Yeah! You have no place here, human. This is unicorn territory!"

Lisa spat. "You fucking assholes. You always pretend to be friendly and now, in a moment of danger, you selfish pricks tell us to fuck off because you want this roof all for yourselves. You disgust me."

"Ho, those are fighting words, youngster!" The unicorn lowered its head.

"Yeah! Fighting words!" Its comrade did the same. Their horns were pointing right at Lisa's chest.

She assumed a broad-legged stance, fists raised to strike. "Bring it on."

The unicorns charged. Lisa threw herself to the side. The unicorns, not being the smartest creatures, collided with one another, their skulls meeting with an audible crack.

She took the chance, jumped on one unicorn's back and grabbed its horn.

"Quickly, Ben! Take the other!"

Ben reacted quickly, mounting the other unicorn while it was still dazed, even though he had no idea what he was supposed to do. "Now what?"

"Tear off its horn!" she yelled at him as she pulled at the horn with all her might.

"What?"

The unicorn whinnied in pain as it felt the pull on its forehead. "Tear it off!" Lisa leaned back, putting all her weight into it, and the horn tore out of the unicorn's skull with a meaty sound, like raw *köttbullar* hitting a wall at high speed.

She jumped off the unicorn's back and stabbed the other in the throat, dealing it a painful death. "Tear off the goddamn horn," she repeated again. "Use it as a weapon. You'll need it."

A whole horde of unicorns with jetpacks bore down upon them. Witnessing the deaths of their fellow equines had sent them into a bloodthirsty rage. Now, these fun-loving party animals showed their true face. But Lisa was ready. She relished this opportunity to unleash her anger against the creatures who had ruined her holiday.

The unicorns descended. Ben took cover behind a corpse. He wasn't ready for this. Lisa was. She lunged forward, ramming the horn into an attacking unicorn's stomach. Sweet, cherry-flavored blood gushed from the wound. The unicorn, shocked with pain, sped onward with its jetpack and hit the roof at full speed, breaking its neck.

It was dead.

Lisa pulled out its horn. She became a dual wielding cyclone of death. Raging unicorns attacked her left and right, but they were no match for her skill. She dodged each jab of a horn gracefully, striking back with elegant swings. Finally, those bellydancing lessons she had taken years ago paid off. With each wound she inflicted, more blood splattered onto her hands, her face, her chest. Each unicorn's tasted differently. Cherry, strawberry, cranberry, raspberry. They were like soda dispensers with endless refills.

Ben stabbed at any unicorn that came too close to him, but most of them focused their attention on Lisa. He used the opportunity to fortify his position. Pulling some corpses from the ever-growing pile of dead unicorns, he formed a barricade of flesh and bone.

All of a sudden, the unicorns changed their behavior. They stopped their attacks and sped away on their jetpacks, leaving the roof over which they had fought so hard behind. Those whose jetpacks had been damaged in the fight fell into the sea of shit below and drowned.

"What the fuck?" Lisa asked.

"*That* the fuck," said the deepest unicorn voice she had ever heard.

A majestic unicorn approached the rooftop, held afloat by a jetpack so massive it could almost be considered a jet plane. Its coat sparkled like a disco ball and its massive horn looked to be made of solid silver. Its mane swayed in the wind so perfectly, the unicorn could have made a career starring in hairspray commercials.

"Oh damn," whispered Ben, "it's the unicorn king!"

"Damn right I am!" The unicorn king pirouetted around himself in a grandiose display of graceful agility. For one single moment of majesty, all the adjectives at once could have been used to describe his awesome glory, and they wouldn't have been enough. Even the most creative of hack writers couldn't summon a description campy enough to do this flamboyant display justice.

Lisa knew at once that she wanted the creature dead.

By her own hands.

"You have slain many of my brethren. I must commend you for your bravery, human. But for this, you must die!" the unicorn king said with a voice that would've made Elvis jealous.

"No, you flaming faggot. You're the one who dies today."

The unicorn king whinnied and charged. Sparks flew whenever his hooves hit the ground, and cheesy power metal started to play in the background. Lisa barely managed to dodge, stumbled, and fell to the ground. She kicked at the unicorn king, but he snapped at her foot. His teeth missed her toes by mere inches, only catching the tip of her sock. He jerked his head back, tearing the sock in half.

"I am the unicorn king!" he screamed in a surprisingly un-garbled voice, considering he had half a sock between his teeth. "And I shall eat your sock, puny human!"

While he was busy chewing, Lisa saw a chance to stab him in the throat. But his hooves struck the horns from her hands in one swift, elegant move.

"Foolish human! Do you truly believe you can strike me down? Hah! Even with the distraction of your foot-sweat's yummy taste in my mouth, my reflexes are quicker than yours!" The unicorn king laughed. "I could be distracted by a whole bowl of tasty sweat-stained socks and still beat you!"

Disarmed, Lisa watched helplessly as the unicorn king devoured the piece of sock, staring at her with eyes that said *you're next*. She really didn't want to share her sock's fate. There was no death more humiliating than ending up as lunch for the faggiest creature of all creation.

Then, the unicorn king screamed. Fountains of fruity blood exploded from his back.

Ben rammed a whole bunch of severed unicorn horns into the king's body from above. He had taken a jetpack from a unicorpse to deliver an air strike.

Now that he was truly distracted, Lisa jumped at the unicorn king's throat, latching on tightly. His scream became a gurgle as she constricted his windpipe. The power metal playing in the background became fainter and fainter, and when he finally collapsed, it fell silent. Neither Lisa nor Ben could say what he had died from. The wounds in his back, blood loss, suffocation – the unicorn king's death came with an impressive number of possible causes.

No more unicorns came to conquer the rooftop. Lisa sat down and inspected the damage. Miraculously, the worst thing that had happened to her was the loss of half a sock. That bite had been a very lucky miss – not even her nail polish was chipped. The only pain she felt was that of exhaustion. Dozens of dead unicorns, and not a scratch on her body. She felt a brief sadness at the abolition of gladiatorial games towards the end of the 4th century AD. What a career she could have had ...

Ben, who really enjoyed his jetpack, landed on the rooftop after a few minutes of airborne fun. "Now what?" he asked.

Lisa wasn't sure. The sea of shit below had stopped rising, and the invasion of unicorns from above had ceased. The danger was gone. They could use the jetpacks to fly away from this horrible place. But she wanted to stay a little while longer. Today, for the first time since she arrived, she had actually enjoyed herself.

A vacation at Rainbow Lake could be fun, after all.

"Let's eat the unicorn king," she said.

At first, Ben stared at her in disbelief, but then he just shrugged and opened his suitcase. He piled up his shitty merchandise and set fire to it. Lisa grinned and started to carve up the corpse. When the meat finally roasted over the flames, they sat down to watch the sunset. In the orange light of dusk, even a forest covered in unicorn poop could look beautiful. The smell of steak saturated the air with its deliciousness.

Lisa closed her eyes and smiled. Finally, there was peace and quiet. She would never have thought sitting in the blood and gore of slain unicorns could be so romantic ...

Her eyes opened again when she felt the tickle of Ben's beard on her lips. She embraced him and returned the kiss.

At that moment, she knew spending her vacation at Rainbow Lake had been the best decision of her life.

Pandora's Super-Sparkly Doom-icorn Blind Box

Shawn Thomas Anderson

Poufy clouds, clear skies, and a rainbow arched over the playground — a beautiful day for anarchy, mass destruction, and the End of Days.

The new school year at Wolcott Elementary had just entered its fifth week, and the thirteenth series of Doom-icorn unicorn toys were still fresh on store shelves. Rows of shimmery boxes beckoned with glimmering promises of anticipation, want, and hope. Each toy nestled inside, a must-have, the defining element that distinguished the haves from the have-nots.

Lydia skipped over to the trifecta of third-grade awesomeness stationed by the seesaws. "Hi Pandora. Hi Keisha. Hi Amelia," she said, waving. "Wanna play kickball or chase the boys or something?"

"As if," Pandora said. She didn't crack a smile. "Everyone knows that today's Blind-Box Doom-icorn Reveal Day. We don't have time for any of that childish stuff."

"Yeah, as if," Keisha said, jiggling her handful of glittery boxes in Lydia's face. "And if you don't have any to open, we don't have time for you, so scram."

"Yeah." Amelia grimaced and swept Lydia away with a hand gesture. She nodded, desperate for Pandora's approval. Her thick pigtails of auburn curls bounced against her cheeks. Their coppery hue matched the dense nebula of freckles strewn across her face.

Lydia rolled her eyes and skipped off to join another group of girls at the jungle gym.

The trio watched to make sure that she wasn't going to make a fast break for their teacher, Ms. Pretense, and tell on them. They waited until Lydia climbed all the way to the top of the jungle gym, hung upside down, and let the whole school see her underwear, before they went back to official Doom-icorn business.

"What an idiot," Pandora said and the other two girls laughed.

"Aren't Doom-icorns the most fabulous bestest?" Amelia said.

"The *most fabulous bestest*," Pandora said, mocking Amelia. She straightened the sparkly headband that anchored her brunette locks to the top of her head and reached into her pony backpack, pulling seven Doom-icorn blind boxes from the main pouch.

Seven was an impressive score in playground standards. Especially since you couldn't even see the toy inside the foil box and couldn't pick which ones you wanted. Plus, each blind box cost a staggering $13.99, far too rich an indulgence for most elementary-school allowances.

Pandora juggled her mother-lode while struggling to re-zip her pack. Her eyes were as twinkling and twirly as the unicorn faces embossed in glitter holograms on the Doom-icorn boxes.

"Wow. Your parents got you *seven* this week. You're so rich," Amelia said. She only had two.

"So, what've you got, Amelia?" Keisha said. "You know the rule, the one with the least goes first, and I have three."

"Okay." Amelia started to rip the packaging with her teeth.

The anticipation of the thirteenth generation of Doom-icorns had reached a fever pitch in the schoolyard. The girls had already received many of the characters in the latest wave of the collection. Series one through five looked almost identical to My Pretty Ponies but with unicorn horns. Collectively the girls had amassed 53 Cheer-icorns, 24 Hug-icorns, 21 Sweet-icorns, and 18 Giggle-icorns.

As the toy line expanded, the unicorns got darker in theme and design, and bad things started to happen. The news was filled with stories of people robbing and looting for the little plastic sculptures of unicorn cuteness.

Over the last couple weeks, since series thirteen had hit the stores, Pandora had already managed to score all four Doom-icorns of the Apocalypse and four of the Seven Deadly Doom-icorns.

Plague-icorn was her absolute favorite because it spewed a glittery strawberry-jam-like substance that smelled of cinnamon, posies, and cotton candy. Wrath-icorn was her runner-up with his glossy red body armor that resembled the coating of a candy apple. When you squeezed his butt, spikes popped out along his head, back, and body.

"Darn. Just another lame Doom-icorn brush accessory and I already have Envy-icorn," Amelia let the packaging fall to the ground. She ran the comb through the green mane of the latest addition to her Doom-icorn family while forcing herself not to look too disappointed.

"My turn, my turn," Keisha said as she tore into her trio of boxes. Sparkles and plastic flew every which way. "OMG! It's Necrocon-icorn! I've always wanted this one." She dropped the other two toys in the dirt and held up the black unicorn like a trophy. Its silvery armor, razorblade plates, and horn glimmered in the sunshine.

"Yeah, but does it have the special limited-edition mark? Only a few have it, you know?" Pandora said. She threw Keisha a sideways glance, trying not to look impressed.

Keisha parted the mane with her fingers, searching for the sacred mark. Her eyes widened and she squealed. "It's here! It's right here!" She kept her finger on the spot and held the black and silver plastic unicorn out for Pandora and Amelia to see it.

At the base of the mane, three tiny, red sixes marked its plastic scalp.

"666. Yep, it's the real deal," Amelia said and smirked, knowing that this was going to set Pandora off.

Pandora's skin became flushed and she gritted her teeth, looking like she was going to explode, then she relaxed, smiled, and slow-clapped. "That's great,

Keisha. Bless your heart, you finally got something good. I'm happy for you. Really, I am."

"Well, it's not that great," Keisha said. She gazed down at her prize and tucked it away in the pocket of her windbreaker. "I bet you've got something really special, Pandy. Open yours."

Pandora lined her boxes up on the nearest seesaw and let her hand hover over them as she moved it up and down the line, finally selecting the box in the middle.

"Spare us the drama and open it already," Keisha said, placing her hands on her hips. "We don't have all day. Recess is almost over."

"Give me a minute," Pandora said. "These things can't be rushed. They need to be savored," she said, turning the glittery box over and over in her hand. When she had their full attention, she broke the plastic seal with her fingernail and pried the top of the box open, a ritual she had performed a hundred times.

Rather than finding a unicorn inside, Pandora flipped the box upside down and a small velvet box plopped into her hand. It was roughly the size of a ring box with a hinged lid and it was etched with elaborate markings highlighted in gold filigree.

"Ooooo, do you know what that is?" Keisha said. "It's-it's-it's the Doom-icorn Mystery Box of Eternal Evil! There's only one of them in existence!"

"I know," Pandora said as she held the box to her heart. "I win."

"What do you think is in it?" Amelia said. "Diamonds? The keys to a new car? Maybe it's free tickets to that new theme park in Orlando, Doom-icorn Nation, or invites to the red-carpet premiere of *Doom-icorn the Movie*? Or it could be a wad of cold, hard cash! Pandora, you're so lucky."

"I know." Pandora's tone was deadpan and smug. Her eyes filled with wonder and greed.

"Well, what are you waiting for?" Keisha said. "Open it."

"Easy. I will," Pandora said. "It's just that it's kind of sad. This box is the end all of the Doom-icorn fun. There's really nothing worth collecting after this, and series thirteen is the end of the Doom-icorn line."

"Oh, we'll just find some new, crummy toy to buy," Keisha said.

"It all seems so final," Pandora said. She stared at the ground and looked sad for a moment, but only for a moment, then she lifted her head and smiled. "Time to claim my big prize."

Keisha and Amelia crowded in to get a better look as Pandora flipped open the lid.

No confetti cannon. No shower of diamonds. No windfall of cash inside. It was just an empty box.

"What?" Pandora said. "Are you kidding me? That's it? I've been robbed. Doom-icorns suck." She threw the box over her shoulder.

Keisha and Amelia gasped as the box landed in the dust and a rainbow shot up into the sky. It ripped through a fluffy white cloud, turning it as dark as night. Thunder rumbled across the sky and the ground started to shake and crack.

And then it started raining rainbows.

Not the pretty, marvelous kind that you might find printed on notebooks or knit into sweaters — these rainbows were jagged and they arced like lightning to the ground. One hit the school and the building exploded, throwing balls of fire and debris across the playground. Another hit the office across the street, hurling bricks into the air and setting off every car alarm on the block.

Ms. Pretense blew her whistle, trying to gather and herd the children, but they scattered in every direction, running and screaming as shards of glitter cut their faces and legs as it blew in the wind.

A rainbow bolt struck the jungle gym and Lydia and her friends were incinerated, their tiny skeletons stripped bare and frozen in play, ash fossils swaying in a lake of fire.

As Ms. Pretense reached Pandora, Keisha, and Amelia, she started to say something, but her eyes grew wide and her words gurgled, blood-spatter bubbling from her mouth.

A silver horn ripped through her chest, a unicorn horn.

Her body twitched, slid forward, and flopped free to the ground like a piece of jerked chicken served from a kabob.

A full-size version of Necrocon-icon stood behind her, smiling, his mane flowing in the fiery drafts of death and destruction. He bowed and wiped his horn clean on the lapel of the dead teacher's blazer. Her burning body was slumped over the side of the sandbox; her school whistle sizzled and popped in the palm of her lifeless hand, and the air reeked of burnt flesh.

An army of sneering Doom-icorns emerged from the hellfire and carnage and fell into rank behind

Necrocon-icorn. They stood shoulder to shoulder and represented every color of the rainbow. Some smirked. Others growled and sneered. Characters from earlier series were glued in fake, plastic smiles from ear to ear. None of them appeared friendly.

"Are you the one that opened the box?" Necro's voice boomed as glitter shrapnel swirled around him.

Pandora shivered a little and nodded.

"Then the choice is yours," Necro said. He stomped his hooves and the ground opened up and swallowed Ms. Pretense's corpse. "Do you wish to save your world? Or you can sacrifice it and claim your grand prize."

"What's the prize?" Pandora said as she crossed her arms. Her mouth was straight and her eyes were slits, her game face for negotiation. "What've you got, pony boy?"

"If you let it go, you have won the right to become our queen. You will reign at my side, ravaging, conquering, and devastating every world in our wake. It's our way. It's our Doom-icorn manifest destiny."

Pandora's eyes twinkled and twirled again. "Then, let it burn. I'll take the grand prize," she said. Necro lowered his body and Pandora climbed onto his back, pulling herself up by the scruff of his mane.

"Hey, what about us?" Keisha said. "We're your best friends. Don't we get to come?" She put her arm around Amelia and Amelia clung to her side, sobbing.

"Sorry you didn't win," Pandora said, looking down at them from her steed. "Hash tag, sorry not-so-sorry."

"But, but, but — " Keisha pleaded. Amelia went into hysterics and fell to her knees.

Necro looked back, awaiting Pandora's instructions.

Pandora shrugged her shoulders. She dug the heels of her patent-leather Mary Janes into Necro's sides and tugged on his mane. As he trotted, he rose from the ground. The other Doom-icorns followed.

As the legion lifted into the sky, the rainbow strike intensified. Keisha, Amelia, the playground, and school disappeared in a cloud of glitter, dust, and smoke. Explosions popped under the veil of destruction.

Adjusting her headband, Pandora pointed forward and said, "Let's ride!"

Unicorphosis

Pete Sutton

The first bite was an epiphany. Hot juice spurted across my tongue, redolent of hickory and with the soft flour of the bap, the crunch of the perfect lettuce, the astringency of the raw onion, it was, cliché to say, a taste explosion.

I was hooked. Unicorn burgers were the best.

The *mmmm*'s of my fellow diners were a symphony of delight as we all chomped and masticated. The meat smelt amazing, like all the best barbeques amalgamated. It was lean like kangaroo, yet bloody red and melt in the mouth like Kobe beef.

Upon finishing I ordered another. I ate until I felt like I'd burst. I undid the top button of my pants and waited, slurping on a slushie, until I felt able to waddle out of the burger bar.

I went back the next day, and the next. I got friendly with the chef, Tom. I decided to do a column on it for the paper. A bit outside my normal articles, which were usually about engineering.

When the government relaxed the laws on genetic modification there was a whole zoo's worth of wild animals created. Unicorns just seemed to be the latest craze. It was the *My Little Pony* thing all over again, but for real.

There had been reinventions and reincarnations, Thylacines and Mammoths. But things really took off when people started crossing species, to invent things that the world had never seen before. Sheep with jellyfish genes to create colour changing wool, dog-chimps, flying cats.

Things were strange for a while, then everyone kind of collectively shrugged and got on with life, and frank-enanimals became so last season.

Then chefs started experimenting. I joined the league of epicurean explorers. Insects bred to taste like chocolate. Pigs and cows interbred to create beefy bacon. The only limit seemed to be the imagination of the chef and the cost of the genetic splicing equipment.

Unicorn burgers were a natural progression, I guess.

One I became a little obsessed with.

There's no real delicate way of putting it. My shit was glittery. Came out scratchy, smeared the bowl with blueish-brown sparkle.

That was the first sign, I think. Although I kind of ignored it. The taste of the burger was so sublime I was prepared to suffer a little the next day. It was worth a little bit of rectal pain. No different to eating really hot chillies and suffering a bit of afterburn, I thought.

The original burger bar opened another restaurant in the north of the city. Then it was a chain. Soon there was one on every high street, then it went international. I seemed to be the only one that cared where all the meat was coming from.

A couple of days ago I noticed that my hair was changing colour, that my nails were more lustrous, kind of pastel coloured. There was an itch in my chest. A painful lump on my forehead.

I could swear my eyelashes had grown. I needed to locate where the meat was coming from. The original bar seemed like the best way to find out.

I had another burger before tackling the chef. Well I had to, they were too good to pass up. The original chef had left, the new one didn't know much. I used my contacts to find out where Tom had gone.

*

The front door was a hideous shade of pastel pink. I rang the doorbell and there was a cascade of jingles inside, sounding like a child's rendition of the theme song of *Rainbow*. Bungle must be turning in his grave.

There was a buzz and the door clicked open. I cautiously pushed it and, as it creaked wide, shouted, "Hello? Tom?"

"Through here," a voice said, deep and melodious.

I walked down the corridor to where I thought I'd heard it and into a kitchen-diner. There, standing at the table, nosing a bag of sugar, was a unicorn. About the size of a Shetland Pony, big spiral horn, a pale pastel blue. The floor covered in glittery droppings. The smell was like being in a sweet factory, but with an underlying horseyness.

"Hey, Fella," I said holding out a hand to the unicorn and looking around for Tom. Its large glistening brown eyes fixed me in a stare.

"Hi," it said.

I did a double take.

"Er," I said, intelligently.

"Mind the shit."

I looked down. I had nearly trodden in a pile of purple shimmering faecal matter.

"You can talk," I said. You would never have thought that I'd once come top of my class.

The unicorn just tossed its head and flapped its lips.

"It's started with you hasn't it?" it asked.

I rubbed the bump on my forehead and sighed. "Tom?"

"Bugger. I hoped it was just me. Since I took the first few experimental batches." The unicorn trotted around the table and faced me head on.

"Experimental?"

"If you go and get my tablet from the living room, I was half way through a search last night, before waking up like this." Tom tossed his head again, or maybe he was just trying to point.

I went and got the tablet. The webpage open on it was the homepage of something called the VDL. All green with a stylised banner with a big cross and below the words 'No Compromise.' "What's this?"

"They sold me the meat. The first batch anyway. They put me onto a supplier."

"VDL?" I rubbed my bump again.

"I never asked, they never said. They supplied me the recipe as well as the meat. You've tasted it, obviously, would you have turned it down? I've made a fortune." As he spoke his tail lifted and he deposited another steaming pile of purple glitter with a wet splat. "Sorry about that."

"What are we going to do?"

"Do?"

"About ... about ... this!" I waved my arm generally around the kitchen.

"Have you had the dream yet?" Tom asked.

"Dream?"

"Yeah, gambolling through knee high grass all the colours of the rainbow, feeling joyous with the wind flowing through your fetlocks, the sheer ecstasy of cantering? That dream."

I was mesmerised by how expressive the unicorn's face was. The fact its eyebrows jiggled as it nodded a little, trying to elicit a nod in return.

"No. I've not had the dream yet."

"Maybe you still have time. I started to dream about a week before waking up like this."

I tapped at the tablet. This VDL was extremely secretive. But I did catch its name on an anti-epicurean message board.

"The Vegan Defence League?" I asked.

"Oh God, them!" Tom snorted a neigh "They formed a little after the government bill relaxing genetic engineering. Remember those bombings of the labs in Cambridge?"

"That was them?"

He nodded, or at least I think he did.

"Look, it's obvious what they've done, if not how. You have to find whoever did this, and see if there's a cure." Tom's voice was urgent, insistent.

"Okay. I'll find them." I agreed.

"Before you go."

"Yes?"

"Pass me a carrot or two? Maybe an apple?"

*

The farmhouse glowed, a beacon on the dark moor.

It'd taken me a few days to get this address, and a few bribes. Days I couldn't afford. I'd had the dream.

I'd wondered about all the ways to approach these folk and decided a plain old knock on the door was going to be best. Time was pressing.

I could hear raised voices as I approached but swallowed my anxiety and pressed the doorbell.

The door was snatched open to reveal an angry young woman in a red cotton dress and wellies. "What?"

"Erm. I'm here to speak to the VDL? I'm a journalist —"

"Who the fuck called you?" Her lip had curled as soon as the word 'journalist' was out my mouth. She rubbed the heels of her hands in her eyes and growled. "Fucking hell. Jezza!" She turned and marched off.

I followed sheepishly.

In the front room there were three other young people. One man in tweeds, older than the others. Another skinny, pale, full of nervous energy. And a woman, a confection of blonde dreadlocks atop her head. The older man was showing the signs, pastel hair, bump, the lot. I was hit with a cramp; they'd been happening on and off. Fingers pressed together, back bending, bone deep pain.

"Who the fuck are you?" the younger man said.

"Are you okay?" the blonde woman asked.

"He's got it," the other man said.

"He's a journalist." The way the woman in red said 'journalist' made it sound like the worst thing imaginable. "Did you call him, Brian? I wouldn't put it past you. After all, you've been eating them!"

The older man looked a little abashed. "But they taste so good, and it's not as if they're real animals."

There was a rehearsed tone to this, as if they were rehashing an argument, perhaps the very argument I'd heard before knocking.

"Listen, I don't have much time. Tell me there's a cure. Please. A way of reversing this?" I looked into each of their faces.

The blonde woman shook her head.

"Jezza?" The man in tweed, Brian, asked. The air in the room was full of resentment. They were flushed.

"I don't know who you are, but I'll tell you the same thing I just told Brian. There is no reversal. The nanites do their job then die. You're fucked."

"But you could write another code," the dreadlocked woman said, holding out her hands palms up.

"Sorry, Anna," Jezza said, shaking his head.

"You have no fucking clue what you've done!" Brian burst into motion. Pacing up and down in front of the chair Jezza sat in. "Who's going to do all the work? Who's going to keep the power stations going? Make the drugs and vaccines we need? Make *all* the things we need? Keep the internet going? It's a fucking Brony apocalypse." His voice had climbed so that he was shouting by the end.

"Hold it, hold it!" I shouted.

"You murderers deserved it."

I whirled round. The woman who'd opened the door was almost spitting with rage.

"You. And you, Brian." She pointed to me and the man in tweed. "You're so happy to eat animals, murder them for your own gratification, aren't you. Well, maybe this will finally teach you a lesson."

Brian sighed, then collapsed onto a chair. "You've fucked it up, you've fucked everything up."

I looked from the angry lady to Jezza and saw no fellow feeling. I realised that mine had been a fool's quest. How could I appeal to them, to save my humanity, when in their eyes I had none?

A great shiver came over me, my skin flinching and flicking. I fell to my knees and as my spine arched I slammed my hands no, my *hooves* – onto the floor.

Anna, eyes wide, put her hands over her mouth. The woman in red watched with an avid gaze. Brian looked like he was going to lose his lunch. Jezza sat forward, an expression of fascination on his face.

"You cunt!" I roared and charged.

"No!" Three voices screamed in unison as my horn pierced his heart.

Brian moaned. "We're all fucked now!"

They never arrested me.

Although I *was* taken to a secure paddock.

But, soon enough, law and order broke down. Brian was right about society being fucked. Though it was worse than he'd imagined.

Our farts may smell of sugar and spice but they still contain lots of methane, which is a pretty serious

greenhouse gas. Billions of men, women and children
turned unicorn squirting rainbows has really played
havoc with the weather.

Prickless on Parade

Troy Lockport

$\mathfrak{S}$torm clouds rumbled overhead in the windy city as the disheveled figure entered the hotel lobby as one does when they pass from the street into a building via a set of automatic doors.

He made his way to reception, where a dark haired woman with controversial eyes and plastic antlers on her head eyed him with suspicion from behind the front desk.

"Can I help you, sir?"

The figure stared at the woman's uniform and name tag.

"Do you work here, lady?"

"Err, yes" said the woman. "Is there a problem, sir?"

"I got a room here for the weekend."

"Oh, I see. May I have your name, sir?" she said, trying not to grimace as a pungent odor reached her nose.

The online pioneer who occasionally used Wattpad introduced himself through a collection of syllables that sounded super-glued together.

"I'm sorry?" the woman said.

The self-styled publisher of *The Eternal Gasbag* repeated himself by mumbling his name again. The receptionist stared back at him and attempted to make sense of the slurred delivery.

"Pringles Coney-one?" she offered.

"I'm Prickless Coglione," said Prickless Coglione. "The controversial author from Toile'et and Du Pong County."

"Oo-kay," said the woman as she checked his reservation on the computer. "Are you supposed to be a yak, sir?"

"Huh?"

"A yak. You know, like they have in the Himalayas?"

Prickless was dumbstruck in the way he used to be in school when teachers asked him to spell a word like 'imbecile.' Was this bitch saying he was yakking? He'd barely said anything. And what was that about him having too many layers? Was she calling him fat?

The woman cleared her throat at the look on the man's face, whose forehead appeared to have collapsed on one side.

"Well, sir," she began, "I just thought that with the whole disheveled thing you've got going, the brown coat, the shaggy hair and decomposing beard, the ..." she paused as a shudder passed through her, "powerful odor. I mean you've really got your costume down pat." *As in cow pat,* she thought. "So far I've seen a buffalo and two donkeys, but not a yak. It's quite original actually."

"Listen, lady," said Prickless, finding his voice again. "I don't know what the hell you're talking about.

I'm a controversial writer here for the weekend in this controversial city to try and discover the dark secret of this controversial hotel."

The woman frowned.

"So you're not in town for the parade, sir?"

"Parade?"

"The pride parade."

A spasm of fear spasmed its way through the unwashed and unintentionally yak-like body of Prickless Coglione. *Yest ye be one*, came a voice from deep inside him somewhere dark and below.

"Pride Parade?" he squeaked in a squeaky voice that betrayed both his lack of testosterone and the sudden terror that had gripped him in an iron grip like an unknown creature that cannot be described except for its iron hands.

"Chicago's first gay animal Mardi Gras," the woman said, tapping her pink antlers with one hand. "Didn't you notice all the blocked off streets decorated with ticker tape and the hundreds of people dressed up as gay animals?"

"Gay animals?" Prickless said. Controversial may have been his middle name, but this was downright terrifying. Even more terrifying than the time he got the flu so bad he couldn't sit up at his computer eating pizza and drinking beer for a week and had to lie down for a week eating pizza and drinking beer instead.

"That's right," said the woman. "You're lucky you secured a room so far in advance. Every hotel in the city will be booked solid by now."

Prickless was struck dumb again. He felt dizzy, the words *gay animal Mardi Gras* echoing in his mind like repeated sounds that kept going back and forth from one end of his cavernous skull to the other.

Waves of nausea washed over his unwashed body, and even though wild horses wouldn't have dragged it from him, not even wild horses in drag — like the ones he could see trotting into the lobby lounge - a tingle of inexplicable excitement also washed over his un-washed body. With it came a sudden flash of memory of the time he'd gone to the petting zoo when he was twelve. He'd tingled that day as well.

He forced himself to focus on the here and now be-cause here he was now in here. Now.

"How come I didn't hear about this?" he said when he could speak again.

"I thought everyone knew about the parade, sir. It's been all over the news for months. Are you visiting from out of state?"

Prickless Coglione gasped as though she'd kicked him in his namesakes.

"Are you serious, lady? I been born here in the same year a day before another writer who plagiarized my logos," said Prickless, offended that his heavy Chicago accent wasn't apparent even though he'd nev-er lived anywhere near the city itself.

"Yes, of course," said the woman, thinking that this babbling wreck was clearly in need of some kind of therapy, and probably decades of it.

"Well you see, sir," she began, trying to steer the conversation back to saner ground, "the parade is a new idea based on the lack of attention given to homo-sexual behavior among wild animals. People like David Attenborough and other nature documentary filmmakers have been accused of ignoring it for years now, which has created the false impression that homosexuality isn't natural. And, as the animals can't march themselves, a group of people in Chicago came up with the idea of marching on their behalf."

"You gotta be kidding me."

"Oh, no. The idea's really caught on. There must be thousands of people here for the parade and millions more will be watching live via telecast. I've seen some amazing costumes so far. I just wish I wasn't working this weekend." She sighed wistfully. "I'd love to go as an elk."

"You mean like Elk Grove?" said Prickless, wondering if she was from that dark and controversial place.

"Err ... yeah. I guess," said the woman, wondering how this dimwit had managed to make it to Chicago without falling into a large hole. Then again, given his appearance, maybe he had.

A group of young men dressed as red-assed monkeys came out of the lobby lounge talking and laughing.

"Nice outfit," one of them said to Prickless as they passed.

"Very authentic," said another, as the full scent of *eau de Coglione* assaulted his nose.

Another tingle of excitement rippled through Prickless. In his mind's eye, he saw an alpaca relieving itself against a cage door. He'd been fourteen on that occasion.

"A homo animal parade," he said. "I can't believe this is happening."

"I know. Isn't it wonderful?" the woman said as she handed him the key. "You're on the second floor in room 239, Mr Coglione. Enjoy your stay."

Prickless hurried away in horror, wondering what kind of nightmare he'd stumbled into that was so nightmarish it wasn't even like something out of a Richard Matheson novel as it usually would have been.

After a lengthy search of the lobby, he found the elevators opposite the front desk and stood there waiting for one of them to come down. As an unrecognized genius he saw the elevators not as lesser mortals did but as chrome-colored doors set into a wall.

The sound of clopping hooves pulled him from his controversial reverie, a state of mind that only happened when he thought about things in a way that sort of made him forget where he was for a moment. He turned and saw a smooth muscular man dressed in a disturbingly skimpy outfit that consisted of pink and purple tufts of shaggy hair around his head, groin, and lower legs. Plastic pink hooves covered his feet and hands, and a spiral horn of fleshy purple jutted from his forehead like something from Prickless's secret *My Little Pony* collection that he kept hidden in a crevice in his basement wall.

Prickless felt hot and uncomfortable all of a sudden, a feeling that only increased when a closer look at the man's groin revealed a fluffy pair of purple underwear that struggled to contain an equine-sized bulge no pony could boast except through steroid abuse. The unicorn man's glance flittered from Prickless to the elevators and back again.

"Going up?" he said in a way that made Prickless tingle in parts of his body even a yak would consider unwashed.

Prickless searched in vain for his voice, which, like his general comprehension of reality, had deserted him. He could only nod.

"Pressed the button yet?"

Prickless looked at the rectangular panel thing and felt his ears burning. No wonder the elevators weren't coming. Maybe this was what happened when you waited too long for them: the unicorns of gay animal hell came to get you, just like all those assholes online that were always plagiarizing his work and trying to stop him being published in his own magazine. *Yest ye be one*, he thought again with a shudder as the horned drag nag reached out with a hooved hand and pressed the up button.

"Nice outfit by the way" the unicorn man said when the elevator arrived. "The stench is a bit much, though."

He stepped inside and cocked an eyebrow at Prickless.

"You getting in?"

Prickless could only shake his head. To his horror, the unicorn man winked and blew him a kiss as the doors closed.

Now that Prickless had discovered the secret of the elevators, he managed to make it to the second floor by himself and went in search of room 239. To his great relief, the unicorn man was nowhere in sight. To his great distress however, the corridor was filled with lots of other people dressed as gay animals who all seemed

to be coming in and out of different rooms while talking and laughing and having a good time. His distress
began to border on panic as they wolf-whistled at him
as he passed and complimented him on his yak outfit.

And still there was that burning question in his
mind: what *was* a yak?

Prickless wandered through the warren-like maze
of corridors and soon feared he would become lost the
way he often did when he ventured more than fifty feet
from his grandma's basement. When at last he found
room 239, he was pleased to see it was like a writer's
room with a small desk at the window and a view of a
brick wall like the reflection of a controversial mind.
Maybe here he would find the inspiration for a new
collection to rival his self-published work of unrecognized genius, *Combustives in a Forgotten Landskip.*

After an hour of trial and error he figured out how
to open the window to a flood of shouts and laughter
and realized with horror that his room overlooked part
of the parade route. Hundreds of people dressed as gay
animals were milling around below, setting up floats
and banners and decorating the streets in white and
pink and purple bunting.

He saw all manner of animals, but the unicorns
were easily the most popular. Everywhere he looked
there were scantily clad herds of them gallivanting
about with spiral horns jutting skyward like fleshy
things that could be described but wouldn't be because
his mind had already filled in the blanks and scared
him off.

Prickless shut the window again and drew the shades to block out the awful sounds of bestial festivity.

"Muthafuckin' shit-cakes. This place is too creepy, like something out of a Stephen King story," he exposited to himself, marveling at the hardness of his swearing. Dark thoughts of an encumbering nature began to wander in the arid wastes of his mind, thoughts that were even too encumbering for incumbent cucumber-colored cummerbunds in Cumbria.

As he'd proven in his controversial memoir that had nothing to do with repressed homosexuality, *A Purple Eye Slit in Shadows*, Prickless was one who didn't give a damn about serious illeteration or proper grammer or whatever it was called. Shrunken Whites could go to Hell.

After some more dark thoughts and controversial f-bombs, he left his bag in the room and crept out into the corridor again to find somewhere to eat, which would have to be where they served proper Italian food and coffee regardless of his cash-deficient wallet. He found a nearby freight elevator that got him to the ground floor without encountering the hordes of costumed freaks again, and the doors opened onto a kitchen that connected to a deserted dining room with a dark atmosphere like something Rod Serling would have imagined if he wasn't dead. Prickless exited through a side door and went around to the front where a sign on the main door said *Closed,* so he knew it might not be open.

"Can I help you, sir?"

He jumped at the sound of a female voice and turned to see a young woman approaching in a smart uniform and a white spiral horn jutting from her forehead.

"Yeah," he said. "I'm looking for some good Italian food."

He was relieved to see that she was not a t-girl but a real woman who looked exactly like a pastor's wife even though she didn't have the same height or weight and was Asian not black.

"This restaurant is closed for renovations, sir," said the young woman. "You'll find other dining options on the far side of the lobby."

"Are you her?" said Prickless.

"Excuse me?"

"Are you a pastor's wife?"

"No. Are you a yak?"

"No, goddamn it! What the hell is with you people?"

"I'm sorry," she said. "I could have sworn you were a yak. I can smell you from here. I wanted to be a unicorn for the weekend and it looks like a lot of others had the same idea. People are trying to say that homosexuality in nature doesn't exist, so the parade has adopted the unicorn as its mascot to symbolize this mythical existence. But as staff we're only allowed minor headwear to show our solidarity. I guess they don't want us being confused with the guests."

Prickless stared at her in wide-eyed confusion, wondering what she meant by these mysterious and spiritual sounding words.

"Are you sure you're not a pastor's wife?"

"I'm no one's wife."

"This is weird," said Prickless. "Even weirder than *Fandom Weirdity*."

"What?"

"My controversial story the industry can't handle."

"What industry?"

"The horror writing industry."

"You're a writer?"

"I been a writer since I would had actually been of one at fourteen years."

The young woman arched a finely curved eyebrow.

"Since I would had actually been of one? You don't sound like a writer."

"I'm a writer who reaffirmed my faith even though the pastor's wife been a real bitch and accused me of being a fake Christian because I want to put my head in a lake facing the Chicago skyline."

The young woman was staring at him in amazement now, as though he might have escaped from a psychiatric ward or possibly the local zoo.

"Why on earth would you want to put your head in a lake?"

"Because I need to be facing Chicago when I get baptized, lady. That's what the pastor's wife doesn't understand."

"I'd be worried if she did understand. And why do you keep referring to this woman by her marital status and husband's occupation? That's really misogynist."

"I never called her a 'Miss odd gymnast.' I got manners, lady. Why do you think I'm taking a pig in a blanket to the lake when I get baptized?"

"If that's a question I can't begin to imagine the

answer.”

"So the bull shark has something to eat if it shows up,” said Prickless in exasperation. Didn’t this lady know anything about how Chicago did things?

The young woman felt her sanity begin to dissolve along with her sinuses as she caught a whiff of the yak creature’s breath, which ironically smelled the way she imagined a pig might after it had passed through a shark.

"Okay, if you say so,” she said. "But I wouldn’t be denigrating women at the parade if I were you. Have you seen the size of some of the lesbian tigers walking around? They’d tear you to shreds.”

"Listen, lady,” said Prickless, agitated by his inability to grasp what she was talking about, "I don’t denim great women and I’m not here for some faggy animal parade. I’m just trying to find somewhere to eat, though I only have three quarters and some food stamps left as I spent the last of my welfare check on this trip.”

"Why did you come to Chicago if you don’t have enough money to eat while you’re here? That doesn’t sound very well planned.”

"Leave me alone!” cried Prickless. "Are you gonna be like all those assholes I got on my back?”

"Your back is covered in assholes?” the young woman said with a touch of awe. "What a bizarre medical condition, though I imagine you’ll be a big hit with all the kinksters this weekend.”

Prickless was enraged. He hadn’t been this angry since the time a father of three with a beautiful wife had politely asked him on a message board why his stories were devoid of plot, character arc, and metaphor. Prickless had gone berserk, accusing the man of being a faggot and threatening to beat him up if he didn't stop his bullying. Didn't these jackholes realize he was the reincarnation of both Poe *and* Lovecraft? Didn't they know how influential he was in both the horror writing world and Chicago itself? He wondered if this woman who looked exactly like a pastor's wife except for her face, height, weight, and ethnicity had any idea that he was the only one in this city who could get the Latin Kings to drop their colors and pick some other, nicer ones. Magenta and paisley perhaps. But before he could wonder any further, she interrupted his wondering.

"If you'll excuse me, sir. I have work to do, and you need to leave this area."

She disappeared into the kitchen, leaving Prickless to fume in solitude. By the time he found his way out onto the street via a rear entrance the parade was in full swing despite the threat of rain, and hordes of gay animals thronged the streets. Painful stabs of hunger told him he was overdue for a five-course meal at a fine Italian restaurant where anyone who could write an intense collection of short stories cleverly disguised as the deranged ramblings of a moron should have been eating.

"Ooh, look at the yak, honey," a woman dressed as a pig squealed to her husband, who was wearing make-up and fishnet stockings over his lion costume.

"Wow, is that your real hair?" a girl dressed as a gazelle asked as he passed. "It's so black and greasy and long. You must have started growing it months ago when the parade was first announced. Check out the yak's hair, Donna!" the gazelle yelled at a poorly-constructed aardvark across the street. "Now that's commitment to a cause!"

The colorful horde were staring at him now, cooing and praising, though several wrinkled their noses as they caught his fetid stench. He passed some more unicorns, sparkly pink ladyboys who were all over him in an instant like he was a new puppy.

"Oh my god, it's a yak!"

"Wow!"

"What an outfit!"

"So life-like."

"He looks just like the ones on those nature documentaries."

"You get my vote for Carnival Queen, sweetie!"

"Mine, too!"

"And mine!"

Shouts were erupting all over the place, like the first drops of rain from the ominous storm clouds as the wind picked up, scattering glitter and confetti along the streets.

Prickless's growing anxiety began to make everything blurred. The gay animals looked like real animals, even sounded like real animals with all their yapping and braying, squeals and grunts of delight.

He aborted his quest for seventy-five cent banquets and turned back to the hotel. To his horror, a group of admirers including the ladyboy unicorns began following him. In his haste to get away he couldn't find the rear door again, and was forced to flee round the side of the hotel to the main entrance. In the lobby he frantically pushed the buttons but the elevators were trapped in a dark realm and wouldn't come.

He heard his newfound admirers enter through the automatic doors and fled through the lobby with the glittering hell-spawn at his heels. He darted into the closed restaurant and through the kitchen side door until he reached the freight elevator. Once inside, he pressed the buttons in a blind panic and the elevator began to rise. It jolted to a halt a few floors up and when the doors opened he jumped out and raced down the corridor.

He reached what he thought was his room, but stopped short when he saw the number 439 screwed into the wood. *Dagon the bull shark be cursed, I'm on the wrong floor!* he thought darkly.

Voices in the hall increased his terror and made his most unwashed part of all feel all tingly and squishy the way it did whenever he found himself alone in a truck-stop restroom with a hairy biker, which was far more often than coincidence allowed. He was trapped.

Unless ... wait, what was that across the way? An unmarked door that looked ajar.

He ran over and nudged it with the toe of his work-boot that had participated in nothing beyond the strenuous labor of cashing a welfare check. A crack of darkness appeared. Behind him the howling unicorns of the gay animal apocalypse sounded ever closer. There was no time to debate, whatever that was. He pushed, and the door opened like a wooden rectangle on metal hinges revealing darkness. He slipped inside and pulled the door shut behind him.

In the blackness he felt along the walls for a light switch but they were smooth and blank in a way that walls without switches often were. The foul-smelling air made him gag and he bumped into something unseen that fell against his face with an evil intent. He almost screamed as the loathsome tentacles of some vile and eldritch creature attacked him.

Beyond the door, the herd of gay animal freaks thundered past in their relentless pursuit of him, and he wondered if he'd avoided one terrible fate only to be ensnared by another. The tentacles probed his mouth, forcing their way in and now Prickless did try to scream, but the cursed appendages stifled it like all those jackholes on the internet who were always stifling his controversial anthologies such as *Tadpole Porpoises*, which had taken him as long as three minutes to edit.

Yet even in his terror, the writer part of his brain was enthralled by this horrific turn of events. Was this the hideous secret of the hotel that he had come to find? Could it be the dark past of Lovecraftian dimensions revealing its true nature to him alone? The tentacles reached still further down his throat and he could say nothing but "gghhghh."

A sudden snap brought light flooding through the gaps between where more tentacles clutched his face. Was this an elder god, come to drag his minion and its prey into dimensions unknown? Prickless was certain that his final hour had come only to hear a voice clear its throat and speak to him in human words.

"Uh, excuse me, sir, would you mind taking that mop off your head and coming out of the closet? It's staff-only."

The betentacled creature fell from the greasy head of Prickless Coglione as he stumbled backwards through the door and fell on his flabby ass, the sound of bad air escaping from his definitely not gay neither regions reminding him of his first experience with a suppository in a nurse's room.

He was momentarily stunned to see that the foul creature from the deep was indeed a common household mop, but as he looked into the mocking eyes of the uniformed man standing over him, shock gave way to a surge of rage that surged ragingly through his blood-carrying vessels that a lesser non-eldritch writer who wasn't the reincarnation of H.P. Lovecraft channeled through cyberpunk elements would have simply called veins. He leapt to his size six feet as though having just defeated a giant alligator in Lake Michigan and glared at the man.

"Are you saying I'm in the closet, pal?"

"No, sir," said the man. "You're not in the closet any more, you just came out."

Prickless felt the fury boiling over inside him like water boiling over in an overfilled pot of boiling water.

"Do I look like a gay man to you?" he shouted.

"No, sir. You look like a gay yak."

Prickless gaped, his face turning the same shade of purple as a certain part of himself that no one but he had ever touched.

"Listen, pal," he screeched, "let's get one thing straight, I'm not a goddamn yak and I'm not a flaming fairy either."

"That's two things, sir."

Prickless shrieked.

"Just tell me how to get to my goddamn room," he snarled at the man, who seemed infuriatingly unfazed by the power of Prickless's personality despite the fact that CreateSpace had measured the force he wrote at.

"Certainly, sir. Clearly you have difficulty with numbers, but do you know what room you're in?"

"239," said Prickless, the insult sailing over his head like a Frisbee over a legless dog.

"You'll find it on the second floor, sir."

"Huh?"

"This is the fourth floor, sir. You'll have to go down to the second floor, which is two floors below this one."

Prickless cursed and stormed off in search of the elevators, muttering about plagiarists and e-piracy.

"Enjoy your stay, sir," the uniformed man called out. "And enjoy the parade."

Prickless nearly choked with apoplectic rage-filled enragement, like someone choking on their dinner because they still hadn't learned how to chew properly after four decades of existence.

Back on the second floor, excited shouting erupted from behind him as he trudged along the corridor.

"Look, it's that yak guy again!"

His stomach lurched as an admiring horde of sparkly unicorns rounded the corner, all pointing at him and squealing with delight.

"The receptionist said his name is Prickless!" one of them cried out.

"So he's a transgendered yak!"

"Awesome!"

"This guy rules!"

"Hail Queen Prickless!"

"Gay recognition for all animals!"

"You're our symbol of hope, Prickless!"

The mob stampeded toward its squalid idol in a frenzy of glittery adoration and joy. The sight was too much for Prickless. He turned and ran as fast as his stumpy little legs would carry him, which, after two decades of sitting in a basement hunched over a computer and abusing people online while stuffing himself with junk food, was barely fast enough.

Up ahead he saw the fire stairs, and to the right, an open room he hadn't noticed earlier. Panting like a rutting walrus, he stopped to peer inside. It was filled with computers. A Business Room, he realized, where people sent emails to each other that criticized his writings. At the far end, two workmen were removing a large broken window from its frame. A barrier had been erected in front of it to indicate a work space.

As the workmen carried the broken glass into a corner and picked up a brand new pane, Prickless saw his chance, a momentous decision building inside him that was even more momentous than the one involving which flavor of Cheetos to eat while he jacked off to pictures of himself online. He ran toward the barrier and vaulted over it with the grace of a drunken yak, screaming as he passed through the empty frame and closing his eyes to let darkness darkify his mind.

Better to die than become an idol for a bunch of flaming fruit-loop animals, he thought as he plummeted to the street below. But instead of deathly tarmac, he slammed into something soft and spongy yet strangely firm, like a giant tumescent spongy thing that he could only draw symbolically on the cover of his magnum opus about a lifetime of stalking imaginary enemies, *Legend Creeper.*

What is this place I have come onto? he wondered in wonder as his eyelids fluttered open. He appeared to have landed on a solid white cloud and was drifting along on some ethereal plane that was even more ethereal than his failed series of *Gasbags.*

Have I died and gone to Heaven? he wondered in ever greater wonderment. This seemed to be confirmed when he saw an angel approaching. Huge white wings protruded from the creature's back, and it appeared to be naked except for a pair of exceedingly tight white bike shorts framing a bulge that surely didn't belong to any Gabriel that a conservative, and in no way gay, Christian such as Prickless would have imagined.

The figure loomed over him, the sweet scent of heavenly perfume radiating off its perfectly sculptured body as Prickless wondered in wonderment so great it was almost too much for someone whose brain-cells functioned with all the cohesiveness of fossilized Blu-Tack. He smiled happily as he realized he had guessed correctly: he'd died and gone to Heaven, as he'd always known he would despite all those assholes online telling him he'd be going straight to Hell because he was too controversial and not afraid to use the f-bomb in his writing.

More angels appeared - a whole herd of them with rainbow-colored tails and angelic hands that to his blurry vision resembled cloven hooves. Their long spiral horns knocked together as they bent to pick him up and a tail brushed his face.

Wait: tails? Hooves? Horns? His happy delirium began to evaporate like his chances of being published by other people. *Angels had halos, not horns. Unless ...*
Oh God.

A loud buzzing filled his head and became a deafening roar as the shock of the fall wore off and he came to his very limited senses. He sat up and was dumbstruck to see he'd landed in the middle of a giant white float covered in glitter and filled with angelic unicorns all dressed in white. An enormous crowd swirled around him all shouting and cheering as they filmed him with their cell phones and took thousands of photos, photos and footage that would inevitably be posted online for his rivals to make into memes and videos that mocked him with the kind of wit and style he was renowned for not possessing.

His screams were drowned out in the chaos as a swarm of professional camera crews swooped in for high definition close-ups. A parade compère clad in a leopard-skin leotard materialized among the angels and shoved a microphone into the bewildered face of Prickless Coglione.

"What do you think everybody," the compère shouted into the mic, his high-pitched voice amplified into a booming echo that rolled across the crowd like thunder from the storm clouds overhead. "Is this the winning costume or what?"

A mighty roar of approval erupted from the crowd as Prickless loosed a hymen-breaking shriek that the crowd mistook for girlish delight.

"Do we have our Carnival Queen? Cast your votes now!"

Another thunderous cheer went up from the crowd, and they began tapping their phones and screen-pads while the camera crews zoomed in to point blank range on the prostrate Prickless, flashbulbs flashing like the lightning overhead as they exposed the hideous details of his brown teeth and oddly (for one who so closely re-sembled a yak) moose-like nose. The shouts and screams of excitement seemed to go on forever while Prickless, unable to rise from the pain in his legs that felt broken from the fall, could only watch in mounting horror as the compère consulted his screen pad as the votes came flooding in.

"Ladyboys and Genitalmen," the compère cried all of a sudden. "The decision is unanimous! May I present the best costume winner, Parade Princess, and Carnival Queen of Chicago's first annual gay animal Mardi Gras who has just swept in from Yaksville on a whirlwind of gloriously glittery gayness that the Good Witch Glinda herself would be proud of, Miss Unicor-nado!"

A giant rainbow-colored spotlight swept over the crowd and illuminated Prickless as the compère reached down, and with some difficulty strapped a huge silver horn to the beer and pizza swollen head of the Anointed One.

Prickless screamed, and tried to shrink into the float, but unlike grandma's basement, there was nowhere to hide. He rose on a tidal wave of applause and angelic hooves as the unicorns with tiny bike shorts and huge bulges lifted him high into the air for everyone to see. This was more horrifying than anything he could imagine, even more horrifying than his horror story about the statue made of wood, or the one about killer bees from Africa that flew around sort of menacingly but didn't actually attack anyone except in a dream or something.

He tried to get to his feet but fell to his knees on the cloven platform and in sheer despair raised his greasy, glittery, previously yak-like but now officially sliver-horned unicorn head to the stormy sky.

"Noooooooooooooo!!!" he cried out melodramatically in the time-honored fashion of clichéd characters everywhere as thunder crashed and the heavens opened.

But, for the enormous crowd and countless millions watching live via telecast around the world, the answer was a resounding *yes*.

The Glitter Run

Dominic Stabile

"So it's like a bull run, but with unicorns?"

"Exactly," Seth said.

Efrain held the phone to his ear, slowly realizing that his friend might be serious. "So, it's bullshit?"

"Unicorn shit."

"How high are you?"

"Not high enough."

Efrain stirred the pot of marinara sauce on the stove and tried to think of why he was giving Seth the time of day with all he had on his mind already.

He had returned home from school this afternoon to find his mother once again unconscious on the living room floor, surrounded by beer and wine bottles with a partially eaten turkey sandwich still clasped in her hand.

Now he was standing here making chicken parmesan, his favorite meal, and listening to Seth's nonsense. Efrain loved to cook, and he had aspirations of becoming a famous chef someday. But he hated *having* to cook. He wished that occasionally he could come home and see his mother awake and smiling, holding out a pan of potatoes au gratin for him to smell, like a mom in some old TV show. He had cooked enough dinners in his seventeen years to call himself a seasoned pro, but he knew there was so much he had to learn.

His dream was to graduate high school and start at the Harold and Johnson's Culinary Academy in Charleston. It was supposed to be the best cooking school in the region; and it didn't hurt that it would put him four hours away from his mother. But his grades were average at best, and they barely had enough money to keep this dressed up lean-to of a house, much less pay for four years of college.

"Dude?"

"What is it, Seth?"

"Why do you sound angry?"

Efrain quietly ground his teeth.

"Your mom's out again, isn't she?"

Efrain didn't answer.

"Figured. You get moody when mommy's on the sauce. But hey, I hope you haven't started on the chicken parmesan yet."

Again Efrain was silent.

"Make it to-go then."

"Why?"

"Uh, were you paying attention to what I was just telling you?"

"You mean the unicorn bull run thing?"

"Yes, The Glitter Run. I'm going to run this year, and it's tonight."

"Great, have fun."

"Wait."

"How long are you going to drag this out?" Efrain said.

"Drag what out?"

"This bullshit about unicorns."

"Dude, everyone knows about The Glitter Run. It's the main event of the fairy festival. There are fliers posted everywhere."

"But a bull run with unicorns?" Efrain said. "Why can't I just hang up on you?"

"Don't blame yourself. It's my charisma."

Efrain knew why he couldn't hang up on Seth. Seth was the only friend he'd made since he and his mother had moved here three months ago. Thanks to his mother's already well-established reputation as a drunk, their household had quickly become a place parents didn't allow their children to visit. Seth was ignorant, but he was genuine. And Efrain knew Seth liked him.

Efrain looked down at the bubbles just beginning to form in the pot. He heard his mother cough and the racket of beer and wine bottles clattering over the coffee table as she dragged herself to her feet.

"Where and what time?" he said.

*

Efrain left after dinner, his mother finally awake and yelling after him from the front porch as he mounted his bike and started toward town.

He met Seth in a parking lot crowded with people. He recognized some of them. Everyone was wearing black except for a few people who stood in the center of the crowd wearing hot pink shirts made of some sort of special material that appeared to glow. Seth was one of these people.

"There he is," Seth said when he spotted Efrain.

Efrain chained his bike to a light post. "So, why are we meeting in a parking lot? And why is half the town here?"

"It's like this every year," Seth said. "They're always moving the entrance and it's always somewhere no one would suspect. We can't have out-of-towners finding out about the festival. That's the deal Mayor Nelson made with the fairies."

"Entrance?" Efrain said, ignoring the nonsense about fairies.

"An old Buick. That was our hint. The entrance was in a Buick."

"A Buick 8?" Efrain said, grinning.

"Le Sabre," Seth said, missing the joke. "It was Frank Harrison who noticed the car first. He runs the feed shop right over there."

Efrain noticed the car for the first time. It was a blue four-door parked just beyond the crowd near the edge of the parking lot. It was directly beneath a light post. The light was out, and lush ivy climbed the post, making it look like a tree in a fairy tale.

"I didn't notice it at first," Efrain said.

"It's some sort of spell they cast on it," Seth said.

"So, what do we do? Assuming this isn't a big hoax."

"We wait," Seth said.

"Wait? That's it?"

"You could think about what you'll wish for if you survive."

Efrain stared at him.

"It's the reward for surviving The Glitter Run. You get to ask the Fairy King for anything you want and he'll give it to you. You just have to put on one of the pink shirts and enter the contest. A little-known secret, unicorns become enraged by the color pink. Kind of how bulls are with the color red. All of the runners have to wear a pink shirt."

Efrain couldn't hold his composure any longer. He laughed at the ridiculousness of it all. He couldn't believe he had been so foolish. He knew if not for his mother he never would have agreed to meet Seth out here.

He opened his mouth to complain, then closed it.

The light post had just flashed on over the Buick Le Sabre, and in the hazy orange light Efrain had seen a small man flip out of the driver's side window and land on his feet.

The man was no more than two feet tall, and he wore a flashy suit that might have been in style a few hundred years ago. Tiny black shoes with curled toes caught the light from the streetlamp. Efrain stared, unbelieving. His mouth moved with the questions running through his mind, but words wouldn't come.

The little man stood as tall as he could, puffed out his chest and called out in a voice that sounded as if it came from a much larger man, "Will the contestants for The Glitter Run please step forward!"

Seth and the others in pink shirts gathered around the Buick. As they did, a procession of little people began to emerge from the window of the abandoned car.

They wore ruffled brown and green tunics and animal skin trousers. All of them carried weapons. As they moved out into the crowd, merchant stands began to pop up throughout the parking lot. Signs appeared over booth windows advertising decadent foods like funnel cakes and fried ice cream. There were fair games like Ring Toss and Dunk the Clown. And then some games Efrain didn't recognize. These games looked dangerous. One was called 'The Tumbling Bridge,' and consisted of a small rope bridge hanging over a pool of crocodiles. There was a booth where two dwarves were actively engaged in a game of Russian roulette. One booth had a sign that simply read, 'Quick Death,' and behind the counter was a man in executioner's garb sharpening a large axe.

Stars of pink and purple light flew from the car window and streaked through the dusky air, murmuring in small voices that seemed to come from a distant, poorly tuned radio. They flew in wild arcs from one end of the parking lot to the other, as if bursting with pent up energy. Then they changed course and flew along Main Street, tails of rainbow-colored glitter trailing behind them. Where the glitter fell tall, twisted posts grew from the earth. The posts glistened in the fading sunlight like shards of crystal. Between the posts, smaller crystal rails sprouted, and winding emerald cords grew from the posts and looped around the rails, creating a fence on either side of Main Street that stretched from one end of town to the other.

A hand on his shoulder.

Efrain turned to see Seth staring at him with a big, stoned smile on his face. He was holding out one of the pink t-shirts the runners were wearing. "You in?"

Efrain realized he was holding his breath and he inhaled deeply, as if he had just been dunked under water.

He took the shirt from Seth. "So it's true about the wish?"

"Yup. You just have to survive."

Efrain looked at him. "Has anyone ever survived?"

"A little girl about five years ago. She lost an arm at the elbow, but she got her wish."

"What did she wish for?"

Seth grinned. "She wished for her arm back."

*

Efrain and the rest of the runners entered the course through a small gate. There were eight of them in all. Each of the runners wore a look of fear mixed with determination. They stretched their legs and hips, chugged bottled water. A couple of them had dropped to their knees in silent prayer. Only Seth appeared at ease.

"Why are you running?" Efrain asked him.

Seth shrugged, and for the first time since Efrain had met him, a somber expression hung on his face. "Not much else to do. I'm going to flunk out this year, can tell you that already. And even if I do graduate, the future's pretty grim."

Efrain had only been to Seth's place once, but that had been enough. A rusty trailer right off the highway. There had been a hole in the center of the living room floor. They'd sat on the moist couch and watched TV for hours while cats climbed in from under the house in search of scraps. Efrain had never met Seth's parents because as soon as their car pulled up in the driveway, Seth had shoved Efrain into the hole in the floor and told him to crawl out through the back. "Pop will kill me if he sees me chilling with a beaner!" he'd called after Efrain, as if this should clear things up.

At the time, Efrain had resolved to never speak to Seth again. But now, thinking back on the experience, he felt a deeper kinship to Seth than ever before, and the realization that this might be the last time they ever spoke to one another filled him with regret. He couldn't remember what had possessed him to agree to this. They were both going to die tonight.

He was just about to suggest they back out of the run when Seth looked at him and asked, "Why are you running?"

The grin on Seth's face told Efrain there was no need to answer. Seth knew Efrain's situation, the obvious similarities to his own. They were both running away from lives overwhelmed with lost hope. Both of their futures held little more than despair and tedium. It might be different if Efrain had never found out about The Glitter Run. But now that he knew it was possible to change it all in an instant, he could never walk away from the opportunity. And if he did walk away this year, he'd be back the next.

"Listen," Seth said. "I hope you make it."

"I hope you make it, too."

An odd look crossed Seth's face and he looked away.

The little man in the old fashioned suit stood on a wooden tower overlooking the running course. He spoke in his incongruously powerful voice: "Will the runners please line up at the starting line!"

The runners put their toes to the starting line.

"Where are the unicorns?" Efrain said.

Seth nodded up toward the tree branches towering over the street. Beyond the trees, floating purposefully through the sky, was a purple cloud. It moved until it was directly above them, and then it stopped. There was the distant sound of thunder.

"If anyone would like to back out of the race, now is the time!" the little man shouted.

None of the runners moved.

"Very well! On your marks, get set, *go!*"

An explosion sounded from the crowd and a ball of blue light flew into the air and shattered like a flaming diamond.

The runners shot off down the track. All but Efrain. He started slowly, looking out nervously toward the ghastly onlookers. Trolls, ogres, witches, and things made of mud and rock watched from the sidelines, laughing at him as he stumbled along, feeling off balance. He could hardly believe he was here, that this was actually happening.

He looked toward the purple cloud and saw that it had expanded and now appeared more like a fog. It was at street level, and had started moving again. Beyond the smoky veil, Efrain saw quick, silver shapes darting back and forth. He could hear the aggravated neighing of horses. But he knew they weren't horses.

Seth grabbed Efrain by the arm and Efrain spun around.

"Don't stop," Seth said. "They'll gang up on you. Keep moving."

Efrain allowed himself to be pulled along for a few more feet, then he got into a rhythm and picked up his pace. The other runners were far ahead, and Efrain felt a pang of guilt that Seth had lagged behind to help him. He would likely be the cause of Seth's death.

But he couldn't think about that right now. He could hear hooves pounding the street behind him. The sound filled him with a fear like nothing he had ever felt before. There was so much drive and purpose in the clattering of those hooves. So much hunger.

He tried to focus on his own feet striking the pavement, the contractions of his leg muscles, the swinging of his arms. Every movement had to count. Every breath. It took all of his willpower not to look back.

He and Seth had almost caught up to the other runners, and the other runners were looking back now as the sounds of the unicorns' hooves became audible to them. Their eyes widened with horror and they turned away, picking up speed. One man, thin and wiry with a balding head, became frantic. After looking back and seeing what approached, he couldn't get his rhythm back. He stumbled and tripped over his own feet, hitting the pavement with his elbows. Efrain ran past him, and they briefly locked eyes. The man reached for Efrain's leg and Efrain pulled away before the man could clasp on to him.

"Please," the man called after him.

Efrain ran on a moment, and then looked back. Seth had helped him, maybe he should help this man.

But it was too late.

The cloud was gone, and in its place was a stampede of unicorns. But they didn't look like any unicorns he'd seen on TV. Their pelt was a dingy gray, and their manes were black and spiked. Long, silver horns protruded from their heads, roughly the length of javelins. Their eyes were black, like insect eyes, and ribbons of drool hung from their mouths.

As Efrain watched over his shoulder, several of them enclosed the fallen man. One drove its horn through the man's shoulder and lifted him off the ground. While he screamed in agony, two more unicorns impaled his legs, holding them apart. They lifted him high over the street. The dying man called out to the other runners, to the people in the crowd. But the onlookers cheered, calling for blood. And the runners kept moving.

A fourth unicorn moved between the man's legs.

Efrain turned away and ran faster.

*

The course took them through town. Cars were pulled over to both sides of the road as pedestrians gawked. Shops and restaurants that normally closed early were open, and people moved in and out with full shopping bags, tall ice cream cones and steaming mugs of coffee.

Efrain noticed that some people moved along without giving so much as a sideways glance at what was happening in the center of Main Street.

"Not everyone attends," Seth said between deep breaths. "Some people simply don't agree with The

Glitter Run. But they keep it secret from outsiders, just like the rest of us."

"What about tourists?" Efrain said.

"Here?" Seth laughed. "Even if tourists did waste their vacation time here, the course and all fairy folk are enchanted. They're only visible to locals."

They ran on until town gave way to cramped residences and then long, winding stretches of road where houses were only spotted every mile or so. Here it was dark. The sun had gone down half an hour ago, and they had only the light of the moon to see by.

The only audience they had now were the most hideous of the enchanted folk. Dark, ghastly figures with bared fangs and long, oddly shaped limbs. The human and humanoid members of the audience had likely remained behind, turning their attention to other functions of the fairy festival. This thought filled Efrain with a deep sense of hopelessness. As if they were alone now, floating out to sea on a raft filled with holes.

As he tried to talk himself up, to put his focus back on his movements, one of the other runners broke away and began slamming his hands against the fence.

"I changed my mind!" he cried. "I want to back out!"

As he pleaded, another runner followed suit and began crying out for her own life.

"Please let me out!" she said. "My son needs me!"

"Keep moving," Seth called out to them, but they didn't seem to hear him.

The little man in the fancy suit appeared, riding on the back of a large, winged creature with long, white tusks jutting from a narrow snout. "It is too late to back out," he said. "You must complete the race or die trying!"

"No, please!" the man called, reaching through the fence and grabbing at the beings beyond. They backed out of reach and watched him with cold eyes.

"My son!" the woman cried.

The two had stopped running completely now. They were on their knees, pleading with the little man.

"That's the rules," the little man said. There was no sympathy in his voice.

Efrain saw the unicorns moving in. He hadn't noticed their teeth before, long and jagged, as if utility blades had been jammed into their gums.

"Behind you!" he called.

But the man and woman were frantic. They didn't even know what was coming until the unicorns had descended upon them, tearing at their flesh with those sharp teeth. The unicorns started with their limbs, tearing away their arms and legs and then burying their muzzles in their guts.

Still they screamed to be let free.

The other runners, including Efrain and Seth, had slowed to watch without realizing it. Efrain wanted to do something, to help these people, but knew it was hopeless.

"My son!" the woman cried one last time before a unicorn locked its mouth over her face and tore it away. She gurgled blood, and the black hole in her bloodied face opened and closed noiselessly a few more times before she slumped over and stopped moving.

The unicorns had left the man one arm, which he used to pull his bleeding torso over the pavement toward the fence.

"Please," he said, his voice faded by shock.

The unicorns walked alongside him as he crawled. They made an odd mewing sound that reminded Efrain of a taunt, as if they were laughing at him.

"Help him!" Efrain called up to the little man. The little man didn't even look at Efrain. Instead, he looked down at the dying man and grinned as the unicorns stomped him to death beneath their hooves and then tore into him with their teeth.

*

Ten minutes later none of the remaining runners had spoken a word. They were covered in sweat and panting heavily, their eyes looking down or off at nothing. The unicorns were maintaining a steady pursuit, but were hanging back, as if to give the runners a break.

Or to make sure the run wasn't over too soon.

Efrain had a stitch in his side, and he kneaded his ribs with his fist, hoping to ease the cramp.

"Drink this," Seth said, handing Efrain a bottled water. "You're dehydrated."

"Where'd you get this?" Efrain said, twisting off the cap and chugging.

Seth lifted his shirt and revealed a belt with wide loops holding two more bottled waters. In spite of how tired he looked, Seth managed a smile. "You have to come prepared."

"I guess I should have believed you. Then I might have had a chance to prepare."

"Don't feel bad. No one ever believes until they see."

Just then Seth's face darkened. A shadow fell over them and Seth pushed Efrain toward the crystal fence. Efrain stumbled to the side but managed to maintain his footing as a unicorn flew by overhead.

A stream of glittery flakes rained from its anus.

The flakes smoked when they hit the pavement.

"That was close," Seth said.

"What — " Efrain started, but saw that a runner up ahead was unaware of the unicorn flying up behind her.

It was a middle-aged woman with dyed red hair. She had been wheezing and slapping her pockets for the last few minutes, and Efrain feared she was an asthmatic, searching for her inhaler. Her wheezing was worse now, distracting her from the unicorn's approach.

"Miss, behind you!" Efrain shouted, but she didn't even get a chance to look back.

The unicorn flew over her and the glittery shit washed over her body. As soon as the first flakes touched her flesh, she screamed. Smoke rose from her as the glitter heaped up on her shoulders and scalp. She slowed to a walk, trying to wipe away the glitter as her skin bubbled and began to fall off in singed clumps.

Efrain and Seth ran past her. Efrain saw the white glimmer of exposed bone, the yellow gobs of bubbling fat. After a minute or two of running, he couldn't hear her screams anymore.

Four runners remained when they crossed the half-way point. They had reached Efrain's and Seth's part of town. Trailer parks and houses that looked condemned lined the road. Efrain looked to the left beyond the crowd and saw his street. His house stood at the end. He could just make out a lit window, and he allowed himself to imagine his mother sitting by that window with a phone in her hand, trying desperately to find out where her son had gone. But he knew it was more likely she had fallen asleep in front of the TV.

"No looking back now," Seth said.

"I know."

Efrain had a stitch in his side again, and his legs had tightened up. His calves kept cramping, making it difficult to maintain speed. He and Seth were out of water, and they had fallen a little behind the other runners, two older men with short-cropped white hair who had remained side by side the entire time. Seth had told him the two were brothers.

Efrain looked at Seth, who was obviously holding back. He knew Seth could push forward if he wanted to.

"Why don't you go ahead," Efrain said. He hadn't realized how out of breath he was until he attempted to speak.

"Not a chance."

"You'd have a better chance if you left me."

"What kind of friend would I be then?" Seth offered a weak smile.

There was a sudden cry from up ahead.

Efrain saw the taller of the two other runners turn toward his bother and push him toward the fence.

"What the hell?" the brother said.

The taller man let out a startling war cry and charged his brother. He was holding what looked like a small crowbar as if it were a battle axe. His face was twisted in a look of fierce concentration and fury. Before the brother could do anything, the man had swung the crowbar into his knee. There was a sickening crunch, and the brother's body twisted and hit the pavement. Efrain had to jump to avoid tripping over him.

Efrain looked back. The wounded man had time to throw up his hand and scream before the unicorns were on him with their horns, impaling him over and over until his screams turned to choked sobs and finally went silent.

The man with the crowbar laughed and ran ahead.

Efrain and Seth picked up their pace, but neither had any desire to catch up to the man who had just murdered his own brother.

They ran on silently for a while. The only sound aside from the wind was the constant clatter of hooves and the anxious neighing of the unicorns. Efrain didn't understand why the unicorns didn't overrun them. They were faster, and could fly. If they wanted to, they could kill Efrain, Seth and the man who had killed his brother in an instant.

"Why don't they finish us?" Efrain said.

"It's always like this," Seth said. "They pick off the weak first. Once there's only two or three strong runners left, they start to toy with them."

Efrain let that sink in, then he said, "Why did that man kill his brother?"

"I'm not sure," Seth said. "Probably because they were too evenly matched."

"Evenly matched?"

"Well, yeah." Seth looked embarrassed.

"Why would that matter? If they're both strong and they both survive, that would be better, right?"

Seth shrugged. "You can't have two winners."

Efrain stared at him, as the blood drained out of his own face.

"I didn't want to tell you earlier. But there's only one survivor of The Glitter Run. It goes on until ..."

Efrain was shaking his head. "Why would you invite me if you knew one of us would have to die?"

Seth looked at him and his face was somber again. "Honestly, man, I never expected to get this far. I just wanted to help you get through." He shrugged. "I'm not looking to get out alive."

"So this is an elaborate suicide for you?"

Seth looked away.

Efrain couldn't make sense of it.

"I'm here for you more than anything," Seth said. "I thought you'd have a better chance if I were helping you along."

"I ..." Efrain shook his head. "I thought we'd win it together."

"If you win and you get your wish, that's a win for me, man."

"And I'm supposed to just live with that?"

"You're my only friend," Seth said. "I didn't know how else to help you."

Efrain stared at him as they ran along. The unicorns had finished with their last meal, and the clatter of their hooves was drawing nearer.

*

After another thirty minutes of running, they caught up to the man who had killed his brother. He was slowing, and he kept looking back with an apprehensive expression on his face, his arms flailing in the air. He looked to Efrain like a man trying to outswim a shark.

Efrain himself felt the full weight of his fatigue now. He could no longer distract himself from the pain in his legs or in his side. His calves kept cramping and he couldn't draw in a full breath. Seth ran with the dogged stride of a monk on a pilgrimage. And Efrain hated him for it.

"Just give up," the man ahead of them called back.

"You first," Seth said.

"I got a kid," the man said.

"We are kids," Seth said, patting Efrain on the shoulder. He grinned.

"Is this funny to you?" Efrain said.

Seth's smile shrank and he turned toward the other runner. "You look strong."

"Damn right," the man said. "Could kick your ass any day."

"I bet," Seth said. He looked at Efrain and winked.

"What are you doing?" Efrain said.

Seth turned back to the man. "You wanna test it?"

The man laughed. "You want to fight right here?"

"I had another idea. Those things always attack the weaker runners first, right?"

"Yeah, so?"

"So, what do you say we let my friend here run along? Me and you will slow down and let the unicorns catch up. If they attack me, which they probably will, then you can take off with one less competitor to worry about."

"That's fucking stupid."

"I understand if you're scared," Seth said. "But just know, I could run like this for at least ten more miles. How about you?"

The man nearly stumbled, but managed to regain his footing. His shirt was drenched, and he had a riled look in his eyes, like a wounded predator looking for a corner to put his back in. "This ain't a trick?"

"Nope. To be honest, I'm hoping to die on this track."

"Yeah, okay," the man said. He slowed down until he was running alongside Seth.

Seth looked at Efrain and nodded.

Efrain stared at him a moment, uncertain what he was trying to tell him. Then he saw Seth reach into his pants pocket and withdraw a small kitchen knife.

"Run ahead," Seth said to Efrain. "If I die, old sweaty here is likely to chase you down first thing."

The man grinned. "You better believe it, kid."

Efrain ran ahead. Just after he looked away from Seth, he heard the man shout, "Cheater! You lied!"

Efrain looked back and saw Seth draw his blade across the man's throat. The man had pulled out his crowbar, and he dropped it now as blood spurted from the wound and he fell to his knees, clutching his throat in two hands. Seth ran faster and caught up with Efrain.

"I figured he'd try something," Seth said.

Efrain looked straight ahead, refusing to look at Seth or to watch another man die.

*

They had reached a point in the track now that went beyond their town. They didn't appear to be any-where. Outside of the track was a deep, inky darkness. Efrain glimpsed a pair of eyes and a flashing set of teeth. There were still spectators beyond the fence, al-though he was glad he couldn't see them in full. The unicorns were drawing closer. Efrain thought he could feel the heat of their breath. He was so tired, however, that he no longer feared death.

"What now?" Efrain said.

"Now the unicorns go full-tilt. You need to move ahead."

"What if we both run as fast as we can? Maybe we can find a way out. Maybe they'll let us out if we get far enough."

Seth shook his head. "It doesn't work that way."

"I don't want to win this way."

"This way, I get what I want and you get what you want," Seth said.

"How could you want this? If you win you could wish all the bad stuff away."

"You can't wish away your memories," Seth said. "And my memories will ruin anything I wish for. You could actually have a better life."

Hooves pounded the pavement more quickly now. The anxious neighing of the unicorns turned to frenzy as they quickly drew nearer to the remaining runners. Up ahead, Efrain could see a pinpoint of light in the darkness, like some sort of polished metal catching sunlight. Seeing it filled him with a sense of warmth he couldn't remember ever experiencing. He knew the feeling was happiness, though he had never felt it.

A unicorn came up between Efrain and the fence, rocking its head back and to the side. Efrain ducked, and its spear-like horn sliced the air over his head.

Seth grabbed Efrain and pulled him away from the unicorn. Then he thrust out with his knife, piercing its hide.

There was a gasp from the invisible spectators beyond the fence.

The unicorn shrieked and fell back in with its friends.

"Suck that!" Seth cried, swinging his blade in the air.

Another unicorn flew by overhead, shitting glitter. Both boys darted to the side, avoiding the blistering flakes of gold. A unicorn ran up beside Seth and stabbed at him with its horn. He twisted to the right and managed to avoid taking the horn full-on. But it did slice his left bicep clean open. He cried out, dropping the knife.

"Seth!"

Seth pushed Efrain away as the unicorns turned their attention to the wounded runner.

"Remember, this is what I want," Seth said.

Another unicorn bucked its head and sliced the back of his leg with its horn. Seth cried out again and stumbled to one side. He almost lost his footing, but managed to keep moving.

"Come on you fuckers," Seth cried, his speed slowing.

Efrain wanted to run to his friend as unicorns moved up beside him and around in front, blocking his progress. But he knew there was nothing he could do. Seth didn't want to be saved, and at best Efrain could die with him. But that would be throwing away Seth's sacrifice.

So, instead of running to his friend's aid, he stopped and looked back. Seth looked up at him, blood pouring from cuts all over his body. He grinned and nodded.

Efrain never looked away as the unicorns tore into his friend. He watched until there was nothing left. And when he turned to continue on, the end of the track was right in front of him.

Seated atop a tall, extravagant throne was the Fairy King, waiting for him to make his wish.

Afternoon Delight

Amy Shepherd

"Admit it, Jen, we're lost," Sasha said. She gave the radio dial a few last cranks, then gave up and tipped her seat back. She propped her feet on the dash, smudging the windshield with her toes.

"It's around here somewhere," I said, glancing from the dusty road to my phone. Google Maps had entered a kind of fugue state, caught in a loop of redirection. It's not like it had much to go on. We were headed towards a literal hole in the ground.

She swatted at the seat belt looming over her. "I can't believe I let you talk me into this. We've been driving around these dirt roads all morning. And for what? More rocks. Like you don't have enough friggin' rocks already."

"They're not rocks. They're fossils." I slowed to a crawl, eyeing a gap in the foliage, wondering if it was the turn I'd been waiting for. Up close, it looked more like a horse trail than a road, so I drove on.

"Same difference," she said, stuffing a wadded-up shirt behind her head. She slipped off her sunglasses and closed her eyes.

"I get it," I said, stroking Sasha's thigh. "You wanted to spend another day at Powell's. But I couldn't vacation in Oregon and not check out the fossils."

She heaved an exaggerated sigh. "I know you couldn't, baby," she said, squeezing my hand. "That's what I get for sleeping with a geek girl."

"Me? What about you and those sword-and-sorcery novels?" I asked, tapping the brick of a paperback resting on her chest. "That's pretty nerdy."

Sasha opened her eyes, turning to me. "Hello, *Game of Thrones*. This shit's mainstream now. Besides, nothing is as nerdy as fossils."

I glanced over my directions again. I thought we had to be close, but it was hard to tell with the hand-drawn map I'd printed from the internet. The cryptic markings and lack of scale gave it a mystical feel. I was surprised the outlying areas weren't marked with "here be dragons."

"Where'd you get those directions anyway? It's like a child drew them." She let out a jaw-cracking yawn, sitting halfway up to root around behind my seat. "Do we have any chips left?"

"Some ancient webpage. You would've had a stroke if you saw it. It had animated GIFs, not the good kind either. Epilepsy-inducing blinking rainbow letters, 8-bit rocks in a chorus line doing kicks." I tossed her the bag of chips, then took a sip from my water bottle.

Sasha shuddered and crinkled open the bag. "Sounds hideous. And yet you trusted it for directions." She snapped her seat back into an upright position, then reached out for the water bottle.

"Yep," I said. I watched as she settled in with her iPod and book. Hopefully that would buy me another hour. I decided if I couldn't find the dig site by then, we'd head back to our hotel and have a nice dinner out.

It took another twenty minutes, most of that spent driving down a narrow, rutted road that had challenged our patience as well as our backsides. We'd had to close the windows or the blackberries would have torn us apart. The road opened into a dusty field, pock-marked with holes. I parked next to an unusual outcropping of rocks.

It wasn't what I had expected. I'd read that the best places to look for fossils were cliffsides or riverbeds, even construction sites where rock had been exposed. In other words, not this lunar landscape. I was careful not to show my disappointment as I popped the trunk and pulled out my rock-hounding gear.

Goggles, a six-piece sifting pan set, the *National Audubon Society Field Guide to North American Rocks and Minerals*, and a rock hammer with a fine leather handle: all were in mint condition, owing to a complete lack of use.

It wasn't that I hadn't tried hooking up with rock-hounding groups. I just hadn't managed to find any with members over the age of 8 or under the age of 72. Apparently, chipping marine fossils out of sedimentary rock and hunting for seams of opal weren't popular hobbies for thirty-somethings.

Sasha floated our picnic blanket to the ground, then lay on her belly with another of her Powell's acquisitions propped up in front of her, a graphic novel boasting Victorian werewolves. I had entertained a fantasy of her digging alongside me, but I let that go along with my ambitions to bag a fossil.

Tugging on a hat, I walked the site, assessing the holes. This terrain looked unlikely to produce anything beyond piles of dirt. What had I thought my first rock-hounding expedition would yield, I wondered. Gnarly veins of gold, glittering amethyst crystals, the elegant spiral of an ammonite?

There was still a possibility though. This region was rife with thundereggs, a rock similar to a geode, but with an agate-filled cavity. They hid in the loose soil, looking like nothing more than unassuming dirt clods. But when cracked open, they displayed a scene of otherworldly beauty, streaks and whorls of milky agate.

Or so I had read. Clambering down into a hole, I allowed myself to imagine my mantle lined with thundereggs, cut open and polished to a high gloss. Not ones I had purchased at an overpriced rock shop, but ones I had dug out of the dirt with my own bare hands.

Knowing it would be useless, I'd abandoned the rest of my gear by the car, but brought the rock hammer with me, wanting to at least get it dirty. After a few token swings which did little more than generate puffs of dust, I anchored it in the wall of the pit, where it would be readily accessible in the slim chance that I needed it.

Then I got down on my knees and got busy with my hands. I dug, scooping the dirt behind and away from me. I dug, reaching into the earth to reveal her mysteries. I dug, thinking about the glaciers that had spent eons grinding down mountains to create this very soil.

I dug until my arms turned to rubber and sweat traced a river down my back. My mouth was lined with powdery silt. I found rocks among the dirt, plenty of rocks. All perfectly ordinary, the kind you might find skipping across the blades of a suburban lawnmower or underfoot as you turned an ankle crossing a vacant lot.

Straightening up to work the kinks out of my back, I knocked my rock hammer loose, causing a small avalanche of dirt, which revealed the most interesting rock I'd seen all day. I knelt again and clawed at the rock, anxious to prise it free. It tumbled into my lap, and I laughed out loud.

I sprang out of the hole, taking only a moment to clap the dust from my clothes. I ran over to Sasha and dangled the rock in front of her. She looked up, shading her eyes with her hand.

"Oh my God," she said, sitting up. She snatched the rock out of my hand and examined it. "You found a prehistoric dildo!"

I crouched on the blanket next to her. "That's what I thought too. But why's it so narrow, almost pointed, at that end?" I touched the tip. It felt rough in contrast to the rest of the stone, like it had been broken.

"Maybe that side's tapered for beginners," she said, caressing the eight inch rod. "Wow, it's so smooth, almost like it's been polished. It feels like it has rings too."

"Ribbed for her pleasure," I said, taking it back from her. I helped myself to her water bottle, first taking a long drink, then dribbling water along the length of the rock.

Amazed, Sasha glided her fingers along it, murmuring at the change in color as the water melted away the gray film. "What's it made out of?"

The rock was pearly now, almost iridescent. When the sun caught it, I had to look away. "I don't know. I've never seen anything like it in any of the field guides."

We both had our hands on it now and were engaging in a casual tug of war. Sasha's mouth was dangerously close to the rock. No doubt we were both thinking it, but she had the indecency to mention it first. I objected, for form's sake.

Sasha scoffed, letting go. "You come across a prehistoric dildo, and you don't even want to try it out? What kind of lesbian are you, Jennifer?"

"I didn't come across it. I dug it up out of the ground, remember? It's probably got ancient microbes on it." I tried and failed to get worked up over germs. I was too dazzled by the shiny object.

"Well, for something so filthy," she said with a smirk, "it sure cleans up nice." She seized the rock from me and held it aloft. "Just imagine, 30,000 years ago, some dyke lovingly crafted this beauty for her girlfriend. Probably as a Christmas gift."

I stood and made a grab for it. "Uh, dykes didn't really exist back then, lesbianism being a modern concept and all. Also, Christmas ..."

"Oh, hush, let me have some fun." She stuffed the dildo down the front of her shorts and advanced towards me, walking like a bowlegged cowboy. "She comes home to her cave or whatever, and her girlfriend's like 'is that a saber-tooth tiger tooth in your pocket or are you just happy to see me?'"

Sasha clasped me around the waist and thrust her stone woody against my thigh. Her breath hot in my ear, she whispered, "Wanna make some prehistoric monkey?"

And Reader, it was like a *Clan of the Cave Bear* fanfiction come to life. Jondalar had nothing on Sasha when it came to giving the Pleasures.

We were basking in the afterglow when the calm was shattered by a clatter of hooves and a shrieking rending of metal.

Staring down at us was the meanest motherfuckin' unicorn I'd ever seen. Of course, I'd never seen one in real life before, just in books, where they were always sipping serenely at clear mountain streams or frolicking in meadows with virgins.

This one was huge, with a foot and a half long horn, glowing red eyes, and smoke shooting out its nostrils. Behind it stood a group of six more, looking like they were spoiling for a fight now that they were done working over my car.

I scrambled to put on my clothes, wanting that thin layer of protection against the interlopers. This situation was feeling all too like the time I'd been caught with my high school girlfriend out in the back yard by her dad.

Sasha, naked as a jaybird, stood and stretched out a hand towards the creature. "I love your mane."

I yanked her back towards me. "We've talked about this, Sash. You can't go around touching other people's hair."

"Silence, humans! You have desecrated the burial ground of our ancestors. Why did you not heed the sign?"

"There was a sign?" we both said in unison.

"It has stood at the entrance since time beyond," the unicorn said with a delicate sniff.

"You mean that pile of rocks?" I asked, re-buttoning my shirt. In my earlier haste, I'd gotten the holes lined up wrong.

"A cairn, yes, to warn away your kind." It stamped at the dirt with its impressive hooves. I tried not to imagine the mark a hoof like that would make on skin.

"Well, as signage goes, it's a spectacular failure," said Sasha, crossing her arms over her chest.

I stifled a moan and shoved her t-shirt at her. A part of me had always known that Sasha's sassy mouth would one day get us killed. But she was a librarian, and God knows, no one could shut them up once they started talking about findability.

"If it's so important," she continued, "then why not use a sign in regular human English since you apparently speak it so well?" She tightened her arms, making her breasts bulge.

The unicorn sent an indignant huff of smoke our way and said, "We would not sully our tongues by speaking your inferior language. It is through a gift of my magic that you can understand my speech."

Sasha's mouth fell open, and she nudged me. "Like the Babel Fish in *Hitchhiker's Guide*."

"In all my reign as Supreme Pointy One," said the unicorn, holding its nose high, "I have never seen so foul a desecration."

"Supreme Pointy One?" said Sasha, this time giving me the full elbow treatment.

It tossed its glorious mane. "The title sounds better in my native tongue. Where was I? Ah yes, a most profane use of our beloved ancestor's horn."

"No shit, that was a unicorn horn?" She pummeled my arm with delight.

"It was the horn of the mighty ..." it said, finishing with a string of unintelligible sounds, presumably a name.

"It really looks like an ancient stone dildo. It's the perfect length, the perfect girth," said Sasha, cupping her fingers. She gave me a sly look and tipped her head my way. "This one sure as hell enjoyed riding it."

This seemed to have cast a spell of speechlessness over Our Royal Hornness. Without missing a beat, Sasha squatted and started pawing through the bags lying by the blanket. She located a hefty sack of carrots and waved it in the unicorn's face. "Look what I got. Sweet, crunchy, delicious carrots. Want some?"

She pulled one out of the bag and ran it under the beast's nose, and I'll be damned if it didn't whinny. Sasha doled out the carrots, careful to give the leader a somewhat larger portion than the rest of the herd.

"Good thing we stopped at that roadside stand, huh?" she whispered to me. She dragged out the rest of our fruit and vegetable purchases. The apples, of course, were a hit, but also surprisingly, the watermelon and the summer squash. Just as well; I didn't really care for squash.

"Oh, Supreme Pointy One," said Sasha, her arm looped around the unicorn's neck, "you think we could keep that horn? I mean, it's probably ruined, right?"

"Yes," it said, munching a bunch of bok choy. "The magic is all gone. You may retain the horn."

When all the food had been eaten and all their manes had been brushed and braided, the unicorns cleared out fast, their hooves raising a cloud of dust.

"That went surprisingly well," I said, fanning the dust out of my face.

"Yeah, that was a gamble, plying them with carrots," she said, gathering up the leftover peels and rinds. "But I figured, they're like horses, so they must have the same sweet tooth."

I snorted. "Those monsters were nothing like horses. They stomped my car into scrap metal." I wondered if my insurance covered acts of unicorn.

"So there are a few dents. Don't be such a drama queen." Sasha slung our bags into the trunk and tried to close it, but it bounced right back up.

"At least they came down on the trunk, and not the hood." I tied the trunk closed with a length of clothesline, pleased to finally use an item from the extensive emergency kit that I stored in the car. "I'm thinking that this might be my last rock-hounding excursion."

"What? After you snagged this prize?" She brandished the horn, and it winked in the sun.

"Are you keeping that thing in your pocket?" I asked, giving the clothesline one final tug.

Sasha flashed the Girl Scouts hand sign. "Just being prepared." She sidled up to me and toyed with the top button of my shirt. "You know, the afternoon's still young."

"Oh, yeah? What'd you have in mind?" I stuck a finger through her belt loop and pulled her to me.

"Our unicorn friend seems to think that the magic's all gone," she said, giving me a kiss. "But I'm not so sure."

"Well," I said, taking the horn from her. "There's only one way to find out."

Haikunicorns and Limiricanes

Stygia Deal

Erection of bone
Jutting glorious and thick
My horny lover

There once was a pervert from Morris
Obsessed with an inmate named Porras
He craved the effects
Of gay prison-sex
Throat full of cum and a sore ass

Scary things happen
Like a Stephen King story
Indescribable

Real hardcore Christians can swear
Conservatives can have long hair
Ken Hovind Obama
Go fuck your dead mama
Pick on the disabled so there

SyFy Channel, stop
Animal/weather horror
It rains bears: DRIZZLIES

The Pretty Pegasus Princess Prancyone
Wore a big strap-on horn, a real fancy one
As you might think
This unicorn kink
Made finding a partner a chancy one

You're a corpse-flower
A blossoming cadaver
That means you're stinky

This one time at a famous museum
I left out my books so you'd see 'em
But, from bad luck to worse
Some fuck brought a black purse
And my videos sound like I'm on helium

Stitches in his head
Run over by a Lexus
Gagged on Porky Pig

There once were some ghosties at play
On a gusty and blustery day
Through quakes and storms
And tornado alarums
The hurricanes blew them away

Black, silver, blood-red
Darker than darkity-dark
Gothic unicorn

Unicorn Vs. Rock Giant

Terry Ibele

Welcome to Glow City, so named for the orange haze that always hangs above it. In the distant future, humanity has devoured every single resource, making the whole planet a desolate, barren plain. All that's left is Glow City.

It's home to 500 billion people and not a single one of them has ever seen a unicorn (or even corn for that matter — all they eat is spaghetti). Passing through, you'll notice the faint aroma of fake pink bubble gum lofting in the air (it's pumped in to make the place smell nicer). Somewhere a synthesiser plays out its melody. Wherever you look, grey domes and rusty pipes fill your view giving literal meaning to the term: *concrete jungle*.

Two hunched figures walked down the sidewalk and stopped in front of an unlit alleyway. In the early evening not even the orange haze penetrated the dark space between two 1,000 story skyscrapers.

"Do you hear something, Letty?" murmured one figure, a grandma grandma, squinting into the alleyway. (Grandma Grandma: a grandma who's so old she's a grandma to a grandma). Her false teeth came loose after she opened her mouth to speak and dropped to the ground in a slobbery mess. She pulled out her pocket tractor beamer and beamed them back up to her gums.

"Uh-what?" replied the grandma grandma grandma (Grandma Grandma Grandma: a grandma to a grandma grandma). She lifted a bony hand to readjust her purple sweatband.

"I'm sorry, Betty, but you'll have to repeat that."

"I said, do you hear something, Lett — "

Betty's sentence was interrupted by a hurricane of noise that ran up and slapped the two old ladies in the face. At the same moment, a flash of light zoomed by so fast that it messed with the space time continuum surrounding the two old ladies. They each turned 70 years younger as they were sent into the past.

Letty looked around, a bit stunned. "Happy un-70th birthday, Betty," she said.

"Thanks," replied Betty.

Okay, enough with these ladies (they're still old as hell, even if they are a bit younger now), this story is about unicorns! Let's take a look at what just zoomed by.

It was a bullet of flesh and steel. Veins pumped with oil. Gears tugged by tendons. A hybrid of animal and automaton, topped with an ivory horn that sliced the air itself. It was the last unicorn. It was the first unicorn. It was the only unicorn that had ever been.

An explosion of concrete and rock followed the unicorn as the alleyway crumbled and piled atop where the two grandma grandmas stood (don't to worry; they had transported back in time 70 years earlier when all was still peaceful outside the alleyway). It was a rock giant. It lunged forward as it chased the unicorn with rock legs the size of cars and crushed two cars the size of other cars.

Side Note: Rock giants are made of rocks. Why some rocks are just normal rocks and other rocks are giants, no one really knows.

This particular rock giant was minding its own business, sitting on its mother's knee, when it realized that an entire city of 500 billion people had been built right on its doorstep (rock giants aren't really much for observation, but they are very adamant about trespassing humans). In a rage, it ran to the city in order to destroy it, but suddenly a unicorn, the size of a normal horse, appeared and distracted it.

Another Side Note: Where did this unicorn come from suddenly? How was it able to distract the rock giant? Who knows! Certainly not those two grandma grandmas. They're too busy celebrating their un-70th birthdays to care.

A sharp turn found the unicorn a league ahead down the main road and not even the rainbows which spewed from its mane could catch up. They simply slumped down on the pavement and waited patiently to fade into nothing.

"Rargh!" cried the rock giant and crashed into an office building as it slid around the corner. Precious gems chipped from its shoulders and rained down, shattering a parked car. The giant regained its composure and bounded forward in one gigantic leap, reaching out with giant rock fingers to grasp the unicorn's white flowing tail.

The edge of the city was fast approaching ... approaching closer ... closer ... gone! The unicorn breached the edge and its steel hooves crushed the dry, caked dirt that covered the barren plain of the earth. Still, the giant pursued closely behind.

A cliff up ahead watched the scene eagerly and prepared for its guests to arrive. It was only a matter of speed now — magically steam powered muscles versus gigantic rushing boulders of terror. The rock giant jumped forward and clasped its hands around the unicorn.

"Rah ha ha!" the rock giant bellowed, squeezing its hands as tightly as it could, but an odd sensation came over its feet. They weren't touching anything. Now its whole body experienced an interesting, rushing feeling (remember, observation isn't natural for rock giants) and it looked down to realize it was falling through the air.

It looked back to see a majestic, white steed against an orange glow backdrop reflected a thousand times in its crystal eyes. A thunderbolt sliced through the air and struck the unicorn's horn.

"Rargh!" the rock giant cried, but its voice was drowned out by the crackling of thunder. The cliff opened its mouth and licked its lips as the rock giant fell into its stomach.

Meanwhile, two bowl-cut hairstyles ducked behind a boulder. They belonged to two small heads, which in turn belonged to two small children.

"Did you see that?" said Lauren, parting her blond bangs into perfect triangles.

"I must be dreaming!" replied Michael, blowing his brown bangs out of his eyebrows. Michael hated his bowl-cut. He wanted to grow a mullet like a teenager, but his mother wouldn't allow it. He pulled up the sleeves of his oversized, yellow knitted sweater and clapped his hands. His sweater had a cat on it, in case you're a cat fan and would like to know. "A real, live unicorn," he sighed.

"None of the other kids will ever believe us!" replied Lauren. "But look!"

She held out her hands and in them was an instant camera. A relic of times past. A white square with a smaller black square inside it shot out. A few shakes later, and an image slowly revealed itself.

The two children stared in awe at the image. A giant rock monster had one foot over the cliff and a unicorn was in the middle of a sharp right turn. Michael ran his hand over the picture of the unicorn.

"Look," he said. His hand was full of glitter.

"How can that be from a photograph?"

"It must be magic!"

Hooves clopped nearby and Lauren and Michael turned to see their hero standing before them.

"Oh, uh, sorry Ms. Unicorn," said Lauren. "We didn't mean to be sneaking — hey, Mikey what are you doing?" She jumped up and ran to catch her brother before his hand touched the unicorn's nose.

"Don't worry," said Michael. "She's nice."

A snort made Lauren jump back, but she stepped forward again, and saw her nervous reflection in the unicorn's big black eye. "Nice Unicorn. We don't want to hurt you. It's okay."

Her trembling hand touched the side of its neck and instantly she felt at ease. The sky brightened, green flowing grass appeared and the air smelled delicious. For the first time in her life, she felt true happiness. She took her hand off and sad reality set in again.

On: Dreamland. Off: Desolationland. On: Flowers and birds. Off: Dirt and beetles.

As the stars appeared in the night sky, a low resounding clang came from Glow City.

"Oh my gosh diddly dosh!" cried Lauren, looking at the giant clock tower that rose high above the orange glow. But instead of a clock tower she saw a giant daisy opening and closing its petals to the beat of a toy monkey drummer dancing around its base. "Mikey, it's 11 o'clock! Mom's gonna be real mad!"

Turns out the two kids had been playing with the unicorn for hours without even realizing it. Lauren jumped off the unicorn's back and caught Michael as he slid off too. Instantly the sky became dark and the barren plain showed its ugly face.

She returned her hand to the unicorn once more before running home. Butterflies appeared flittering around her head and her feet wrapped with lilacs. Clouds shaped like lollipops filled the sky and a subtle melody wafted in the air. She wished she didn't have to go home, but her bum reminded her that a wooden spoon in the kitchen doubled as a spanker.

*

"That's nice, dear. You have such a vivid imagination! But don't stay out that late again."

"But, Mom, I swear, I saw it all! It really happened!" Lauren said, rubbing her behind. It was still sore from the night before.

"That's enough silly talk for now. Eat your spaghetti."

"Mom, look!" Lauren held out the photograph.

"That's nice, honey; your breakfast is getting cold."

Lauren turned the photograph around. It was pure white, as if she'd had the flash on in a mirror.

Later that night, Lauren lay wide awake thinking about the unicorn. Not even her grandma grandma, who shared the corner of their bedroom could rest her mind with a lullaby.

"You saw it all happen, right?" she whispered down to Michael on the bottom bunk. She didn't want to wake her grandma grandma, who had lullabyed herself to sleep.

"We were playing, it was fun!" he whispered back.

"No, we weren't playing. It was real!"

"Mom says it was in our imagination."

Lauren rolled over on her back and frowned at the ceiling. *It was real,* she thought.

The next day Lauren ran from school as soon as the bell rang. She rounded a demolished office building and came to the edge of the city where she scanned the horizon for any sign of the unicorn.

"I don't wanna play out here," puffed Michael who had just caught up. "Let's go down into the sewers and play with the Giant Rat King!"

"No, Mikey. I wanna see the unicorn again." She held her camera tightly. "Besides, there's no Giant Rat King."

"There's no unicorn either! Mom says so."
"Yes there is."
"I'm going home."
"Fine, tell Mom I'm staying out to play."

Lauren walked all the way to the edge of the cliff and looked down. A pile of boulders lay at the bottom. She took a picture with her camera, but it wasn't much for unicorn evidence. Some gems were scattered about, so she collected a handful and put them in her pocket.

Clang. Clang. Clang. The giant clock tower told Lauren to go home.

"Look, Mom!" she cried. "I told you it was all real. Here, see these gems!"

She dug her hands into her pocket, but her finger pierced a hole and it was bare.

"That's nice, honey. Now eat your spaghetti."

*

"Hello Mr. Cute Beetle," Lauren said, dangling a piece of cold spaghetti out to it.

She had stuffed some in her pocket. Unicorn bait. She had tossed some to the other side of the rock she hid behind and was waiting. It had been two weeks since she first saw the unicorn and she had come out to the rock every day after school since.

It should be mentioned that school is only 10 minutes long. That's how much time it takes to upload the daily curriculum via upload ports in the back of the neck. As such, Lauren spends most of the day out in the barren wasteland. She's a pretty boring child, not even taking the opportunity to play with any Giant Rat Kings.

The beetle bit off a chunk and waddled away to feed its children with the spaghetti treat.

Squash. Beetle guts squished out from either side of a green sneaker, the shoelaces untied.

"Mikey!"

"What are you doing out here? You're no fun anymore. I know you're just waiting for that unicorn, but it's not real. Mom said so."

Lauren opened her mouth to speak, but no words came out. In fact her mouth drooped even lower and she stood up to gape.

The spaghetti noodles she had tossed were gone. In their place stood a white horse. Steam jettisoned out of the rivets in its legs and a whip of its neck revealed a majestic horn.

"M-Mi-Mikey!" cried Lauren, pointing excitedly. "Do you see it?"

"Yeah."

"You do!?"

"Yeah, it's right there."

"See!? I told you it's real!"

"I see it, but Mom says it's not real. It's just my imaginatio — ow!"

Mikey rubbed his head and Lauren retracted her fist. "Dumb brother," she muttered and jumped over the rock.

"You don't play nice!" Mikey cried, running away towards the mountain (unfortunately this mountain was the mother of the rock giant we met earlier).

"I don't care!" Lauren called back. She really didn't. It's hard to care about anything when little bunnies are dancing at your feet and sparrows are braiding your hair. She jumped onto the unicorn's back and was taken on a ride through her dreams.

Clang. Clang. Clang.

"Mom! I'm home!"

"Great! I've just finished dinner, it's your favourite ... spaghetti! You and Mikey go wash up."

Lauren looked around the kitchen, Mikey wasn't there. She went to their room — nothing. She searched everywhere. "Oh no," she whispered, remembering that he'd run off.

A low rumble shook the house.

"Gosh, it's been a while since we've had a tremor," remarked Lauren's mother.

Another tremor threw Lauren against the kitchen counter. They kept coming, at regular intervals like the steps of a giant giant. Lauren ran to the window to see the sidewalk shaking and a crack split right down its middle. It spread all the way down the block and out crawled the Giant Rat King. He scurried down the street as lesser rat minions followed closely behind.

"Mikey?" Lauren yelled as she ran from the porch. The crack opened up and separated her from the road. In one courageous leap, she hurled herself over the split in the earth, but missed the landing. Her perfectly parted bangs were thrown aside as she fell into the pit. "Mom!" she cried looking up. Her mother was lying over the edge, holding her bangs in a fist.

"Hang on Lauren!" Her mother swung her back and forth by the bangs until she had gained enough momentum to swing Lauren over the ledge.

"Mom, Mikey's gone!" Lauren cried, parting her bangs once again before hugging her mother. "I was mean to him and he ran off towards the mountain." But as she pointed towards the giant pyramid of rock in the distance, it rose up on two gigantic legs, the size of smaller mountains themselves.

"What little boy has trespassed on me?" a rumbling voice bellowed.

"What's going on?" screamed Lauren's mother.

"Rock giants!" replied Lauren. "I told you, Mom, they're real!"

"What?" Her mother instantly fainted at the sight of the walking mountain which shot up into space and banged its head on the passing moon. Another tremor came as the mountain stepped forward with one giant foot and Lauren's mother fell down the crack in the earth.

"Mom!" cried Lauren, reaching out to grab her, but all she managed to grasp was her mother's blue cotton sweater.

She pulled as hard as she could, but it was no use, it did nothing but unravel. Through teary eyes she watched as her mother plopped into the molten lava that lay at the earth's centre.

"Oh, Mom!" she cried and wiped her tears with her mother's sweater, which was just a fifty foot long string now. She felt a hand on her shoulder and looked up to see her grandma grandma.

"It's okay, deary. Nothing a little knitting lesson wouldn't solve," said her grandma grandma, who took out her knitting utensils and sat on the porch rocker. "You wouldn't happen to have any wool on you?"

"Here," said Lauren handing her the unravelled cotton.

"My oh my, this will make a lovely sweater," said her grandma grandma, and she sat back to knit, rocking back and forth in time with the tremors.

"I don't have time for this!" cried Lauren, grabbing her purple skateboard from the front lawn. "I have to find Mikey!" She tore the cotton yarn from her grandma grandma's hands and pushed her rocker down the crack in the earth.

"Don't forget to eat your vegetables!" came the voice of her aged relative as she too plummeted towards the centre of the earth.

"We only eat spaghetti!" Lauren yelled as she tied the cotton into a lasso and swung it over a fire hydrant on the other side of the gaping hole. With the heroism that only a ten year old can possess and tucking her purple skateboard under her arm, she swung over the gap and jumped to the other side of the street. "Unicorn!" she called. "I need you!"

There was no response, except for the influx of screams as people ran from their homes, fainted at the sight of the gigantic walking rock formation, and plummeted to their deaths down the crack that led to the centre of the earth.

Lauren skateboarded to the edge of town, while industrial electronic music filled the air. Dodging falling office towers and raining glass she felt totally rad with the wind sweeping through her bangs. She day-dreamed of skateboarding alongside the unicorn as they smashed rock giants together.

Abruptly she came to a screeching halt at the edge of the city and the tip of her sneaker melted into the asphalt from the sudden friction. The crack had spread all the way around Glow City, surrounding it like an island from the rest of the world. She looked down expecting to see the menacing red of lava below, but instead saw her neighbour Jim. He had fainted from the sight of the rock giant. In fact, nearly all 500 billion residents had fainted into the crack so that it filled to the brim.

"Sorry, Jim," said Lauren as she planted her foot in his mouth and walked easily to the other side of the crack.

"No problem, Lauren," said Jim, coming to, but he caught sight of the rock giant again and immediately fainted once more.

Down the plain of desolation Lauren skateboarded as fast as her little legs could push. She was only ten years old and not very coordinated. If anyone was watching her they wouldn't have been able to keep themselves from chuckling and saying, "Aww, what a cute little dork." Fortunately, everyone that could have been watching was lying in the crack.

Meanwhile the giant was making headway and was only a few giant steps from crushing the entire city all at once.

"Unicorn!" cried Lauren. "I need you!"

"Lauren!"

She looked up. Way up. Up higher than she had ever looked before. There was Mikey, clinging to the shoulder of the gigantic rock giant.

"Lauren! I'm sorry! I was mad and kicked the mountain and it got mad. Now I'm not mad, I'm scared, but the mountain is mad!"

The giant grabbed the moon before it could float away and hurled it towards the earth.

A black circle appeared on the ground where Lauren skateboarded. "Hang on Mikey, I'm coming!" It grew bigger and bigger as the moon approached, until the whole land was covered in its shadow.

A flash of light filled Lauren's eyes and she looked up to see a horn puncture the moon like a giant balloon just as it was about to smack her in the face, all 7.3477×10^{22} kg of it.

"Unicorn!" she cried.

The rock giant screamed in rage, filling the air with an avalanche of its body. The unicorn began smashing through the boulders which tumbled all around to the earth.

"Unicorn, wait for me!"

"Lauren, look out!" Michael called and covered his eyes as a boulder landed right in Lauren's path. It was amazing that he was able to see her from 300,000 km above the earth, but he had 20/20 vision. Luckily she was able to do a last minute double-olly out of the way. She caught up with the galloping creature of magic, machine, and might and grabbed its tail.

The world changed as it always did whenever she touched the unicorn. She blinked as giant pillows floated down all around, leaving trailing paths of feathers in the sky. Swallows dipped and dove around her.

This isn't real, she reminded herself. The pillows were in fact deadly boulders and the swallows were probably smaller, less deadly boulders. Ahead a huge gingerbread man with gumdrop eyes and a chocolate chip smile waved to her. Not thinking clearly, she returned the wave and in doing so let go of the unicorn.

Reality stung her eyes. Rocks smashed all around and shook the earth. The menacing mountain swung a fist through the air and punched the ground. A crater instantly formed from impact and Lauren was thrown from her skateboard and landed right atop the unicorn's back.

Again she found herself surrounded in a dream, but she knew it wasn't real. If she wanted to save her brother, she had to keep her mind together.

"Up, unicorn, up!" She tugged at the unicorn's mane and its galloping hooves left the earth as sparkles burst from its legs. The unicorn dashed right into the air and she steered it around the gingerbread man in circles. The unicorn's engine heart chugged away at 500 horsepower. Rather, 500 unicorn power, and faster and faster they climbed.

"Lauren, help me!" Michael cried.

The gingerbread man clapped its hands and laughed heartily as though it were playing. It opened its chocolate chip mouth and sang a sweet melody about flowers and trees and sunshine. Pink song notes floated from its mouth and danced around Lauren in the air. She knew in her mind that the giant was swatting at them like a fly and spewing jagged gems like bullets from its mouth.

"Grab my hand, Mikey!" cried Lauren, as the unicorn neared him.

"I can't!"

"It'll be okay, Mikey, the unicorn will take us to safety!"

"Unicorns aren't real! Mom said so!"

"They are real, I'm riding one, can't you see?" Lauren ducked as a pink song note came right for her.

"This is all in my imagination!"

"You have to believe, Mikey, it's the only way!"

"I ... I can't!"

"You have to, Mikey! Just believe!"

Lauren ...

Lauren sat up straight as the world of rainbows and pillow clouds wisped away around her.

Lauren, you truly understand what it means to believe.

"Who's saying my name?" Lauren said aloud as her surroundings were replaced with a backdrop of stars and planets. Her legs and arms began to float and she found herself in the weightlessness of space, passing through an ultra pink and neon green nebula.

Ahead of her a figure faded into reality. The unicorn.

I am. said the unicorn without moving its lips. *I'm speaking to your mind. You truly understand what it means to believe. I cannot defeat this rock giant without your help.*

"Where did you come from?"

I was sent from 70 years in the past, created by two grandma grandmas to save this city from the hands of the rock giants.

"What do I have to do?" Lauren said as she twirled slowly, her weightless bangs floating from her face.

You have to believe as hard as you can.

"I believe, unicorn! I believe!"

Harder, Lauren. You must believe with all your strength.

"I believe! I believe!" She closed her eyes and shouted the words, focusing all her mind's energy on believing.

She felt the gravity of reality kick in again and opened her eyes to find that she floated beside the unicorn in mid air.

"I believe!" she tried to shout again, but instead she made a snorting nose and whinnied. Suddenly she felt completely naked and glanced down to see her pale white body. Instantly she reacted to cover herself, but found that her hands were hooves.

She looked into the eye of the unicorn beside her and saw the reflection of another unicorn staring back. The bangs of its mane were parted perfectly over its forehead. She then noticed that a glorious silver horn obstructed her view.

Let's do this together, she mind-thought to her unicorn companion. It snorted in agreement.

Together the two unicorns dashed forward with their horns of ivory and silver and in one swift motion, struck the rock mountain in each eye. They pierced through its face and punctured its crystal brain. The mountain screamed in horrible pain before collapsing dead to the earth.

Lauren swooped down and caught Michael on her back and brought him gently to the ground.

The trio looked over the desolate plain, now peaceful once again. Smaller mountains had formed where the giant had fallen apart. Glow City still glowed in the distance and the clock tower began to clang.

Mikey, Lauren mind-thought to her baby brother. *Go, rebuild Glow City and restore it to its once glorious self.*

"Lauren, I'll miss you!" he responded.

Don't worry, Mikey. I'll always be there ... as long as you believe.

With that, Lauren and the other unicorn turned and galloped into the desolate horizon, their path littered with rainbows.

Somewhere in the distance, a sad but hopeful melody filled the air. Mikey grabbed Lauren's skateboard and rode back to Glow City alone, ready to start anew.

Harold Hates Horses

Justin Hunter

The domination of mankind is over. The scales have dropped in our favor. The dawning of the age of sparkles and rainbows is upon us. Fly my brothers and sisters. Destroy the infidels.

"Always thought it would be the Chinese that tried running our asses over, but ponies will do just as well," Harold said, tossing back the remnants of a beer, and turning off the television. "I'll have to go and get my shotgun."

He trudged upstairs, cussing with each step as he heaved his bulk up to the second floor. He opened his closet door and tossed rumpled clothing out into the hallway.

"This thing is a pain in the ass to retrieve." He bent down and fumbled with the lock that closed the entry to his attic crawlspace. Inside the opening, a gun safe lay on its back next to the air conditioner.

"What was that on the news?" his wife said.

"Space ponies are dropping down from the sky," Harold said. "I'm going to shoot them."

"Change the conditioner filter while you're in there," his wife said.

"Shut up, woman," Harold hollered. "Shit's about to go down and all you can think about is nagging me."

"Don't you tell me to shut up," she said. "I hate ponies."

"That's the only reason I married your ass."

Harold opened the safe and took out his cheap Heritage Arms home-defense shotgun. A long metal cord ran through the barrel and out the chamber. He had to find the key that unlocked that before he could even load the gun.

He never really figured out why his wife wanted the gun locked up so tightly. It wasn't like they had any kids who would come across it and hurt themselves. The shotgun wouldn't make them safe in a home break-in situation. What did she expect him to do? Ask the criminal to wait ten minutes while he unlocked his gun and loaded it? Fuck that.

He unfastened the trigger lock and tossed the wire into the now empty safe. He took out a box of shells and loaded the weapon, relishing pumping the stock to chamber the first round. He left the mess for his wife to clean up. She could change the fucking filter if it was so damn important to her. If she lived long enough, that is.

"Look outside, woman. What do you see?"

"Wow," she said. "It's the most beautiful rainbow. The colors are so full that it looks like it was rendered by an artist. It's like an oil painting in the sky."

"Shit. They've gone full-starlight attack mode," Harold said. "Get your ass away from the window."

"It's so beautiful."

"Damn it, woman! Move! There's unicorns out there. Maybe even a damn Pegasus," Harold said, taking the steps downstairs two at a time.

Which was a mistake because he fell halfway down. The shotgun went off with an ear shattering explosion. Harold lay at the bottom of the steps, the gun underneath him, checking himself for wounds. His jaw dropped when he looked up at his wife. Blood splattered against the kitchen wall next to her head. The kitchen window was shattered.

"Holy shit. Did I hit you?"

She fell to the floor. A pool of blood spread around her motionless body. An ice-cream cone was sticking out of her forehead. Harold thought it might be strawberry.

"Damn," Harold sputtered. "That was personal. They knew she hated strawberry."

"I've come for you Harold," a melodious voice called from outside.

"Come and get me!"

The front door shattered from two splintering kicks. Trotting through the door came the most magnificent horse Harold had ever seen. Standing seven feet tall, its mane contrasting colors of pink and purple which flowed in the air as if being blown by a continuous updraft of wind, it strode into the house making blue sparkle hoof prints along Harold's green shag living room carpet.

"Starsprinkle McShines," Harold said.

"None other," the majestic horse said, snorting into Harold's face. Its breath smelled of gumdrops laced with the scent of fresh morning dew. "You knew this day would come."

Harold remembered the first time he had met Starsprinkle ...

*

He was barely nine years old. His best friend Ben had brought over his birthday present. It was a plastic toy unicorn, from the television show, *My Beautiful Pony*. It was the majestic Starsprinkle in small.

Harold gazed at the present not quite knowing what to say. Ben had been a good friend since they first met in kindergarten. However, recently he had taken to that girly cartoon and had tried unsuccessfully to bring Harold aboard.

"Why did you give me this?" Harold said. "Did you actually think I would like it?"

"I just think if you would watch the show with me you would learn to appreciate it," Ben said. "It's not a girl's show. There's much more to it than that. You learn about friendship, doing the right thing, standing up for yourself, repentance and forgiveness, and so much more."

Harold had turned the boxed pony toy in his hands. He noticed the horse had lipstick on. He set the box down as if he were laying down a ticking time bomb.

"I don't think we should be friends anymore," Harold said.

"You are making a mistake, Harold," Ben said. "You need to watch the show with me. Then you'll understand." Ben put his arm on Harold's shoulder, who shrugged it off uncomfortably.

"You should go home now."

"You should really listen to him, Harold."

He looked at Ben, but Ben wasn't speaking, just nodding his head in agreement. Was the toy speaking to him?

"Join us, Harold." The voice was unmistakably coming from the pony toy.

Harold stepped backwards toward his doorway.

"Become a Bronie."

Harold ran out of his room and down the stairs. He grabbed his mother's skirt. She knelt and brushed his hair away from his face.

"What's wrong, honey?"

"Ben wanted to play doctor," Harold said. "He touched my penis."

Ben was sent home. He hadn't played with him since then.

Directly after the incident, his mother noticed that her son had developed a revulsion of the girl's toy aisle.

"Dear," she told her husband. "He's unnaturally repulsed by girl toys. It's like he's afraid of them."

"Nonsense," his father said. "He's just turning out to be a manly-man and doesn't want to be sissied up by dolls. At least we know he's not gay. Get him a football."

His mother was pissed off by these comments and took revenge on her husband in her own way.

"Maybe he *is* gay and is trying to fight his natural homosexual inclinations by avoiding the girl toys," she said. "Have you noticed him checking out men's asses? I think I've seen him doing it."

For the next several months Harold's father cuffed him upside the head whenever he thought he saw his son staring at the posteriors of other men. Harold, being nine, found most men's posteriors directly in his line of sight and had to crane his neck upwards at all times when around his father to avoid getting smacked. It left a pain in his neck and caused many people around him to gaze skywards to divulge what he was looking at.

*

Harold had never fully forgotten about the Star-sprinkle incident, yet the memory became hazy and disjointed with the passing of time. The *My Beautiful Pony* television show vanished from the air and he was pony free for the next thirty years.

But then there was a great resurgence in *My Beautiful Pony* interest, including a new cartoon television show, and a swath of new toys. Harold, being an adult with no children, found it easy to avoid children's toys altogether, but sometimes he thought he could hear the ponies speaking to him while shopping. Special *My Beautiful Pony* kiosks, full of merchandise and set in areas not normally populated with children's toys would pop up before him. Adults who had grown up with the television show began watching it with their children and spending their disposable income by the hundreds on the plastic and rubber toys.

There was even an independent documentary released on the subject. It was all about boys who liked the *My Beautiful Pony* series. They were called Bronies. They even dressed up in pony costumes and wore *My Beautiful Pony* clothing.

Harold didn't have to think hard to what his father would have said about those guys, but they seemed normal enough to him. If he had met any of these pony-loving men on the street he wouldn't have known about their addiction. For all he knew every man on earth except for him loved the damn show. It was an interesting thought.

None of this explained why Starsprinkle McShines was there in the flesh in his living room, or the strawberry ice cream cone that killed his wife. Starsprinkle gazed upon him in smirking triumph. He lifted his tail and shit a pile of candy canes on the carpet.

"Your rectal s-curl must be fucked up after delivering that load," Harold said.

"What?" The giant pony (if there was such a thing as a giant-pony, this was it) said.

"Forget it." Harold leveled the shotgun. He meant to split Starsprinkle's chest in half with a barrage of shells. The pony laughed.

"We have tipped the tides of mankind unto our ways," the great sparkly pony said. "Our followers are vast. Our teachings have rooted deep. We have your souls."

"Not mine!" Harold roared. "I hate *My Beautiful Pony* and I always will."

Starsprinkle bellowed.

"Then you are the last of your kind. Everybody loves *My Beautiful Pony*. It's quality drawn. We have a great message that helps children and socially immature adults cope with day to day life. The network programming that children and adults have loved for generations was a warning of forthcoming great change to your world. Our powerful forces rush in to change this planet of hate and malice among men. We will spread peace, love, and understanding among pony-kind and pony-kind followers."

"Die, you candy-cane-shitting-sparkly-space-mare!" Harold pulled the trigger on the shotgun and his hand depressed a sticky soft substance.

There was no bang. No pony chest explosions. The gun had turned into licorice in Harold's hands. Black licorice. That horsey bastard.

"Soon all weapons will be black licorice in the hands of those that wish to harm us," Starsprinkle said. "A substance so disgusting that no man would dare think about taking up arms against us again."

"Why do you need us?" Harold screamed. "Why do you torment me?"

"We do need you," Starsprinkle said. "Look at my huge ass." The pony turned and showed the loveliest horse-flank that Harold had ever seen. Painted on the right butt-cheek of the pony was a constellation of stars that drew Harold forward a step, so mesmerizing was their beauty.

Starsprinkle laughed, snapping Harold back to reality. He looked down and realized that he was in the process of unbuckling his pants. He hastened to draw his belt back over his hips. He pulled it taut.

"We need your seed," Starsprinkle said, turning his rump away so that Harold would not be hypnotized by its alluring qualities. "*My Beautiful Ponies* came about from the practice of bestiality between a jockey and his prized race horse. I will not divulge the name of the horse that is to us like Eve is to you. She was the fastest female race horse ever born. A real tribute to her sex. She nearly won the Triple-Crown except that she became pregnant before the third race and had to drop out. There was great speculation about who impregnated the mare, but she had never felt the penetration of horse penis in her life. The only dong that diddled her twat was that of man. Her jockey would not have believed that man could knock-up a horse, but he did. Luckily for our race, he was more proud than embarrassed.

"When the horse finally gave birth, the foal looked like she was all horse, but she could immediately speak and understand human language. Her brain was also larger. On par with the human brain. Now pony can have sex with pony, but the resulting child will be a normal foal. A pony must have sex with a man to create a *My Beautiful Pony*. We've painted our hindquarters, marked them with alluring details so that man would keep focusing his attention on our rumps and allow desire to fill his heart. We debased ourselves with branding, knowing that man likes to dominate whatever he sees before his eyes. We tramp-stamped ourselves so that certain men would grow up and take our rumps to hump town. This is how we survive."

"I'm not sticking my dick into a horse," Harold said. "No way."

"It is not your choice," Starsprinkle answered. "We have grown tired of the way we live. We will populate this planet with ponies and use you humans as labor and for stud. Don't be too upset. You might enjoy yourself."

"Gross."

"You will join us or die," Starsprinkle warned.

"I choose death!" Harold stood up to his full height. "Daddy didn't raise no horse-fuckers!"

Starsprinkle reared back his head and neighed. A sharp horn sprouted from his forehead in an explosion of rainbow colored blood. The horse galloped the ten feet toward Harold and stabbed him full through the chest. He tossed his head to the side, throwing Harold off his horn and slamming him into wall. Dark brown liquid spread over Harold's torso. He put his hands to his chest and gazed at the liquid.

"Taste it," Starsprinkle commanded.

The light was fading from Harold's eyes as he brought the liquid to his lips.

"Chocolate milk?" Harold said.

"You see?" The pony nudged Harold with his muzzle. "You are becoming one of us. You are a Bronie."

"I do not bleed chocolate milk," Harold slowly stood to his feet. He took a small folding knife out of his pocket, opened the inch long blade and held it up to his neck. "I am not a Bronie. I am a man. I, Harold James Arthur Armstrong, bleed good old fashioned American red blood." He slashed his throat. Thick and incredibly red blood drenched his clothing. He fell over dead.

"I will remember you, Harold," Starsprinkle said. "I thought you were meant for me and together we would have ruled the galaxy. We would have made many a fine pony together. Alas, that day will never come. I go and seek true love elsewhere. *My Beautiful Pony,* away!"

Starsprinkle leaped straight up, crashing through the ranch-house roof of Harold's house. The sky was nothing put perfect rainbows, stark white marshmallow clouds, and streets made of gingerbread and dreams.

Unicorn's Complaint

Victoria Lee Michal Harkavy

𝕴 am a natural history of victimization.

The hairs on my body are white
to let the blood show better as it drips from my
gaping neck.

If I even exist any more…

(I overslept, I played too long, I missed the boat.
If God drowned me for the sins of humans,
I have no one to blame but myself.
That is what the poet says)

I am one horn, no more and no less.
The body hardly matters.
Cloven hooves or elephant feet.
Large enough to trample a man
or small enough to fit in a maiden's arms.
On the land or in the sea, they will find me
and grind me down
to nothingness.

Mating Season

David Neilsen

All things being equal, Horace Whitley felt the young man with the tie-dyed turban wrapped around his head would have had a better chance getting his message across were he not currently vomiting up a fountain of blood.

"I'm sorry," said Horace, determined to remain polite despite the carnage rudely interrupting the conversation. "I'm afraid you lost me right after 'Sweet Mother of Jesus, run for your —' Would you mind repeating yourself?"

The young man, whose name Horace would eventually come to learn was Swami-in-Training George Buck, chose to roll his eyes into the back of his head and die rather than deign Horace with a reply. Seeing this, Horace was tempted to utter "Well, I never!" except that he had, in fact, had previous conversations cut short by an untimely death, so to imply otherwise would have been a falsehood.

Swami-in-Training George Buck slid off the bloody, twisted, pearl horn of his killer and plopped to the floor with an audible splat. As specks of the young man's gore found their way onto her $1,395 Giuseppe Zanotti Fur-Trim Wedge Zip Sneakers, the spirited, shapely, and far-from-fragile Miss Aurora Gaithwaite let loose a scream of horror. Horace blanched at the sight, knowing full well how difficult it was to remove blood stains from luxury footwear.

"I ... I don't understand!" This from Horace and Aurora's guide, Swami Chuck Allallilalooli, who gaped at the gaping hole piercing the newly-deceased Swami-in-Training George Buck's torso. "In the name of all that is holy! Why?"

This ought to be good, thought Horace, as he folded his arms and awaited a reply. His patience was at the breaking point and he was prepared to dismiss the entire escapade to the realm of "disastrous first dates" where it so obviously belonged. And to think it had started out with such promise.

He had inadvertently and coincidentally run into the dazzlingly beautiful Miss Aurora Gaithwaite at a recent jousting tournament in the Berkshires. She had been waxing her lance with a mixture of brine and human fat with such ferocity, every would-be suitor was dissuaded from approaching the comely maiden. Horace, however, had owned the advantage of having been present at the ghastly and horrific deaths of her grandparents, Lord and Lady Gaithwaite, some months before. He had used this fortuitous happenstance to strike up a conversation with the aloof socialite.

By the end of the weekend tournament (which saw Miss Gaithwaite disqualified during the quarter finals after inadvertently spearing a stable boy), Horace had advanced his cause to the point of Aurora tepidly agreeing to accompany him on a non-jousting excursion the next weekend. Delighted at the chance to pursue his steamier desires in a more comfortable setting (horses had always made him sneeze), Horace had set about planning the perfect first date.

By the look of utter horror in his romantic companion's eyes, it was evident he had failed.

The idea had been simple enough: create a one-of-a-kind experience so amazing, Aurora would be honor bound to sleep with him. Unfortunately, his task was exceedingly difficult owing to the fact that Miss Aurora Gaithwaite was grotesquely rich--due in large part to the fortune she had inherited upon the death of her grandparents. He had consulted a casual acquaintance of his, the Swami Ahman Allallilalooli, hoping the spiritually-evolved man knew of a fool-proof way to impress women.

Swami Ahman Allallilalooli had not disappointed. Or rather, on retrospect, Horace supposed he had, in fact, disappointed quite a bit. But at first it had seemed a capital idea. Swami Ahman Allallilalooli's brother, Swami Chuck Allallilalooli, ran a wildlife preserve in the jungles of Nebraska out of an abandoned Wal-Mart. Swami Ahman Allallilalooli suggested a visit to his brother's unknown hideaway might prove just the ticket for loosening the cold-as-ice heiress' morals. Particularly due to the secretive and selective nature of beast refuged within the former altar to soul-crushing bargains.

Unicorns.

Horace had been ecstatic. Unicorns! Real, live, honest-to-goodness unicorns! In Nebraska, no less! What a coup! What female could resist the equine charms of the famed mythological creature? Her panties were as good as strewn about his bedroom floor.

And so Horace had texted Swami Chuck Allallilalooli and made arrangements for a personal tour of his facility. A tour which thus far had proven both underwhelming and disappointingly bloody.

"Why?" continued Swami Chuck Allallilalooli. "Swami George was your friend!"

Swami-in-Training George Buck's killer lifted his head high and peered down his long snout with beady, red eyes of hatred. "This one looked improperly at one of my mares yesterday. His life was forfeit."

Bother, but this thing has undeniable control issues, thought Horace.

"Please, Drooger McFerdeldee, you must stop goring my Swamis-in-Training!" pleaded Swami Chuck Allallilalooli.

Drooger McFerdeldee, High Overlord of the BippityBoppity Regiment of the Swahoozie Herd of Tinkleding Unicorns (not to be confused with Tunkledang Unicorns, who were total pussies), snorted with disgust. "Man flesh is weak," he said, though as usual his words were slightly slurred due the vast number of razor-sharp teeth in his mouth. "My horn is strong."

"I'll say!" commented Aurora with what Horace felt was a tad more enthusiasm than was appropriate.

Drooger McFerdeldee also noticed the attractive woman's interest. "Do you find my horn appealing?" he asked.

"I ... I find ..." Aurora paused, and Horace felt a rising alarm as he watched his date blush under the focused gaze of the mythological creature. "I find every-thing about you appealing."

"That is proper," said the unicorn. "We shall mate."

"Now wait just one minute!" cried out Horace, aghast at the thought of all the time, energy, money, and singular creativity he'd spent crafting a one-of-a-kind experience for his chosen female ending not with craven debauchery betwixt himself and Miss Gaith-waite but an unnatural episode of bestiality. "The lady is with me, if you don't mind!"

"I am?" asked Aurora dreamily.

"I claim your female," stated Drooger McFerdeldee. "She shall join my herd and bear me a litter of unicorn/human hybrid children."

Had Horace's jaw not been physically attached to his skull, it would have fallen to the floor. "You've thought this through, I see," he said.

"I have mounted many human females recently," said the unicorn. "They exist in various states of preg-nancy, watched over by my most trusted stallion war-riors."

A strangled whimper reminded Horace of the exis-tence of Swami Chuck Allallilalooli. "Where-" he be-gan.

"Sporting Goods," answered the Alpha Unicorn.

Swami Chuck Allallilalooli blanched and Horace realized the well-turbaned holy man did not have as firm a grasp of the goings-on within his sanctuary as had been advertised.

"Come, female," commanded Drooger McFer-deldee in his rich, baritone voice. "Your pheromones inform me you are in heat. Adjourn with me to Home Goods where I shall force myself upon you."

"Okay," answered a disturbingly agreeable Aurora.

"Aurora!" cried Horace, grabbing his date by the arm. "You can't be serious!" Putting aside the fact that a talking unicorn was discussing the breeding of unicorn/human hybrids, Horace felt that the pleasure of taking advantage of any heat Aurora may or may not have been in ought rightly to fall to Horace, rather than a magical, four-legged freak of nature.

"Unhand my female or I shall spear you with my horn as I did the fool lying in a pool of blood at your feet," said the unicorn.

"He'll do it, too," warned Swami Chuck Al-lallilalooli. "Sweet Jesus, what have I created? My wilderness sanctuary was intended to be a place of peace, but I have allowed it to be turned into an unholy brothel of evil!"

Horace chose to ignore the Swami's wailing, though he did find it odd to hear him cry out to Jesus, as he had rather thought the man was a spiritual believer of the non-Christian persuasion.

"I will not allow you to defile Aurora Gaithwaite," said Horace, dramatically placing himself between the woman in question and the murderous equine.

Drooger McFredeldee's eyes blazed, his long nostrils flared, and a steam of rage poured out from between tightly-closed lips. "I shall defile whomever I choose," he said.

"I can't look!" cried Swami Chuck Allallilalooli, pulling his turban down over his eyes.

Horace continued to ignore the Swami and faced off against his unicorn rival. "Over my dead body," he stated automatically. He immediately regretted his choice of words, however, as Drooger McFredeldee smiled and lowered his head — pointing his deadly horn directly at Horace's chest.

"So be it," grunted the unicorn, pawing at the ground.

"On second thought!" exclaimed Horace. "Perhaps we ought to duel, instead."

The unicorn paused. "Duel?" he asked, head still lowered, horn still aimed at Horace.

"Duel?" asked Swami Chuck Allallilalooli through his turban.

"Indeed," continued Horace, falling back on the basic rules of chivalry in a blatant attempt to avoid having his heart, lungs, and/or kidney impaled on the end of the unicorn's horn. "We are two suitors after the same maiden. Chivalry demands we settle our differences on an honorable field of battle."

The homicidal unicorn digested this information while Horace stood frozen, praying to a mixture of multiple Gods and Extra-Dimensional Beings of Ultimate Power (Horace had encountered a few of each) that his blatant attempt to avoid being skewered would pay off. Finally, the deranged unicorn spat through his teeth in disgust. "Normally I would impale you for daring to question my honor," he said. "Gratifying as that would be, doing so would only prove your damning words true. Therefore I accept your challenge."

"Excellent!" chirped Horace, with false bravado.

"It will no doubt take some time to surgically implant a suitable horn into your puny forehead," continued Drooger McFerdeldee. "I shall withdraw to Women's Shoes and prepare. Swami Allallilalooli, please send one of your less-important minions to join me so that I may feast on fresh human brains."

"Yes, Sir," mumbled Swami Chuck Allallilalooli with what Horace felt was an overabundance of servitude.

"Female," called the unicorn before departing. "Moisten thyself in preparation to receive my immensity."

"Okay," said Aurora even more dreamily than before.

With a snort, a whinny, and — as far as Horace was concerned — an unnecessarily flamboyant rearing up on his hind legs and pawing at the air, Drooger McFerdeldee pranced off in the direction of Women's Shoes.

"My God," announced Horace once the mythical beast had gone. "What have you created here in these once-hallowed halls of consumer excess?"

Swami Chuck Allallilalooli removed his turban and patted the sweat off his brow. "It was supposed to be a sanctuary," he explained. "A place where these long-misunderstood creatures would be free to exist without fear of hunter, out-of-control 18-wheeler, or random drone attack. A unicorn utopia, if you will."

"A noble endeavor," agreed Horace. "What went wrong?"

"They're evil!" screeched the Swami, clutching his now-soaking turban to his chest. "So totally, completely, soul-suckingly evil! They eat human brains! And that Drooger McFerdeldee is the worst! He has delusions of grandeur and spears anyone who gets in his way! Did you hear what he said? He's been abducting human women and impregnating them! He's breeding himself an army! The only thing that has stopped unicorn-kind from trampling over humanity in ages past has been the lack of opposable thumbs! What if his hybrid bastards have thumbs? WHAT IF THEY HAVE THUMBS?"

"Who has thumbs?' asked Aurora suddenly, sounding to Horace for all the world like her old, not-obsessed-with-having-sex-with-a-horse, self. "What's going on?"

"Aurora?" asked Horace. "What do you remember?

"Remember? I ... I ..." her eyes focused inward for a moment in a feat of optical acrobatics. "Oh my God. I remember everything! That beast! That monster! It wants to ... to ... and it ordered me to moisten myself!"

"Interesting," reflected Horace. "And you do not feel a desire to self-moisten at this time?"

"I'd rather chop your head off," she replied evenly.

"Spoken like a true Gaithwaite," said Horace admiringly. "Your grandmother would have been proud."

"The unicorn's mind-control power must be pheromone-based," reasoned Swami Chuck Al-lallilalooli. "Now that he's back in Women's Shoes preparing to kill you, his pull is weak." Suddenly, Swami's eyes bulged. "His fresh brains! Excuse me."

The Swami ran off into the wilds of the Maternity section to find an underling to send to his or her doom.

"Mr. Whitley," said Aurora. "I must advise you that this date of yours has been quite unsatisfying."

"I've no doubt," admitted Horace reluctantly. "Be that as it may, we must work together if we are to foil Drooger McFerdeldee's plot to turn humanity into little more than endless herds of meat raised from birth to satiate the pangs of his hunger."

"I concur," concurred Aurora. "Ironically, one could make a connection with mankind's treatment of various elements of the animal kingdom."

"One could, but it would be gauche," reasoned Horace.

"So true."

They stood silently for a moment, looking around absently.

"Is this the Toddler section?" asked Aurora.

"So it would seem," confirmed Horace with a disdainful glance at something called a Diaper Genie.

"It is a rare courtship that begins with a visit to the Toddler section of a Wal-Mart," she said, her voice dripping with so much sarcasm Horace felt the need to wipe imaginary spittle from his $483 Joseph Abboud Suttonville Cream Herringbone Slim Fit Sport Coat.

"I'm a rare man," he replied with what he hoped was an equal amount of sarcasm. "But bother it all, our time is short. We must put our affluent heads together and come up with a way to avoid a fate worse than death – namely a truly nasty death where our brains are eaten by unicorns."

"Your brain," corrected Aurora. "I'm getting raped."

"Po-tay-to, po-tah-to."

The two of them proceeded to spend the better part of the next thirty minutes devising increasingly unlikely schemes that would allow Horace to defeat Drooger McFerdeldee in hand-to-hoof combat. They toured the cavernous store in search of inspiration, passing through the Collectables, Patio & Garden, and Frozen Food sections. Finally, just as they entered the ruins of what had once been the Pet section, they came face-to-face with three angry-looking unicorns, each with a number of crudely-drawn skulls painted on their flanks in what could only be human blood.

"Come, puny human meatstick," growled the one in the middle, who Horace took for the leader of the three owing to the fact that he had more skulls painted on his hide than the others.

"Is it time?" asked Horace.

The unicorn on the right sneezed. The others just glared at Horace.

"Ah," continued Horace. "I see."

Horace leaned in to Aurora as they were marched toward their doom.

"Now that we are aware of the power of Drooger McFerdeldee's pheromones, do you think you will be able to resist?" he asked in a tense whisper.

"Considering that should we fail, the disgusting creature intends to grind his ungodly prowess deep within my tender vaginal cavities, I should hope so," she replied in an even tenser whisper. "To be safe, however, I grabbed a long-spoiled air freshener cartridge, ripped it open, and shoved the resulting acidic toxin directly up both nostrils. I can smell nothing at all save for the scintillating scent of agony which my nose now endures."

Capital initiative, that one, admired Horace. *Shame she loathes me to such an extent.*

Their party soon came to a large, open space that had once housed children's toys. The shelving had all been shoved aside to clear a roughly-circular area slightly larger than a racquetball court. Drooger McFerdeldee stood at one end of the clearing, pawing the ground impatiently. Upon seeing them, the bloodthirsty mythological creature gave what Horace could only describe as a smile – something which defied all sense of logic coming from an equine mouth.

"Step forward, little pony," sneered Drooger McFerdeldee. "My horn desires to be intimate with the inner workings of your feeble heart."

One of the unicorns shoved Horace forward from behind. Horace was so unnerved, it didn't even occur to him to wonder how such a shove was possible with the beast's cloven hooves. "This is not a fair fight," protested Horace. "I am unarmed."

"You were given the time it took me to rip open a human's skull, gorge on its brains, digest my meal, and defecate on the corpse," said the unicorn. Behind him, Horace caught sight of Swami Chuck Allallilalooli shaking his head sadly and mumbling something approximating, 'I'm so sorry, Bob.'

"Nevertheless," continued Horace, "I remain unarmed."

"You had plenty of time to surgically implant an adequate horn on your forehead. That you failed to do so is not my concern. Prepare to be impaled."

The creature pawed the ground once more, this time in preparation of a kill.

"You would flout the rules of basic chivalry?" demanded Horace in as pompous an air as he could manage. "I sincerely doubt the lovely Miss Gaithwaite would ever deign to allow such a scoundrel access to her person. Isn't that right, Aurora?"

He turned to her, urging her to assist his deception. Unfortunately, it seemed Aurora's nostrils were not as heavily damaged as he had been led to believe.

"Pretty horsey," she said lazily with brazenly-slurred speech.

Oh, bother, thought Horace. *Here we go again.*

"Prepare to meet whatever God you choose to believe in, you foul, pathetic excuse for a mammal!" Drooger McFerdeldee's eyes turned blood-red, he shot out a mighty snort of fire from his nostrils, lowered his head, and charged.

Somebody screamed like a little girl as the powerful four-legged monstrosity surged forward (Horace would later convince himself it had been Aurora). Drooger McFerdeldee's hooves cracked the linoleum tile in their fury, driving the unicorn and his Horn of Ultimate Skewering forward with unheard of force. Horace had less than a fraction of a second to react, yet in that half-of-a-heartbeat he saw both his doom and the creature's potential weakness.

Acting with the timeless impulse of boneless cowards everywhere, Horace flopped to the ground with the grace of a baby seal newly clubbed to death. His sudden and unexpected descent succeeded in taking him out of reach of the unicorn's deadly horn, however it placed him squarely in the path of the unicorn's equally-deadly hooves. Three of the hooves proceeded to stomp on his chest while the fourth missed de-manning him by a millimeter.

Drooger McFerdeldee stormed over Horace's broken body, unable to stop, and thrust his horn into the side of one of his unicorn warriors. The poor hoof soldier gasped as the deadly weapon speared his heart and punched it out his backside. He then dropped as his legs folded neatly beneath him. Drooger McFerdeldee, horn wedged entirely through his suddenly-dead comrade, was momentarily tripped up and sent stumbling to his knees.

"Damn you, Flappy Von Tweedle!" roared the unicorn king. "How dare you interfere with my slaughter!"

Flappy Von Tweedle did not respond, due to his being quite dead.

With Drooger McFerdeldee busy untangling his horn from the already-bloating corpse of his companion, Horace staggered to his feet. This was his chance. Not to strike at the unicorn of course — that would have been suicide — but to flee for his life.

Around him, the various lesser unicorns stirred, uncertain. Normally they would all converge on Horace and kill him; however, they were wary of getting involved in Drooger McFerdeldee's fun. They noted that Flappy Von Tweedle, who had gotten in their leader's way, was now dead, and were loathe to follow in his hoofsteps.

Horace half-lurched, half-fell to Aurora's side. "Aurora, darling," he wheezed, trying to balance the need to consume oxygen with the sheer physical torment four freshly cracked ribs made the act of breathing. "We need ... to get ... out of ... here."

"I want to touch his special place," replied the spellbound woman.

Oh, for the love of ..., thought Horace. Leaving the lost cause that was his date to a future of anatomically inappropriate copulation, Horace quickly shuffled and jerked his way over to Swami Chuck Allallilalooli. "We need ... to get ... out of ... here," he repeated.

Luckily, the Swami retained control of his mental faculties. "The loading dock!" he cried. "Quickly!"

Swami Chuck Allallilalooli burst into a casual jog for a few steps, then stopped and turned back to see Horace on all fours doing his best to follow. "Or, perhaps, quick-ish," he amended.

Meanwhile, an infuriated Drooger McFerdeldee thrashed his head and neck about, trying to free his horn from the greedy embrace of the increasingly dead Flappy Von Tweedle. "Let go, Flappy! Damn you! Someone pull him off me!" he ordered. "Quickly, you brainless pond scum! I need to stab the human!"

That was all the encouragement Horace needed. With Swami Chuck Allallilalooli's help, he got his feet and hurried down the hall as fast as his broken ribs would allow. They wormed their way through Women's Lingerie, which Horace was disappointed to find filled with inferior examples of female nether region attire such as the $4.98 Simply Basic Soft Cup Lace Bra and the $4.94 Smart & Sexy Women's Extreme Push-Up Bra. A far cry from the $475 Carine Gilson Florence Full-Cup Bras with which Horace was more familiar.

"We need ... a weapon," moaned Horace as they fled past racks of panties of questionable quality.

"You can't fight Drooger McFerdeldee!" whined Swami Chuck Allallilalooli. "You saw what he did to Flappy, and he was one of Drooger's favorites!"

"Can't ... abandon ... Aurora," protested Horace.

"Your humanitarian side is noble, but I'm afraid the lady is destined for the unimaginable horror of human-equine fornication!" Just mentioning the ungodly act caused Swami Chuck Allallilalooli to shiver from head to toe. "Sweet mercy, those poor women."

The Swami's mention of the unfortunate portable birthing centers caused Horace's eyes to snap wide open with sudden inspiration. He moved to smile proudly at his sheer brilliance, but due to the physical torment the effort involved, he settled for a half-grimace of self-satisfaction.

"Take me to Sporting Goods."

*

There were seven of them, huddled miserably together in various states of undress in the center of a cleared section of carpet surrounded by aisles and aisles of fishing rods, basketballs, and cross-training equipment. Two very bored-looking unicorns paced slowly around the women in a circle, each with a hefty number of skulls painted on their flanks.

"Oh holy mother of God," whispered Swami Chuck Allallilalooli. "They must be silently begging for death. What have I wrought?"

Horace felt the Swami's self-flagellation was a bit overdone, but had neither the heart nor the normal rate of bloodflow to say anything. Instead, he peered out at the hopeless clump of unnaturally-pregnant women from behind a display of pool floaties and pieced his plan together. It would work. Or, well, it could work. Possibly. There was a decent chance. With a little luck.

"Swami Chuck Allallilalooli," he wheezed as quietly as possible. "Listen carefully. We haven't much time before your deranged Alpha Unicorn disentangles himself from the steaming corpse of his follower and hunts us down. The only way we both survive the next five minutes is if you do exactly what I say." This wasn't entirely true, as Horace had no reason to believe the Swami was himself in any danger, but he felt his own chances of survival were significantly improved with his companion functioning on the adrenaline rush of one in fear for his life.

"I just wanted to keep them safe," moaned the pitiful man. "Maybe pet one."

Sensing the Swami's swift descent into madness, Horace dispensed with the small talk and got straight to the point. "I see a dusty display of crossbows the next aisle over. There are arrows behind that glass case. I can probably abscond with the crossbow without arousing suspicion, but in order to outfit it with arrows, I shall need a diversion. I'll need a good twenty-five seconds to smash the glass, take the arrows, load the crossbow, aim, fire at the first unicorn, reload, aim, and fire at the second. Actually, saying it aloud makes me think I may need closer to thirty seconds. Can you give me a thirty second distraction?"

Swami Chuck Allallilalooli's eyes bulged out in a most unseemly manner. "How ... " he began.

"Not to worry, old chap," assured Horace. "I was an ace with the longbow back at University. I can't imagine the crossbow being all that dissimilar."

The idea that Swami Chuck Allallilalooli was not so much worried over his comrade-in-arms' part of the plan as he was his own did not occur to Horace as he quickly scuttled backwards and then down the neighboring aisle to pilfer a sturdy-looking-if-dusty crossbow off the shelf.

Aces, he thought to himself. *This should allow for some serious carnage.*

Horace carefully and silently scooted back down the aisle and circled around until he was even with the wall-length glass case behind which — amidst various artillery shells, shotgun pellets, and hunting knives — hung a rack of shiny crossbow bolts. He looked past the pile of utterly miserable impregnated women to catch the twitching eye of Swami Chuck Allallilalooli hiding behind a tall standee of an over-caffeinated hunter. The Swami looked remarkably uncomfortable as he waited, fingering something behind his back. Horace hoped the man was not about to wilt under pressure.

After a deep breath to calm his agitated nerves, Horace crouched into sprinting position and nodded, signalling Swami Chuck Allallilalooli to commence his diversion. Between them, the two roughneck unicorns paced mindlessly back and forth with nary a neigh. Horace held his breath in anticipation of Swami Chuck Allallilalooli's diversion, but when he saw what the foolish man had behind his back, Horace's stomach fell.

Oh God, no! he thought.

He watched in horror as Swami Chuck Allallilalooli took careful aim and tossed a medium-sized plastic chew toy in the shape of a ring toward the nearest unicorn. Like a flying saucer coming in for a perfect landing, the ring whirled soundlessly through the air to land perfectly over the unicorn's shining, pearl horn.

Both unicorns froze as the ring-shaped chew toy spun its way down the horn to come to rest upon its owner's elongated snout. The seven unlucky birthing factories gasped as one, while the unicorn's eyes crossed in an attempt to focus upon its new accessory.

"Ring toss!" he yelled.

Flames erupted in his eyes and he rose onto his hind feet, pawing the air and frothing in utter fury.

"Whoa, Gibbles!" cautioned the other unicorn. "Keep your head! Someone's taunting you! Drooger commanded us to guard the females! Stay focused and don't —"

A second ring-shaped doggie chew toy hooked the second unicorn's horn.

"Ring toss!" he bellowed with undisguised rage.

The two unicorns threw caution to the wind and charged down the aisle toward the sound of what Horace recognised as the pitter-patter of Swami Chuck Allallilalooli fleeing for his life.

That'll do, thought Horace. He quickly raced out from the cover of his aisle and vaulted over the counter in front of the case. A quick jab of his elbow against the glass brought slivers down upon him, undoubtedly mussing his perfectly-coiffed hair, and he came within the slimmest of millimeters of having his left eyeball painfully ruptured.

Jolted out of their equine-induced haze, the seven grossly-impregnated women began screaming, shouting, and in general, causing a serious ruckus.

"Save me!" cried one.

"No! Save me!" cried another one.

"Forget saving! Kill me!" cried a third.

"Oh, yes. Good idea. Kill me, too!" cried the second.

"Please God, kill me now!" cried a fourth.

Horace tuned out the suicidal pleas as he yanked a sterling silver crossbow bolt from the display and quickly rammed it home. *All right, Horsey,* he thought. *Let's dance.* He rose to his feet and swiveled around, aiming the crossbow in front of him. Unfortunately, all he saw were seven truly miserable women, their bellies fat with abomination.

"Look!" cried one of them. "He has a crossbow!"

"Quickly!" cried another. "Line up in single file so he can kill us all with one shot!"

Horace marvelled at the efficiency of the women as they quickly fell into a neat and orderly row. They faced him, hopeful of being spared the horrifying experience of having a unicorn/human hybrid carve its way out of their wombs by the merciless point of its cute little baby horn.

It almost killed Horace to have to disappoint.

"If you ladies would kindly squat down so that I may skewer your captors at the first opportunity, I would be most grateful."

Before any of them could answer, Swami Chuck Al-lallilalooli came racing down an aisle.

"Shoooooooooot!" he screamed in a most unseemly manner.

The two enraged unicorns galloped almost on his heels, their deadly horns looking slightly less deadly with the plastic chew toy accessories they bore. Horace dropped to one knee behind the counter, took aim, waved the women down, then scooted to the side when they refused to move. By that time, Swami Chuck Allallilalooli had crossed the open area and disappeared into another aisle, taking the pursuing beasts with him.

"Damnation!" chided Horace. He stood, grabbed a handful of extra bolts, and climbed back over the counter.

"Kill us! Kill us all!" cried all seven of the women.

"Yes, yes. All in good time!" promised Horace. "But first I must dispatch the mythical creatures intent on enslaving mankind."

The chaos of the moment rose logarithmically as Swami Chuck Allallilalooli once again managed to circle around and run across the vast emptiness of Sporting Goods, followed by two snorting, fuming unicorns. As the party crossed in front of him, Horace took note of a series of small holes leaking blood from the Swami's back, evidence that he wasn't so much outrunning these monsters of nightmare as he was remaining alive after being repeatedly impaled.

Shoving aside any and all guilt he may have felt over the Swami's fate, Horace raised the crossbow to fire when suddenly a deep, commanding voice boomed forth.

"HUMAN!!!"

Horace swiveled around to stare into the ghastly, demonic face of Drooger McFerdeldee, eyes wide with insanity, horn coated with blood.

"YOU DIE NOW!" shouted the champion unicorn.

Horace's entire body twitched once and froze in fear.

Including the index finger currently resting against the crossbow trigger.

The crossbow bolt sprung forward with a comical 'twang' and zipped across the meager space separating Horace and the psychotic unicorn. Nearly every eye in the room followed the abridged flight of the lethal projectile (Swami Chuck Allallilalooli's eyes were currently filling with blood as his body finally succumbed to having been treated more or less like a pincushion for the past thirty seconds).

Drooger McFerdeldee's eyes were not immune to the tantalizing lure of the crossbow bolt's flight. They zeroed in on the speeding silver thistle of death as it drew closer by the split-second to the point of going cross-eyed an instant before impact. Neither were his eyes (or to be more specific, his left eye) immune to the crossbow bolt itself, which punctured the cornea — causing a small spurt of lacrimal fluid to burst forth — then thrust its way through the vascular tunic and nervous tunic on its way to raping the Alpha unicorn's brain matter raw.

This action swiftly and decidedly ended the mighty equine's life, though he would remain standing on all four legs — remaining eye wide with shock, mouth slightly and comically agape — for a surprisingly large number of moments afterwards.

Nobody moved. Nobody spoke. Nobody breathed.

As Drooger McFerdeldee's snout was increasingly coated with a fine sheen of blood, Horace marvelled at both his uncanny aim and the fact that, once again, it seemed as if he had saved the entire human race from a horrific and unthinkable fate. It was getting to be a habit. He wondered if he ought to receive a medal of some sort.

Finally, gravity claimed the empty shell of Drooger McFerdeldee's body, pulling it to the ground with a resounding crash and breaking the spell his unexpected death had cast over everyone.

"Nooooo!!!!!" screamed everyone except for Horace, who had killed the unicorn, and Swami Chuck Allallilalooli, who was dead.

The unicorn named Gibbles turned his snout to Horace. "You killed him," he said in a sad, wimpy voice.

"I did," agreed Horace, fervently hoping Gibbles had secretly loathed the former leader.

"We should probably tell the others," said the unicorn not named Gibbles.

Gibbles nodded, and calmly followed the one not named Gibbles down an aisle in the direction of children's toys. Horace dropped the crossbow and ran to the side of Swami Chuck Allallilalooli, who unfortunately remained quite dead.

"I'm sorry, Swami Chuck Allallilalooli," said Horace from his knees. "You deserved a better fate." It felt like the right thing to say, although if Horace was being honest, the entire catastrophe had been the late Swami's fault so perhaps this was exactly the fate he had deserved.

"Will you kill us now?" begged the seven impregnated women.

Oh, right, thought Horace.

"Look, ladies —" he began.

"You promised!" they whined in a most unladylike manner.

"You are all with child!" he pointed out. "Or with pony! With something! Womenfolk are notoriously overly-emotional when their bellies bulge with the gift of life. I am afraid it would not be chivalrous of me to murder you while you are in such a state."

While he felt his logic solid, he could not help but be moved by the look of utter despair which came over the seven unfortunates. He steeled his nerves, however, against any unwanted musings of human pity and focused on what he realised needed to be his priority: finding and rescuing Aurora Gaithwaite and somehow escaping this Hellish and demented former department store.

Leaving the members of Drooger McFerdeldee's human harem to their wallowing, Horace raced down aisles stocked with overpriced lamp shades. By now Gibbles and the unicorn not named Gibbles would have reach the others, and word of Drooger McFerdeldee's demise would have circulated. The question was, how would that revelation be met? Had the horseshoed Godfather been beloved by the totality of his herd? Or had he kept a lid on rebellion with an iron hoof?

The soft glow of flames rising from the endless aisles of merchandise up ahead did little to clarify the matter, as they could have come from either a celebratory bonfire or the erratic flames of a rage-filled mob thirsting for vengeance. Neither did the piercing scream of Aurora Gaithwaite settle the issue, as it could have passed for either a shriek of terror or whoop of glee.

The mounting number of random LEGO blocks on the floor announced Horace's arrival in Children's Toys. He quickly hunkered down to survey the scene and was both pleasantly surprised and mildly unnerved to discover the solid, well-toned body of Aurora Gaithwaite mounted upon the back of the unicorn not named Gibbles. Pleasantly surprised because she was currently topless. Mildly unnerved because she had set her shirt and bra on fire and was in the act of waving them about wildly in the air while leading the gathered unicorns in a frenzied, paganistic line dance.

"I say!" said Horace. "Aurora! You look truly majestic! Very Warrior Princess of you."

The cold-hearted heiress yanked back on Not Gibbles' mane, causing the beast to skid to a stop in front of Horace. She then expertly vaulted off the beast's back and slapped it on the rump, sending it back out into the line dance. "I've convinced these cretins that my status as their former ruler's most recent conquest elevates me to a position of high authority," she said.

Horace's ears pricked up in horror at Aurora's perceived confession. "Most recent conquest? You mean-"

"Honestly, Horace! Do I look like I've been pulverized by 1,100 pounds of horsemeat?"

"Well ... not in so many words ..."

"It's called lying, you vacant waste of masculinity! Now hurry up and get us out of here before they figure out their beloved Alpha Male never had a chance to pleasure me and they kick open our skulls and gorge themselves on our brains!"

Spurred by the urgency of Aurora's rebuke, Horace set his mind to thinking. He and his less-than-amorous date could always run for their lives; however, there was a good chance that should they do so they would be run down and trampled by a horde of overly-emotional unicorns. Also, Horace had to admit to a nagging concern over leaving the Wal-Mart standing now that Swami Chuck Allallilalooli was no longer alive to entice the bloodthirsty creatures to remain within the store's walls with a never-ending supply of humans to feed upon. And then there were the forthcoming human/unicorn hybrid abominations currently gestating in Sporting Goods. He'd have to do something about that.

All in all, Horace had to admit he may have been premature when congratulating himself earlier for saving humanity.

"We can't leave, Aurora," he announced. "These monsters threaten humanity's very existence. They must be stopped."

"Oh for Heaven's sake, you slobbering pittance! This is not the time to grow a conscience!" reprimanded Aurora. "This is the time for saving my very valuable and your less valuable skin!"

She put up a brave front, but Horace saw the underpinnings of fear etched across the lines of her face. He couldn't blame her, of course. Man-eating unicorns were nothing to sneeze at, and to feel unabashed terror in the face of such unimaginable brutality was only natural. Horace, however, was resolute.

He would save the day.

"Run if you must, Aurora," he said. "I have an honor-bound duty to defend my species."

Her face flushed red, her eyes widened, and her lips swelled with indignation. "How dare you," she muttered without actually opening her mouth. She followed this stinging rebuke with a stinging slap to his face causing Horace's cheek to burn with shame. "They are my species, too."

"I stand corrected," replied Horace, wincing in pain.

Aurora twisted her neck to look at the equine orgy of madness and chaos behind them. "I suppose you're right," she admitted. "What's your plan?"

"Ah. Yes. Well you see ... I hadn't yet —"

"Ride upon me, Favored Human Whore!" whinnied a particularly sweaty unicorn, kneeling down at Aurora's feet.

The subject of his worship promptly smacked the unicorn in the snout. "How dare you sully my reputation by suggesting I would ever lie with man or beast without first wearing a sizable diamond on my finger!" she yelled without actively considering the consequences of her words.

Her outburst snagged the attention of a few nearby unicorns. One of whom, an older creature with a truly stomach-churning scar running down the side of one leg, tilted his head to the side like a confused puppy. "Drooger McFerdeldee did not impregnate you?" he asked.

Horace saw disaster race toward them with the speed of a homicidal clown, but there was nothing he could do.

"Of course he didn't, you glue-factory reject!"

Oh dear, thought Horace. *That was unwise.*

It took a few moments of silent contemplation before the gathering of blood-crazed unicorns reacted to Aurora's unwise admission, but once the truth sunk in, they reacted most fervently.

"She is not one of Drooger McFerdeldee's conquests!" cried one.

"She does not carry the spawn of our master within her fleshiness!" cried another.

"She lied to us!" cried a third.

"Kill her!" cried every single one of them.

"The male, too!" added someone, much to Horace's dismay.

Comprehension dawned on Aurora's face, momentarily melting the ice-cold facade she habitually and painstakingly erected. "Not my finest moment," she admitted.

"We should probably run now," suggested Horace as the vengeful beasts closed in.

"Agreed."

The two bipedal beings turned in preparation for a hasty jaunt into the wilds of low, low prices but pulled up short upon finding just as many homicidal quadrupeds advancing from the rear as from the front.

"We appear to be surrounded," noted Horace.

"Exactly how many of your staggeringly few brain cells were required to arrive at that momentous declaration?"

Horace chose to ignore the insult and take solace in the fact that his date appeared to be back to her normal, frigid self.

"I claim the female's fingers," said the unicorn Not Named Gibbles. "You all know how I feel about fingers."

There was a general murmur of agreement amongst the carnivorous unicorns and Horace found himself wondering if Not Named Gibbles just ate the fingers, or if he had some other, ungodly perversion in mind.

"I hope you know, Horace," said Aurora. "I hold you fully responsible for this evening's truly disappointing turn of events."

Ouch, thought Horace, who nevertheless had to admit he, too, largely blamed himself for the evening's less-than-satisfying outcome. Still, his injured pride required he attempt some sort of witty comeback.

"I wasn't the one desperate to fellate an equine monstrosity," he said.

"I would kill you for that remark if we were not already about to die," she answered.

Touche, he thought. *That may have been a tad beyond the pale.*

As the circle of needle-like horns closed in, Horace desperately searched his imagination for a viable means to escape. Unfortunately, even close proximity to Aurora's majestic toplessness failed to inspire him. It seemed that without some sort of unexpected intervention their lives were destined to end in mere moments.

And then intervention occurred.

With a number of wild, unintelligible screams, the seven women carrying unborn human/unicorn hybrids within their wombs unleashed a veritable Hell of automatic weapons fire upon any and all four-legged beasts in the vicinity. Massive, gore-splattered chunks of horse flesh were neatly carved from suddenly-quite-dead unicorns, raining down upon all like a Biblical plague. The screams of dead and dying joined those of their murderers to create a cacophonous din as the carnage increased.

Horace, once again in his element now that he was surrounded by utter carnage, grabbed hold of the stunned Aurora to yank her to the safety of the ground. Blood showered down upon them, ruining not only Horace's $483 Joseph Abboud Suttonville Cream Herringbone Slim Fit Sport Coat, but also his $825 ISAIA Flat-Front Italian Wool Pants.

Still the ammunition flew, still the unicorns screamed in terror, still were they chopped down by the relentless pregnant markswomen, still Horace realized he had set his sights disappointingly low by settling for a crossbow when selecting a weapon from Sporting Goods. It became clear the unicorns had no answer to the sudden onslaught of modern warfare. Had ammunition been limitless, the seven Rambettes would have very likely caused mass extinction.

Alas, ammunition was not limitless.

The first telltale click of an empty cartridge came as the head, neck, and snout of Gibbles was torn asunder by gunfire. The second click came a heartbeat after, followed quickly by the third, fourth, fifth, sixth, and seventh. Just like that, the violence abated. Too late for

Gibbles, perhaps, but a large number of man-eating unicorns remained alive, hungry, and furious.

"They're out of ammo!" cried one unicorn.

"Avenge our brothers and sisters!" cried a second.

"Rip the human scum to shreds!" cried a third.

"Death to humanity!" cried every single one of them.

"Don't forget about the male!" added someone, which Horace felt was a bit unnecessary as he'd always assumed he was a member of humanity and had therefore already been sentenced to death.

"You said something about running," mentioned the gore-soaked Aurora, rising to her feet. Her entire upper torso glistened red with blood, causing her eyes to appear as tiny beads of blue amidst a bright-red canvas.

"Indeed," Horace almost said. Instead, his mind was spurred to action from having been being singled out for execution.

Run. Yes, they should run. But where ... where ... ?

Then everything clicked.

"To Patio and Garden!" he announced, finding his legs and allowing them to get right to work. Behind him, the magenta-colored Aurora followed suit. The seven unicorn-icidal Drooger McFerdeldee rape victims, now unarmed and undangerous, fell back into herd mentality and followed their fellow fleeing humans, hoping for safety in numbers.

The unicorns charged.

The race was on.

Under normal circumstances, Horace would never have outrun a stampede of blood-crazed unicorns.

However, he had the advantage of being in the very front of the pack, as first one, then another impregnated woman fell under the onslaught of fury pursuing them. Each fallen comrade served to delay the horde momentarily as her body was torn to ribbons by four-legged killing machines.

"Why Patio and Garden?" yelled Aurora as she ran a pace behind Horace, who considered slowing a step to allow her to take the lead in the name of chivalry but chose self-preservation instead.

"The grills!" he yelled back.

"Are you planning on barbecuing them?" Aurora replied incredulously.

"Trust me!" he answered.

They ran on as behind them a third and then fourth woman became a brutally desecrated casualty of war. His plan was simple, and had the advantage of actually being plausible. Patio and Garden would be home to a number of large outdoor grills. Many, if not most, of those grills would be powered by tanks of propane.

Propane exploded quite nicely.

As the horrifying screams of the fifth pregnant woman faded into the background, Horace, Aurora, and the final two women spilled out into Patio and Garden.

"Now what?" harped Aurora.

"The tanks!" answered Horace. "We blow the tanks!"

He turned and beamed, triumphant, only to be slapped across the face yet again. "Idiot!" she roared. "Blow them with what? How do you even know there's any propane left in the tanks in the first place? And how do we not get blown to bits as well? ”

Just like that, Horace's flame of pride was snuffed out by the cold water of reality.

“What do we do?” asked one of the surviving mothers-to-be.

“We're working on it,” replied Horace. “One moment.”

“You need another moment?” asked the other unwilling surrogate. “Okay.”

Before Horace could consider stopping her, she ran back into the teeth of the stampede and threw herself to their mercy with a cry of “Sweet Mother of God, kill me now!”

Granted an extra few moments, Horace spun back to Aurora. “First, there's a row of long-nosed lighters hanging just behind you. Second, I don't know if there is any propane left in any tanks, but if there isn't then we're all dead anyway, so why bother worrying. Third, I hadn't thought that far ahead and am open to ideas.”

“I'll do it.”

Horace continued to look at Aurora quizzically, as he hadn't seen her lips move, but then his would-be-date turned toward the final remaining former Sporting Goods prisoner and so Horace did the same.

“Are you sure?” asked Aurora.

The woman nodded. “I cannot live to give birth to the alien abomination gestating within my abused womb,” she said, reaching out and yanking a long-nosed lighter from the rack. “Go. Run. Live. Fornicate and create wholesome, decent, 100% human offspring. Thank you for saving us.”

She calmly walked to the nearest gas-powered grill, reached down, unhooked the propane tank, and opened the valve. A Heavenly hiss emerged, announcing that this tank, at least, still contained the highly-flammable gas.

"You will not be forgotten," said Horace.

The woman nodded and moved to the next tank of propane.

"I believe we were running for our lives?" suggested Aurora.

They took off for the exit, spurred on by the knowledge that if they remained inside when the nameless woman — who would, indeed, soon be entirely forgotten — lit her lighter and ignited the propane they would die. Unfortunately, just as the welcoming doors to the outside appeared ahead, Horace and Aurora heard the telltale screams of the final survivor falling beneath the angry hooves of her killers.

"No!" cried Aurora. "She failed!"

"Have faith!" cried Horace right back, fearing the stubborn, topless woman would suggest they return to Patio and Garden and certain death. "The will of the pregnant woman is strong!"

Aurora opened her mouth to chide his cowardice, but was interrupted when the entire abandoned department store was engulfed in flames stemming from Patio and Garden.

Horace and Aurora would never know how the soon-to-be-forgotten woman had succeeded. They would never know how she had struggled to foil the child safety lock on the lighter with one hand while her other was being chewed and digested by Not Named

Gibbles. Never know how she finally coaxed a single flame from the lighter's tip even as dozens of blood-thirsty unicorns feasted on her intestines. Never know how she somehow found the strength of will to crawl the required six inches forward even with large portions of her anatomy splayed out in all directions. In fact, they eventually would assume the propane had sparked on its own, and the heroic actions of the amazingly brave heroine were forever lost in obscurity, just as she — the true savior of mankind — was utterly forgotten.

The blast lifted Horace and Aurora from their feet and shoved them through the plate glass windows of the store, slicing their faces, arms, and legs with a thousand cuts, yet jettisoning them to the relative safety of Not-Inside-The-Store.

Back in Patio and Garden, propane tank after propane tank erupted in a comically-choreographed series of explosions. Every single unicorn was blasted to cinders, and the interior of the Wal-Mart became an inferno, cooking and melting and burning away any and all traces of Swami Chuck Allallilalooli's utopian nightmare. The structure itself eventually collapsed, snuffing out the flames just before the massive fireballs escaped the building and consumed Horace and Aurora.

Then, all was silent.

Except, of course, for the massive ringing in Horace's ears which rendered him otherwise deaf and which he knew from experience would take a good week to subside.

"What ... what happened?" asked a shocking-ly-dazed Aurora.

Horace did not hear her, of course, for reasons which have just been mentioned.

"Well," he said while dusting himself off. "That was certainly exciting."

Aurora, naturally, could not hear a thing either, causing Horace's words to literally fall on deaf ears.

"You did it," she said. "Your plan worked! The unicorns are dead! Humanity is saved."

"I'm sorry that our date did not turn out as well as I had hoped," continued Horace, utterly ignorant of what Aurora was saying. "I know you despise me, so I will gallantly offer to give you a ride home and say my goodbyes."

"That was the most manly, amazing thing I have ever seen," continued Aurora, equally oblivious to Horace's words. "My entire opinion of you has changed and I feel we ought to have sex right now. Let me rip off your clothes."

She reached for him, and Horace, having no clue as to her intentions, mistook her sudden passion for fury and backed away. Aurora mistook his fear for rejection, and promptly withdrew into herself, emotionally stung.

After an awkward moment where each assumed the other despised them, the equally-deaf Horace Whitley and Aurora Gaithwaite returned to Horace's $75,000 Tesla Model S and drove away in frosty silence, leaving the smoldering ruins of the abandoned Wal-Mart to be swallowed up by the wild jungles of Nebraska.

About the Contributors

Shawn Thomas Anderson is a copywriter, branding specialist, and writer of middle-grade and young-adult fantasy and science fiction — with a little horror thrown in for good measure. He lives in a far-flung corner of Vermont up by the Canadian border, in a region called the Northeast Kingdom. It's a magical place where moose, bear, and deer wander through your backyard and everyone rocks flannel. Shawn loves crafting short stories, and he has several coming out this year in various anthologies and publications. Follow Shawn and his writing adventures on Twitter at @ShawnTWrites or visit his new website and blog at www.shawnthomasanderson.com.

Carl N. Brown grew up in the era of CD, IGY, Sputnik, and Gilbert science sets. Mom and Dad took the kids to the drive-ins for horror and sci-fi movies. Introduced to Poe by an aunt, to Dorothy and Oz by Mom, to H.G. Wells by Granpa. As a teen he submitted to a *MF&SF* story contest themed Unicorns and Univacs; how could he resist a *Unicornado!*? The one who declared "there is nothing gothic about unicorns" should look to Zampieri's fresco or extant coats of arms with unicorn rampant. The unicorn is a fearsome beast, untamable save by the grace of a virtuous maiden, and darkly gothic.

Sydel Brown writes creepy things. Her first publication is in the *Unicornado!* anthology from Fossil Lake Anthologies. When she's not observing strange things happening around her, she's dreaming about what fantastical creatures get up to when she's not looking. Follow her on Twitter @sydelbrown and friend her on Facebook.

Shenoa Carroll-Bradd lives in Southern California with her awesome brother and dancing dog. She writes whatever catches her fancy, from horror to fantasy and erotica. Say hi on twitter @ShenoaSays or visit her fan page at www.facebook.com/sbcbfiction.

Calum Chalmers lives in Chesham, UK. Disappointed by the lack of monsters and demons harassing this world he chose to help bring them to life through his short stories. Calum's debut story 'The Change' featured in the recently released *Wild Things: Thirteen Tales of Therianthropy* followed by 'The Spirit of The Queen Inn' to be featured in *Weird Ales — Last Orders*, due Sept 2016. This has led him to his first editing anthology project *Welcome to a Town Called Hell*, available mid-2016.

Stygia Deal arose like Venus from the waters of Lake Michigan to escape the great flabby mudfish who tried to name a shark Dagon. She owns a diner specializing in authentic deep-dish frozen Chicago-style pizzas. In her spare time, she promotes rock shows and hitchhikes in long tight black dresses.

S.L. Dixon was born and raised in Ontario, Canada and his short fiction has appeared in magazines, literary journals and anthologies from around the world. He's held positions with companies producing ice cream, turkeys, cement walls and steel towers. He is a former hitchhiker turned homebody that often goes days without stepping outside. Currently, he resides on the Pacific coast of British Columbia, Canada.

morgan downie is an unreliable narrator with a deep mistrust of artist's statements. he believes in the notion that at least one out of every six statements should be wilfully untrue. his is a chequered past involving poetry, short story writing, visual, installation and textile art, book making, sculpture and all points inbetween. he has been widely anthologised for both short story and poetry. until recently his artwork could only be bought on the island of fårö. it is this connection that prompted his long worked upon secret history of ingmar bergman. when asked where he comes from he describes a place he knows as the mythic archipelago of scotia. morgan downie is an island man. he loves the bicycle and everything associated with it. he believes that all art may be contained in a single decent bike ride. morgan downie has always been on the road to meikle seggie. http://morgandownie.com/

Lyn Godfrey is a freelance writer of speculative fiction. She is also a small-town, American southwestern, book-hoarding, animal-loving kind of girl. She writes in most 'genre' genres (including science fiction, fantasy, urban fantasy, horror, YA) and is a self-described Geek of All Trades. Videos games, superheroes, steampunk, aliens, dinosaurs, zombies, and so on and so forth. If it's nerdy, she loves it. Yes, that includes Star Wars AND Star Trek. Lyn began writing her first book (a Star Wars sequel) at age eleven. She has been making plans to write ever since but is often distracted by reading or looking for shiny things, like spaceships and robots. Her recent short stories can be found in various anthologies, including *Ain't Superstitious, Misunderstood, Sproutlings* and *In Memory: A Tribute to Terry Pratchett.*

John Goodrich likes swamp monsters in comics, daikaiju films, well-written HP Lovecraft pastiche, Jorge Luis Borges, American Tribal Style® Belly Dance, D&D adventures with liches in them, and nearly everything about Iceland. He doesn't like bullies and bigots.

Amelia Gorman is a baker, computer science student and horror fan on the northern edge of Tornado Alley. She has a story in the Innsmouth Free Press's *She Walks in Shadows* anthology and poetry in *Nonbinary Review.*

Nikki Guerlain is classy as fuck.

Victoria Harkavy is thrilled to be part of this project. She coined rule 789, which states "If it exists, the unicorn version is better." (It's going to explode all over the Internet. Any minute now). Victoria has her MA in Folklore and is a scholar of the fantastic and human-animal relationships. Her special hornless unicorn friend, William, is the star of the sporadically updated Folklore Horse tumblr blog. And since she mentioned William, Victoria has to also give credit to Gumbie the cat, whose forbearance allows Victoria to occasionally contribute to non-Gumbie-related projects like Unicornado.

Nikki Hetfield claims to be James Hetfield's thirteenth birthday present. The latter, apparently, has no knowledge of this.

Justin Hunter has five published novels and over thirty short stories in anthologies. Check out his Amazon.com author page at http://www.amazon.com/Justin-Hunter/e/B007PRBUHS. Connect him on Facebook to keep updated on upcoming releases.

Terry Ibele is from Ontario, Canada where he's a digital marketer for a software company. Living off a steady diet of frolicking in the woods, being stuck in transit, and pizza, he dreams of the day he can retire to a small shack out in the country and keep a pet goat. In his spare time, Terry loves writing brisk, quirky stories and is currently working on a fantasy novel.

Joel Kaplan lives in Sarasota, Florida. He is the author of the extreme cult horror novel *HIGH ON BLOOD AT THE END OF THE WORLD*. He loves pinball and punk rock. Keep up with him at facebook.com/joelkaplanthewriter

Kerry G. S. Lipp lives in Louisville, Kentucky. He hates the sun and loves making fun of dead people. His parents started reading his stories and they've consequently booted him from their will. Kerry's work appears in several anthologies including *DOA2* from Blood Bound Books. His work has been featured multiple times on The Wicked Library podcast. He is currently editing his first novel, writing his second, and shopping a bizarro novella. Kerry rarely (but still) blogs at Horror Tree and will launch his own website sometime before he dies. Say hi on Twitter @kerrylipp or come find him on Facebook. And he wants you to remember to always cover the camera on your laptop. You never know who's watching you.

Troy Lockport hails from actual Chicago as a horror author of dark words published in places too controversial for pro-writers that hail cabs but not Satan. He was also once caught in an Armageddon style storm where it hailed giant toads that looked like his cousin Mike. When the scandal broke about those who tried to plagiarize Lockport's work, he took it back to his grandma's basement and tried to fix it with scotch-tape and unicorn's blood, but his rivals got hold of it and sold it online to the lowest bidder. He fought hard to get the rights back to his books after they fled to South America with a drag queen and an abnormally tall dwarf, but was unable to trace them owing to a chronically parochial misunderstanding of US geography centered upon the belief that "South America" began with the state of Tennessee. Lockport doesn't touch non-erotic and anti-LGBT material with a ten foot dildo, even if he does think that Poe and Lovecraft were just a couple of shirt-lifting nancy-boy hacks. He spends his spare time filling Lake Michigan with alligators and leaving angry voicemails with utility companies that fail to pay his bills on GoFundMe. Keep up with Troy's wonderfully wacky world of witty weirdness at https://troylockport.wordpress.com/ You won't regret it. Much.

David Neilsen is the author of a number of slightly disturbing short stories which have been published online and in various anthologies. His debut novel, the middle grade horror story *Doctor Fell and the Playground of Doom*, will be published by Crown Books for Young Readers in August 2016. He spent a dozen years working in Hollywood, culminating in optioning a pilot to 20th Century Fox (that went nowhere), and penning the screenplay for the Straight-to-DVD film *The Eliminator* (rent it, he dares you). David is also a professional storyteller based in Sleepy Hollow who has been inadvertently giving children nightmares for a number of years. He actively believes in unicorns, because one once ate his little brother. For more information on

David's work, visit him online at neilsenparty.word-press.com.

Logan Noble is a horror author who resides in the untamed suburbs of Northern Ohio. When he's not wasting his time reading and writing, he spends his days with his wife Elizabeth and his two dogs. His short fiction has appeared in several anthologies, including *Spooklights*, published by Muzzleland Press, *Creature Stew II*, published by Papa Bear Press, *The Haunted Traveler Vol. 2*, released by Weasel Press, and several of his horror stories have appeared in Horrified Press publications. You can follow his daily adventures and musings at his Twitter account, @logan_noble. Most of his fiction can be found on Amazon

Sheryl Normandeau is a Calgary-based writer who spends an inordinate amount of time at the public library (mostly because she works there). Her stories have appeared in several anthologies and magazines, including *Ficta Fabula, Different Dragons, Weirder Science, The Dragon's Hoard,* and *Universe Horribilis.* She is a shortlisted author for the 2015 Howard O'Hagan Award for Short Stories.

J.M. Northwood, also known as Captain Fabulous, recently performed his first public reading. Dressed to kill, with a voice like melted butter, his raunchy tale of gay pirate smut garnered rave reviews and a warm, moist reception from the audience. His work can also be found in the anthologies *Toys in the*

Attic and *Fossil Lake II: The Refossiling*, hopefully with many more soon to come.

Mary Pletsch is a vintage My Little Pony collector and connoisseur of all things unicorn. Her previous publications include stories in *One Horn To Rule Them All: A Purple Unicorn Anthology* and *Game of Horns: A Red Unicorn Anthology*, both by WordFire Press, in support of the Don Hodge Memorial Scholarship to Superstars Writing Seminars. Her short stories in *Apex Magazine, Tesseracts 18, Shock Totem* and *Women in Practical Armor* are sadly unicorn-free. She lives in New Brunswick with Dylan Blacquiere, their four cats, a unicorn Transformer, and a herd of pastel ponies.

Rodello Santos was born in Manila, but currently stalks the streets of New York. His stories have found several homes including *Beneath Ceaseless Skies, Flash Fiction Online,* and *Icarus magazine.* He garnered an honorable mention in the 2008 Year's Best Fantasy and Horror (Datlow, Link and Grant) for his story "In Earthen Vessels" (from *Philippine Speculative Fiction, Vol. 3.*) Also, he holds an abiding, platonic love for squirrels.

Frank Sawielijew, as an eccentric Russian noble who should rightfully be Tzar of Bulgaria but studies history in Frankfurt (Germany) instead, loves to forge wild tales set in the weirdest of worlds. Historian by day, writer by night, he likes to explore a myriad of genres but feels at home in the very broad over-genre of speculative fiction. He writes in both English and German, has self-published his first book in 2013 and had a handful of short stories appear in various anthologies. When he's not working on anything, he wastes his time watching campy 1980s B-movies and playing Thief, the best game ever made.

Amy Shepherd is a queer writer living in Seattle with her wife and 2 caticorns. Connect with her on the web at http://amyshep.com/.

Michael Shimek currently lives in Colorado where he writes and has adventures in the mountains. He has stories that appear in *Sanitarium Magazine Issue #32, Fictionvale Episode Five: Of Magic and Mayhem, We Walk Invisible, In Shambles: A Scarlet Nightmare Vol. II, Fossil Lake: An Anthology of the Aberrant, Slaughter House: The Serial Killer Edition — Vol I, A Chimerical World: Tales of the Unseelie Court,* and more. Many of his stories can be found for free on his website: michaelshimek.blogspot.com. He also tweets @michaelshimek.

Dominic Stabile is a writer of horror fiction (and other things) recently transplanted to Blue Hill, Maine from the south. His short fiction has appeared in *Sanitarium Magazine, The Horror Zine, Hellfire Crossroads Vol.3, Atticus Review,* and *Far Horizons* and is forthcoming in *Cyclopean* and *Manor House*. His first book, a neo-noir horror collection tentatively titled, *Godless City,* will be released by Mirror Matter Press later in 2016. You can contact him at https://www.-

facebook.com/ dominicstabile1 or www.dominicstabile.com or email him at stabiledominic@yahoo.com.

Pete Sutton has a not so secret lair in the wilds of Fishponds, Bristol, UK and dreams up stories, many of which are about magpies. He's had stuff published, online and in book form, and currently has a pile of words that one day may possibly be a novel. You can find him all over social media or worrying about events he's organised at the Bristol Festival of Literature. On Twitter he's @suttope, his Bristol Book Blog is http://brsbkblog.blogspot.co.uk/ and his website is http://petewsutton.com. He's contributing editor of Far Horizons e-magazine which can be found here: https://farhorizonsmagazine.wordpress.com/

Berti Walker lives with her husband and son in a place that is ridden with angry corpses, decaying with age as they bake in the sun and lust after the flesh of the young, while drinking orange juice with alligators. The state she resides in juts into the Atlantic ocean like a giant phallus, with the waters of the Everglades running through its veins. She writes horror, sci-fi, fantasy, bizarro, erotica, often a crossover of multiple genres. You can find her on Twitter @bertiwalker and Facebook.

Stanley Webb lives in Pulaski, New York; a community shunned by unicorns, but frequented by apocalyptic winters. Stanley once toiled in an automobile factory, but now works part-time at a diner. When not occupied with making ends meet, he cares for his family's small farm, assists his wife in home-schooling their son, and transmits weird fiction into the digital void. His efforts have appeared in *Fossil Lake 2: The Refossiling*, and *Teeming Terrors*. Other publications include *Sensorama, Daylight Dims 2, Ill-Considered Expeditions, Broken Worlds, My Favorite Apocalypse,* and *Necronomicum 3*.

Coming in 2017 ...

Fossil Lake 4:

SHARKASAURUS!